CATRINA'S RETURN

ANNEMARIE BREAR

ALSO BY ANNEMARIE BREAR

* * *

Contemporary

Long Distance Love ✓

Hooked on You ✓

Where Dragonflies Hover (Dual Timeline)

* * *

Short Stories

A New Dawn

Art of Desire

What He Taught Her

Catrina's Return

ANNEMARIE BREAR

CHAPTER 1

S cottish Highlands
1899

CATRINA ALLOWED her shawl to slip further down from her shoulders while she gathered wildflowers. The warmth of the sun, so rare in this part of the world, peeked out between scattered clouds, caressing her back. Spring in the highlands was late this year and if she'd been forced to spend another day inside the house she'd go mad.

From the height advantage on the side of the mountain, she could see for miles. Before her lay a carpet of heather and wildflowers of purple, yellow and green, which covered the steep rugged slopes down to the valley and the close-knit hamlet she rarely visited. In the distance, snow still capped the highest peaks, giving the air a clear, bracing feel. Catrina breathed in deeply and smiled. The end of winter always signalled renewed energy and her body simmered with the need to run and skip, to remember the girl she once was.

Then she frowned, she'd never be that girl again. How could she after all that had happened?

'Miss Catrina!'

Turning, Catrina spied her maid, Lettie, clambering up the incline, her brown skirt hitched in one hand. She waited until Lettie was close enough so she didn't have to shout. 'What is it?'

'You've a visitor, Miss.'

'Mr Henley?'

'Nay, I would've said if it were him.' Lettie paused to take some deep breaths. 'Why do you walk so high up? Mad it is, total madness.'

Ignoring Lettie's mutterings, Catrina headed back towards the cottage nestled in a hollow half way down the mountain. 'Is it someone from the village?' She worried, wondering who would come to her door. She never had visitors. Side-stepping an outcrop of lichen covered grey rock, she looked towards the cottage wishing she could see through the thick stone walls and know who was inside.

'No one from the village.' Lettie stumbled down the sheep ruts behind her. 'It's a gentleman.'

Catrina jerked to a halt and Lettie nearly tripped into her. 'A gentleman?'

'Aye.'

'Why did you not say so immediately?' A shiver of anxiety flickered through her body. 'He's not lost perhaps?'

'No, he asked for you by name, so there's no need to look at me like that, Miss. It's not my fault, I was a bit shaken hearing the knock at the door. Nobody comes to the cottage, but Mr Henley, and I knew he weren't due to arrive for a few days yet.'

Catrina was both apprehensive and curious as to who had arrived. No one knew she lived here, except for those in the village and none of the males down there could be classed as a gentleman. She hurried over the small rises and dips that years of harsh weather had carved into the mountain, wanting for once that she lived on level ground. After flinging open the small wooden gate in the walled garden behind the cottage, she weaved between the vegetable beds that she worked on earlier. At sunrise she'd been up digging and planting the beds ready for the summer crops. Geese honked out of her way, offended by the intrusion.

At the back door she hesitated, puffing, and glanced at Lettie. 'Did he say nothing at all?'

'Only that he wished to see Miss Catrina Davies.' Lettie opened the door, which led into the stone floor scullery and then through to the small, yet comfortable kitchen, which was her domain. Lettie turned in the act of taking her apron down from the hook on the wall. 'I must say he seems very... important. Do you think he's come from your old home?'

Catrina flinched. She'd had no contact with her family for three years. She slowly pulled out the pins securing her straw hat. It wouldn't be someone from home, surely? How would they know where to find her? Unless something had happened to Hugh...

Seeing her concerned face, Lettie patted her arm. 'Nay, Miss, don't worry. It might be something and nothing.' She smiled, her plump cheeks dimpling. 'Go on through and I'll set a tea tray.'

Summoning her courage, Catrina slipped off her shawl, tidied her hair and smoothed down her skirt of light green and white stripe. On impulse, after washing off the dirt from the garden this morning, she had dressed in one of her best day dresses, as her way of welcoming the fine weather and the hope of spring. She was thankful she at least looked suitable for visitors, even if she didn't feel it.

From the kitchen, Catrina stepped down the narrow dark hall to the front sitting room. Her footsteps faltered in the doorway as movement near the fireplace caught her attention. A tall man dressed in dark trousers and a long black coat stood with his back to the door. On the chair by the window sat his hat and gloves. This touch of manliness was foreign. The only man to have been in this room for years was Hugh Henley. She glanced around the room once more to check if anything else was different, but nothing showed out of the ordinary. Her embroidery lay on the side table, a handkerchief on top of the book she'd been reading last night.

Suddenly the gentleman turned around to face her. Catrina stood rigid, shocked. Travis. *He was here.* Her focus dimmed, and all went black.

* * *

WITH A MUTTERED OATH, Travis Millard left his place by the fire and knelt at her side. For a moment he couldn't touch her. She didn't seem real, even this cottage, swallowed in the middle of nowhere, didn't seem real.

Three years he'd been subtly looking for her without anyone knowing. She had haunted him in all that time and now, to have her lying before him, frightened him. Perhaps he should have sent a note ahead of his visit?

A pain encircled his chest as he stared at her. Her beauty had matured since he last saw her. Her figure had become finely toned over the years. When he had turned and seen her standing in the doorway, he'd glimpsed the composed and elegant woman she had always been. His heart had contracted, the old love returning tenfold.

He hadn't expected to feel anything overpowering, in fact, he'd hoped all his affection for her had been in his imagination, and any real feelings had died, but he'd been wrong. He could deal with his own emotions, but he hadn't expected her to react to his presence so severely.

What *had* he imagined, smiles of welcome?

His mad dash to Scotland now seemed foolish, an obsessive decision that went against his nature, not to mention his better judgement. Years ago, his grandmother said he was a fool, *soft*, where Catrina was concerned, but she didn't know the half of it. How could he tell her that Catrina's disappearance had left a hole inside him that nothing could fill?

But that didn't mean Catrina returned his sentiments. What had possessed him to come here? Hadn't Catrina made it clear that whatever they once shared was long forgotten? She'd disappeared without a word to him. She couldn't know how much her actions hurt him, and neither would he let her know.

So why had he come? Why stir up old wounds?

He sighed, not wanting to know the answer.

Her eyes, the colour of rich honey, which matched the deeper chestnut of her hair, fluttered open and she frowned. Travis had the urge to kiss her fully awake, but then his reason returned, clamping down on any immature desire. As beautiful as she was, he had to remember what she apparently was, an old man's whore.

CHAPTER 2

'Did my father send you?' Catrina murmured, sipping the sweet tea Lettie had brought in. Her hands shook as she sat in her chair by the fireplace and stared at the low flames licking the wood. The astonishment of having Travis in the cottage made her tremble. He was the last man in the world she expected to seek her out.

'No, he didn't.'

'Why did you come then?'

'I don't know why.' He stood looking out of the window, his hands clasped behind his back, his teacup ignored. 'It was brainless of me really. But then most whims are, aren't they?'

Catrina gripped the porcelain saucer, willing her stupid heart to slow its frantic rate. Travis looked older, and his eyes spoke of him being a little wiser. Yet, his face was still as handsome as ever, creating the same stunning effect on her. 'Who-who told you I was here?'

'I overheard a conversation last week between two gentlemen at one of the clubs in York.'

'A club?' She frowned, the Travis she knew wasn't a member of any gentleman's club.

'Yes. I find myself mixing in those circles now. I took up my grandfather's membership. Anyway, one of the older men spoke of travelling to the Highlands to see his Catrina.'

'I see.' She studied his broad shoulders with a familiar jolt of yearning that dismayed her. Had she not put all this behind her? He was dressed in tailored cut wool of the most expensive kind, the kind her father and brother wore. Why was he dressed so? She'd never seen him wear such clothing, nor did he ever have the need, not as her father's estate manager.

Puzzled, she gave him a cutting look. 'The Highlands are full of women called Catrina.'

'But less called Catrina Davies, I suspect.' He grimaced. 'I took a gamble on gut instinct. It's never failed me before. However, I did manage to learn some details, which made me believe it was you they spoke about. Even now I can hardly believe it turned out to be true – to be you.'

'Mr Hugh Henley is one of the gentlemen, I gather?' She sighed. Why had Hugh mentioned her? He was normally so good at keeping his own counsel. And how ironic that the one time he did mention her, Travis was within hearing distance.

'Yes. Though I did not know of him at the time, but I did know of his friend, Mr Digby. Apparently this Mr Henley was just passing through, and stopped for some refreshments. I think Fate played its hand, do you?'

'So it seems.'

Travis twitched the lace curtains aside as though something of interest outside had caught his attention. 'Fortunately, Mr Digby has a loose tongue when he's drunk too many brandies.' He released the curtain and glanced at her. 'Lord knows who else he's gabbled to about you.'

'I can imagine what he told you, but I don't care.' Her cup

rattled on the saucer and she quickly placed it back on the tray.

Travis turned from the window, his piercing blue eyes held her still. 'Digby spoke of your situation. He thought it a big joke. A Davies brought low. Oh yes, he revelled in that.'

Her voice caught in her throat. If only he didn't have the power to render her witless. 'I assure you, it's not how you think.'

'You're not old man Henley's mistress?'

'No!' She shot to her feet, her cheeks burning. 'No, I'm not.' She covered her mouth with her hand, horrified at the thought of spilling her secrets to this man, the one man who had turned her head, the one who she had foolishly thought would give her the happiness she craved.

'I don't believe you.'

'I speak the truth!'

His top lip curled in revulsion. 'Does he pay well? I'm told you've made him very happy over the years.' He glared around the room, his expression hard and unreadable. 'He has a fine establishment here, keeping you away from society.'

'You know nothing about it.'

He took a step forward. 'He doesn't keep you? He doesn't put a roof over your head, food in your belly?' Travis gave a derogatory laugh.

'I don't have to explain anything to you. Get out.' She lifted her chin. 'You are not welcome here.'

'Now I know why you are not talked about by your family.'

'As I said, you know nothing and neither do they.' Loathing for him clouded all thought. This man, who she had once thought she even loved, was now a stranger. His mere presence threatened the fragile contentment she'd carved out for herself after fleeing her family home. She'd dreamed of meeting him again, foolish dreams where he took her in his arms declared undying love for her. How idiotic of her. The dream had turned into a nightmare, and the long-suffered pain began to rise once more.

'Then tell me, Miss Davies.' He smiled sarcastically, folding his arms and leaning against the windowsill as if he had all the time in the world. 'What is the story from your lips and not Digby's?'

'I'm not answerable to you or anyone.' She turned away to gaze into the fire. Why did he come here? What reasons did he have after all this time? What good would it do?

'Why did you leave without word?'

She tensed, hearing the restrained hurt in his voice. Or had she imagined it? 'I had no choice.' Straightening her shoulders, she pushed away the awful memories of that time when she had fled in the darkness of predawn and left everything she loved behind.

'Why didn't you come to me?'

'You were busy,' she snapped, and then wished she hadn't.

He was beside her in an instant, gripping her elbow and spinning her around to glare into her eyes. 'What do you mean?'

'I arrived at Estella's wedding, Travis, and I saw that you were, you were...' She hung her head. The image of that afternoon never faded, never stopped tormenting her. But it was only one of the many things that made staying at home unbearable. It was only one more incident of that dreadful day when her heart and spirit broke.

'I don't understand. Tell me!' His fingers bruised her tender skin inside her arm. 'I deserve the truth.'

'You deserve nothing,' she sneered. 'How dare you come here and assault me in my own home.' She snatched her arm away. 'Leave at once.'

'You can stop ordering me about like some lackey, Miss

Davies,' he snapped. 'I don't work for your family anymore, and I'm not leaving until I have some answers.'

'What gives you the right?' Her eyes narrowed with hate. 'How is this important to you?'

'I want to know why you left. Your actions hurt many people. Your father and brother most of all.'

'But not you?' She flared, hating the mention of her half-brother, Phillip. He would have been the most happiest to see her go.

'Would I be here if it didn't affect me?' He gave her a long look. 'Why?'

'Because of you and…and… Oh, leave me alone. You should never have come here,' she spat, all the hurt and anger she'd buried for years surfaced with such force she thought she'd explode from it.

'You left because of me? I don't understand?'

'I saw you in the barn, half naked, kissing another woman, fondling her, laughing. You were having the best of times.'

'Another woman?' He blinked in surprise.

'Yes, at your cousin's wedding celebrations.' She glared, desperately wanting him to tell her it was all a lie, that she had imagined the whole thing. On top of what she'd suffered at home, seeing Travis's cheating ways had been the last straw.

Travis stepped back, frowning. 'Estella's wedding?'

'Yes! She is the only cousin you have!' Was he stupid?

'I cannot remember much of the occasion.' Silence stretched as he thought. 'I think I was awfully drunk that night. I suppose it was the effects of relief. After years of being in my care, Estella, with her wild temperament, her attraction to unruliness was now safely married and happy. My role as the authority in her life was finished. And I was glad.'

'Glad enough to forget me with a wedding guest who is known for her loose ways? Why did it have to be Myrtle Willis? You knew how much I detested her. The whole village knows of her as a trollop.' Catrina remembered the soul-destroying view of Myrtle running her hands through Travis's hair, kissing his neck...

'I have no excuses for my behaviour. I'm sorry it happened. I had drunk too much. I was missing you and confused about what we were going to do.'

'I had only been away for two weeks.'

Travis's expression hardened. 'You said you'd be gone for a few days. What held your interest at your uncle's home so much? Perhaps his nephew, Randolph?'

'Don't talk nonsense! Randy is like a brother to me.' A better brother than the actual one she had.

'That's not how he saw it. His eyes followed you whenever you were nearby. I used to watch him. At first his devotion to you amused me, he behaved like a puppy, but when I realised he wanted you as a man wants a woman, my amusement turned to anger. It was no longer funny.'

'There was no need to be annoyed. As I said, Randy is—was like a brother to me.'

'I couldn't compete with him, a wealthy man.'

'You didn't have to compete with anyone.' Her anger seeped away, leaving her deflated. Why were men so dim-witted about such things?

'I heard he married last summer.' Travis watched her carefully.

'I'm happy for him then.' She raised her chin and stared with open honesty, though inside she cried for another family event she had missed.

'So, what was the reason you didn't come home before Estella's wedding? Everyone was expecting you, especially me.'

She blew out a frustrated sigh, annoyed that he had to press for every scrap of information. 'The reason I was delayed returning home, and why I missed your cousin's wedding was because Uncle Hector had fallen ill. He said I soothed him by being there, so I stayed. Or do you wish to believe your own thoughts on the matter and prefer to think the worst of me and Randolph?' she scoffed.

Travis stiffened, his eyes narrowing. 'I cannot be blamed for having doubts. After Arthur Seaton...'

'Arthur Seaton?' She laughed without humour at the old memory of one of her brother's friends, the one friend of Phillip's who'd treated her with respect. 'He was a complete gentleman towards me. He always has been, despite the rumours that he and I shared something more than friendship. When we were caught in that rainstorm we did nothing but talk in that old stable.' She tilted her head to study him. 'But, if I knew then what I do now, I should have chosen Arthur and saved myself years of pain.'

His eyes widened, and he jut out his chin. 'Everyone on the estate and in the village believed you should have picked him as your beau. But Arthur is as dull as a grey day, and you knew it. The Catrina I remember, the untamed girl with the wicked laugh never looked twice at Arthur.'

'No, I looked at *you* instead,' she bit out. 'Yet, you doubted me, and you doubted Arthur when we spoke the truth.' She shook her head at the regret of it all. The gossip had been violent and insulting, and Phillip had been the worst at stirring the nest as usual. 'My Father worried constantly that I'd fall for someone unsuitable. Little did he know he was right and that I'd fall for one of our staff.' Catrina laughed mockingly, recalling the terrifying times when all she'd wanted was to marry Travis, but knew that such a simple act would cause even more scandal.

Travis scowled. 'As I recall you didn't reject any interest I showed in you. In fact, you seemed very keen for us to become closer.'

'Yes, well, looking back, I realise I was desperate.'

'Desperate?' His voice became low, lethal sounding.

'I'd turned two and twenty. I thought I had lost my chance to marry. I threw myself at you.' It was true in some respects, but deep down she'd loved him and knew they'd make an excellent couple despite the differences in their stations. At that time, they seemed to have one mind.

'Why me though? You could have had any man.'

'I didn't want those who had offered to court me. None of those men inspired me to like them, never mind instil affection.' She fought a shudder as images of her brother's hideous friends and acquaintances tried to kiss and fondle her at parties. Phillip always surrounded himself with nasty people, whose wealth and status allowed them to get away with anything.

She blinked rapidly. The old wound was being ripped open again and she had to be strong. Now wasn't the time to think of those times. 'I was foolish, Travis. I see that now. An estate manager was never the right sort, even if you were a respected doctor's grandson. My father would have been horrified and put a stop to it, and rightly so.' If she was brutal perhaps he would leave.

'So, I dreamed the bond we shared? It was all a fabrication?' His eyes became the colour of ice blue, like that of deep frozen water. 'I was your bit of fun for the summer?'

She shook her head. 'No. I won't lie or pretend about that. For that whole summer I only thought of you.'

'As a true suitor, an equal? I don't think so.'

'No... well, yes, but also as a friend.' She stumbled over the words. It wouldn't do any good now to tell him how much she loved him then. 'You were a man I admired.'

'But you left.' His accusation grated on her raw nerves.

'After seeing you with Myrtle, I believed I had...' she paused, selecting the right words, 'I believed I had misjudged you. I felt as though you had made a fool out of me, and you had. I couldn't stay and be laughed at. Catrina Davies, Sir George Davies's daughter, who couldn't even get the attention of her father's estate manager. How tragic.' She shuddered, imaging the gossips' tongues wagging.

'I see.' His stiff manner made him appear as though he was carved from stone.

She swallowed. 'The whole village had seen us spending time together. My brother had some idea about our relationship and many times he'd confronted me about it. Rumours and tittle-tattle were growing. That's why I went to Uncle Hector's house in the first place. To clear my head and let the rumours die.'

'Why would the gossip concern you, if you planned for us to marry? Or perhaps you had changed your mind?' A nerve clenched in his jaw.

'I made a decision at Uncle Hector's. I was coming home to talk to you about us not marrying. I couldn't hurt my father.' She glanced down at the patterned rug at her feet, remembering how nervous she was that day. 'It was late when I arrived in the village, but I still went along to the wedding, hoping to see you. Some of the guests looked at me oddly. You know what they are like.' She shrugged one shoulder as if unconcerned, although the opposite was true. 'I knew they didn't like me being amongst them. I wasn't one of them, even though they'd all known me since I was born. They whispered behind their hands while I looked for you and doubts began to plague me. I had to see you before I went home. I had to make certain you understood how hard it was for me.'

'I did,' he said softly.

'Everyone at the wedding was so happy, laughing and

dancing, drinking and talking, and I had fantasised about a similar wedding for us, but knew it could never be...'

She thought back to that warm August evening, the wedding was held in the home and garden of Estella's groom, Mr Baldwin, a well-to-do solicitor of the village. 'Estella told me you were down near the barn with the men, tapping another barrel. I went down there and saw the men, but you weren't amongst them. I found you in a horse stall.'

Travis spun away, raking his hand through his dark hair. 'I was young and stupid. It's what young drunk men do, especially when goaded by a room full of friends. It meant nothing. Myrtle is the same with all men.'

'Yes. Everyone knows what Myrtle is. That's why I was so upset. I thought you loved me,' she whispered, her heart breaking all over again. 'We spent the entire summer together. You must have known how I felt. I let you...We kissed...'

'Yes, I know.' His expression softened. 'That's why I was so shocked when you simply disappeared like that. Why didn't you speak with me about this?'

'It didn't matter. The damage was done.' She sucked in a deep breath. 'I came to you that night because I was troubled by what the future held. I'd been away, and before that, Estella and your grandmother monopolised your time. It all seemed to be slipping through my fingers. I panicked.'

'What happened at the wedding was not important. It meant *nothing* to me. Myrtle has a reputation of being...fun. I was ready to relax and enjoy myself.' He swore under his breath. 'If I had known you needed me, that you had come home, I would have come to you immediately. I missed you. Surely you knew that from my letters?'

'Did you really want to marry me, Travis?' She blinked back tears. 'Throughout that whole summer I was so happy. I ignored the rumours about you, but that afternoon they came back to mock me.'

'What rumours?'

'Amelia Kirkham was to be your intended bride, your grandmother told me that quite clearly and often.'

'My grandmother spoke too freely. I never wanted Amelia. That was just her and Grandmother's wishful thinking.'

'And I was too emotional and confused to know any different.' She couldn't tell him of what she endured at home, which only compounded matters.

'Do you think I would have used you so ill? Did you think of me as being capable of such cruelty? I respected you too much to play you false, Catrina.'

'I didn't know what to think, especially as we had so many obstacles to overcome.'

'The only obstacle was your family allowing me to marry you.'

She nodded. 'I was left alone with my thoughts when I went to visit Uncle Hector and the days grew into weeks.' She sighed at the remembered agony of being away from Travis, but also at the peace of being spared Phillip's taunts. 'I wanted you as a woman wants a man, but it was wrong to do so. I brought shame upon myself and my family. My reckless behaviour had been fun until I learned the consequences. I was thoughtless and a child in many ways despite my age.'

Travis ran his fingers through his hair. 'I know we should have simply stayed friends, but you were so engaging and beautiful, easy to talk to—'

'And I encouraged you that we should become involved. I insisted.' She bowed her head. 'It was wicked of me. I cannot believe how I managed to do it, to be so determined. But the thought of becoming an old spinster was unbearable at the time and no other man tempted me. Once I saw you, I was lost. No other man came close to you. No wonder my father despaired of me ever finding a husband. Father thought me too choosey and joked that he'd never have me off his hands...'

'You should have stayed, Catrina.' His voice was low, compelling.

'I couldn't.' She couldn't tell him the main reason why she left. Closing her eyes, she tried to block the memory of that night, of what happened to her when she raced home from Estella's wedding celebrations - the night her innocence was cruelly taken from her.

'Your family made excuses to everyone, saying you'd gone to stay with an elderly aunt in Cornwall, but your leaving upset your father dreadfully.'

'I know, and I'm sorry for it.' Ashamed, she looked away. Her father would have suffered, but not Phillip. He'd have found another unfortunate to bully. 'There are many things I am sorry for.'

'I suppose that includes your involvement with me.'

'Yes.'

He took a step closer. 'I don't regret a minute of it.'

Warmth crept up her neck at his admission. 'It would never have worked for us. I'm sorry I persuaded you to abandon your reason and indulge me in the folly.'

He took her chin gently and turned her face towards him, his eyes were soft and tender. 'The fault lay with me, not you. There's no excuse about my actions. I didn't use you, Catrina. I wanted the very same things you did.'

'I know,' she whispered, desperately wanting to lean into his arms. The touch of his hand stirred memories that even after all this time were unbearably painful. 'But we were wrong to do so.'

'Why? Simply because we weren't of the same class?'

'You know as well as I do that it counts for nearly everything.'

'I wrote to you while you were at your Uncle's. I told you that we'd work it out somehow.'

She had to steel her heart against him. She edged away slightly, and he dropped his hand. 'Yes, you wrote, but your letters weren't enough. It was all too hard.'

'The assurance of my feelings weren't enough?' He stared incredulously at her. 'What more could you ask for?'

'A happy life without any unpleasantness from my family, your family, people in the village, no whispers...' She closed her eyes and turned away. 'I wanted the world to accept us. The very thing I couldn't have.'

'You could have had me, Catrina,' he murmured, 'as I only wanted you. The rest wouldn't have mattered.'

She glanced back at him as he made for the door. 'You're leaving?'

He grabbed his hat and gloves. 'I need time to think. I'll be back in the morning.'

'Why?' She was exhausted. She hadn't talked so much for a very long time and tiredness consumed her.

Travis stared down at his hat. 'I'm not sure.' He looked at her for a long moment. 'You haven't even asked why I no longer work for your father.' Quietly he walked out of the cottage.

Catrina hurried to the window. Leaning her head against the cold glass, she watched him step down the steep rocky path that led to the winding sheep tracks heading for the hamlet below.

Why had he left her father's employ?

CHAPTER 3

*A*fter a weary night of tossing and turning, of half formed dreams and hours spent staring at the ceiling, Catrina rose late. Lettie brought up a breakfast tray and opened the red velvet curtains. Outside the window, another sunny day brightened the mountains. Catrina picked at the boiled eggs and toast, her stomach clenched at the prospect of seeing Travis again.

A night of worry had brought her no closer to the answers for her questions. Obviously, much had changed in Travis's life in the last few years. While she remained stagnant in the Highlands, he had come into money. He'd once mentioned a trust he would gain, and clearly it had come to him since she'd been away. Her mind drifted back to the life she once led.

When she was a girl, Travis and his family had come to live in the local village of her father's estate, but he had gone away to school in York as a youth, only returning home the year he was hired by her father.

She knew of the Millard family; his strict grandmother, Ailsa and wild cousin, Estella. They lived in the large house

19

down the lane behind the blacksmith's shop. Ailsa was the widow of Doctor Millard, the onetime village doctor, and whom Catrina barely remembered for he had died not long after their move to the village. The rumours had been that the doctor lost his fortune in speculations, and a doctor of reduced circumstances couldn't afford to live amongst his wealthy clients. Catrina remembered snippets of her father mentioning Millard as an acquaintance and when he learned of the fellow's misfortune he offered him the post as village doctor.

Estella became a companion to the vicar's wife, the dainty and sickly Mrs Holton. Both Estella and Travis had lived with their grandparents since children when their individual parents died unexpectedly. The school in York had given Travis a good education, and being the grandson of a once wealthy doctor allowed him to be above the common labouring man, but not high enough to be an appropriate suitor for her, the daughter of Sir George Davies, Esq.

However, that didn't stop her when, that summer, she had despaired of ever marrying a decent man she could love, and Travis Millard entered her life. That summer, three years ago, he arrived at *Davmoor Court*, her family's county house in Yorkshire, and became the dependable man her father employed. The man, her father said, was intelligent, honest, discreet and hard working. That Travis had rejected all offers from suitable patrons to pursue a life in more exalted circles did the rounds of drawing rooms for months. No one understood why he wanted to be an estate manager, least of all, his grandmother.

During his first few months at *Davmoor*, Catrina became aware of him as he oversaw the work of the house's east wing extensions. Tall, handsome and with an easy manner, he had come to her to discuss the project when her father and Phillip left for business in Dublin.

It wasn't just his good looks which first attracted her to him. Travis held himself in a way completely different to the men she knew. Phillip's awful, bragging friends were rude to her, and at Phillip's insistence made her feel nothing more than a butt for their vulgar jokes. In contrast, her father's elderly acquaintances, those who were widowed and seeking a new wife, a ready-made mother for their children, all fawned over her. They treated her like she was made of spun gold and didn't have an intelligent thought in her head. Marriage to someone in either group was unbearable to consider.

Travis did the opposite of any man she'd ever known. He came to her with ideas or problems of the building plans. He discussed every aspect of the construction with her. He asked for her advice and suggestions. Most of all, he made her laugh. While walking the grounds together, out riding, or sitting on the terrace surrounded by plans, he talked and laughed, making her feel a part of his life. No one had done that before. No one had cared for her opinion, or simply listened to what she had to say. It was refreshing. It was lovely.

She fell in love with him before she was aware of it. And then men who hoped to have her hand in marriage grew dim on the edge of her conscience. They became a backdrop to her life, like players on a stage, but at the centre was Travis.

Then she became aware of the rumours about them and fled to her uncle's home to think on what to do, and make the biggest decision of her life. Marriage to Travis would have been fraught with difficulties, too many to deal with. It wouldn't have been fair to either of them. She decided instead to go travelling, forget him and see the world.

Returning to Davmoor, she witnessed him in the arms of that trollop, Myrtle, and knew her decision had been the correct one. She'd gone home and stepped into the middle of one of Phillip's infamous parties...

A knock interrupted her memories. Catrina pushed the tray away and climbed out of bed as Lettie entered again. 'Yes?'

'Mr Millard is here, Miss.'

Catrina stared out the window. Lost in her thoughts she hadn't seen him arrive.

'He came the back way, Miss, over the brow. I saw him when I went to hang out the washing.'

Catrina nodded and sighed deeply. Trust Travis to do the unexpected. 'Inform Mr Millard I will be a few minutes. Ask him if he wants refreshments while he waits.'

'Yes, Miss.'

When Lettie left the room, Catrina discarded her night-gown and washed. She donned a fresh chemise and a front fastening corset then stared at her clothes. 'Lord, what does it matter what I wear?' Disgusted at her vanity, she yanked out the first garment closest to her. Dressing quickly in a white blouse with white lace at the collar and cuffs, and a dark blue skirt, she then brushed out her hair and tied it up into an unflattering bun at the back.

At the door, she stopped and, racing back to the dressing table, pulled out her hairpins and brushed it again. This time, she gathered it up onto the top of her head less tightly and secured it with pearl combs. She added pearl earrings to her ears and a dash of perfume to the throat. So armed, she left the bedroom and headed downstairs.

Travis sat in her chair by the low fire, drinking tea. Half hidden by the door, she watched him replace his cup and saucer on the tray and then lean forward, his elbows resting on his knees. The sadness on his face tightened her chest. Why did he seem so miserable?

'Good morning.' She walked into the room, a small, hesitant smile on her face.

He stood and bowed his head. 'Good morning. I hope you slept well?'

She raised her eyebrows, noticing the worn look on his face. 'About as well as you it seems.'

Smiling, he sat down again as she took the chair opposite. 'The hamlet boasts an inn, but the inn doesn't boast a comfortable bed.'

'There isn't the need for it, I suppose. Visitors are rare up here.'

'Is that why you came here?'

Her hand faltered in pouring out some tea for herself. Straight to the point yet again. Travis wasn't one for polite chatter, she remembered. She glanced at him from under her lashes. 'I didn't care where I was. But the remoteness proved to be what I needed.'

'How did you meet Henley?'

'At the train station in Stirling.' She added sugar to her cup and stirred. 'The rain had soaked me through and I'd caught a dreadful cold. I'd been travelling aimlessly for three days. My mother's family came from near Stirling, but I had forgotten the town's name. Not that there was anyone I would have called on. I do not know them. Anyway, Hugh saw me, coughing and shivering, in the waiting room on the station and took pity on me.'

'How noble.'

She jerked at the sarcasm in his voice. 'I will not, under any circumstances, allow you to disrespect Hugh. He saved me, helped me when I was at my lowest point.'

'How is keeping you here, helping you?'

'It's what I wanted. To be so far removed from everyone and everything I knew. I was ashamed of myself, beside myself with humiliation.'

'Because of me.'

'When I left Estella's wedding, people were laughing at me. They knew you were with Myrtle. The men at the barrel made crude remarks and gestures. I was mortified.' She left her chair and went to the window. It was wrong of her to let him think he was the blame for her departure. But how could she tell him of what happened once she arrived home?

'It could have all been avoided.'

'Do you think so?' She gave him a brief smile of amusement. 'My father and Phillip would have been against our marriage. Also, I knew I wasn't what your family wanted for you either. Your grandmother certainly believed I wasn't right for you. She told me once that you needed to marry a young woman who'd not challenge your every word, unlike me.'

'I don't know why she'd say something like that. A biddable wife would have me bored within weeks.'

'For some reason she is very much against us, the Davies family. Do you know why she resents us so strongly?'

'No. Besides, their opinions didn't matter to me.'

'It mattered to them though, to all of them. I might have been Sir George Davies daughter, but in your Grandmother's eyes I was nothing and she made that plain to anyone who would listen.' Her smile turned sad. She moved towards the fire as he rose and walked to where she'd been standing. Catrina nearly chuckled at how they coordinated their movements like human chess pieces.

With his long fingers, Travis lightly touched the petals of the flowers in a vase that stood on the small table. 'My grandmother likes to control everything. She's had free rein with both Estella and myself because our sets of parents died young and before their time, especially mine. Why do you think Estella is so wild? It's all because of Grandmother. Estella never wanted to be a companion. She wanted to go to the cities and sing in theatres. My grand-mother was disgusted at the idea, and rightly so.' He sighed resignedly. 'It's always been a battle of wills between those two with me in the middle once Grandfather died. Even Estella's marriage was fraught with difficulties. She was with child, you know. It was a terrible time...' He gave her a long stare. 'But you should never have listened to Grandmother.'

'What is past is past.'

The minutes ticked by. Catrina remained by the fire absently watching the flames lick the apple wood logs. How was she going to overcome this? Travis coming here had stirred up too many memories, too much pain. How would she return to the humdrum life of only a few days ago?

She looked at him over her shoulder. 'So, why did you come here, Travis?'

'To see if you really were the Catrina of whom Digby spoke.'

'Well, I am, and we have spoken. Now you can go home.'

'Are you Henley's mistress? The truth now.'

'No, I am not, nor have I been. But are you content with the truth or do you prefer lies?'

'I believe you. I'm sorry I didn't before. I was shocked to learn of you through Digby, I suppose. His tale was sordid and I'm sorry I fell for it. I know that some gentle women become mistresses, and to think you had...'

She waved towards the door. It was too difficult having him so close. She couldn't think straight. 'We've said all there is to say. Please go.'

He jerked away from the window and stepped towards her with the fluid movement she remembered. 'And what if I wish to stay here a while longer?'

She lowered her lashes to hide the yearning in her eyes. He still had the power to melt her. How easy it would be to hate him, but it was impossible. The love she felt for him had never vanished. 'There is nothing for you here.'

'I beg to differ.' His eyes darkened as though drugged. 'There is much here I want.'

'No…'

'Yes.'

'It's too late, Travis. So much has happened. We're different people now. We always have been.'

'Once that was an issue between us, but not now. Our roles have changed.'

'We don't know each other like we used to, if we ever did.'

'So, we'll begin again then.' He smiled and took her hand, the contact sending shivers along her skin. 'We might have matured a little more, become a little more wiser, but underneath we're still Catrina and Travis.'

'We cannot.'

'Oh yes we can, my lovely. I've waited years for you.'

'No, you haven't.' She raised her chin and glared at him. She didn't believe him. 'I wouldn't have crossed your mind at all until you overheard the conversation between Hugh and Digby.'

'Not true.' His hand slid gently up her arm, across her shoulder and around behind her neck. 'You've haunted me constantly. I searched for you.'

His touch flamed her awakening desire, a desire that had lain dormant for so long. She could not become entangled with him again. It was too late, too much had passed. 'You must go, Travis. I cannot do this.'

'Why?' The caressing of his hand stopped. 'Why can't I taste you again?'

'And open old wounds?' She stepped away, needing breathing space. 'I think not.'

'Is it because of Henley?'

Catrina gave him a long look. 'There are many reasons.'

His lips tightened until they were edged with white. 'Why didn't he marry you?'

'He already was.'

Travis jerked back. 'I see. That makes sense now. He hides you up here away from the world and—'

'That's not true. You haven't any notion of what it's been like. His wife was frail, but they were still devoted to each other. I am like a daughter to him. Why won't you believe what I say?'

'He's ruined your reputation. His friends think you are his mistress. Even those in the hamlet down there became abrupt yesterday when I asked where you lived.'

'With you coming here twice in as many days will add to their beliefs.' She sighed. 'They speak mainly Gaelic and I don't understand a word of it. It makes communication difficult.'

Silence stretched between them broken only by the sparks crackling up the chimney. Travis came and sat back down, and she sat too. They both stared into the fire. Then he spoke, 'I was young, Catrina. Imprudent. I was making my way in the world. First, I planned to work for your father for a few years and then I wanted to spread my wings and perhaps use my brains to make some money, be my own man. I wanted land of my own, lots of it. Perhaps not in England, I entertained thoughts of going to America, Canada or even Australia. When you entered my world, it threw me. All my ideas grew intertwined with having you as my wife. I didn't know if I could do it, or if it was even possible to do it.'

'I can understand that.'

'I was terrified I wasn't good enough for you. How could I be? An estate manager and you, Sir George's daughter. It wasn't possible I thought. Yet, my heart didn't listen to my head.'

'Nor did mine.'

He gave her a brief smile. 'I laid awake at night wondering how we could be together and make everyone happy. I didn't know the answer. You couldn't live in my manager's quarters, not after being in the *big house*. And as a manager I couldn't suddenly live in your father's house and eat at his table. Your brother, Phillip would never have stood for that. It was all such a mess.'

'I know.' She wanted to reach out and take his hand, but she kept her hands folded in her lap.

'I made a mistake, one terrible mistake.'

'Really?' Her sarcasm made him frown. 'Just one?'

'Yes. I should never have kissed you. If I hadn't we might have been able to salvage at least a friendship out of all this and you'd still be at home where you belong.' He stood abruptly. 'That is what hurts me the most. That you have been denied your rightful place with your family.'

'It was my choice.' She scrambled in her head for the right words, to say anything but what actually happened. 'I... I wasn't happy at home. I saw my life as being Father's and then Phillip's hostess until he married, and I hated the thought of it. I was never Catrina, but only Father's daughter and Phillip's spinster sister. A Davies, true, but a lesser one.' She bowed her head. And after the incident at the party, staying truly hadn't been an option.

'Is that why you've not come home?'

She sighed heavily. 'Partly.'

He looked intently at her, as if trying to see into her head and read her mind. 'What happened between us is long forgotten by the village. Nothing would have been said had you returned after a few months away.'

'I haven't gone home because I didn't want to return to the emptiness that I left. Yes, I miss my father, but I couldn't live there...' Not anymore. And to see Travis go about his life would have been too painful. She hadn't wanted to grow old alone and be pitied.

He jerked to his feet. 'I must go.'

Her head snapped up at the sudden decision. 'Go?'

Like a repeat of the day before, he collected his hat and gloves and went to the door. 'I'll be back tomorrow.'

'Travis?'

He turned. 'Yes?'

'Why did you leave my father's employ?'

Smiling, he twirled his hat slowly in his hands. 'I'll tell you tomorrow.'

CHAPTER 4

ravis kept her waiting impatiently until after the midday meal before he appeared on the track coming up the mountain. Annoyed, more at herself than him, Catrina pretended to be busy when he knocked on the door. The last thing she wanted was for him to think that she'd spent the day waiting for him to arrive. Determined to show indifference towards him, she was on her knees before the cabinet in the sitting room, spilling out its contents over the square carpet rug. Books, newspapers, an old sewing basket, balls of wool, playing cards and numerous other items covered the floorboards.

Catrina glanced up as Lettie showed him into the room. 'Oh, Travis. Forgive me, you've caught me in a muddle.' She smiled sweetly and waved at the surrounding mess. 'I was searching for something, and the time has flown by without me realising it.'

He reached out a hand to help her to her feet, his eyes cold. 'Shall I return another time?'

'Heavens, no. You're here. Why make the climb twice in

one day?' She stepped away from the cabinet's debris and smiled at Lettie. 'Tea, please.'

'Actually,' Travis tilted his head, 'Perhaps we could go for a walk. The day is rather lovely out.'

'Excellent idea.' This time her smile was true. A walk outside in the fresh air was far more acceptable than being trapped in the sitting room with him for an hour or more.

They left the cottage and walked up the steep slope behind the cottage, stopping only when they reached the top. In all directions the mountains soared, interspersed with deep dark gullies, the sides of which, if hit by the sun, were covered in purple heather and green bracken. On the horizon, the sapphire blue sky met with the steel grey of the sea.

'What a magnificent view.' Travis stood, hands on hips, surveying the landscape. He smiled at her, which made him look younger, more the man she fell in love with. 'It makes you feel like you're on top of the world here.'

'Yes.' Catrina breathed in the pure cold air. In the shadows of the rock crags, snow still lingered, but alpine wildflowers were doing their best to burst into flower for the brief time they had without ice cover.

He gazed into the distance at the jagged skyline. 'If you must spend time away from home, then here is a good a place as any.'

'True.'

'Do you get lonely?'

'Sometimes. However, Lettie is my constant companion, a dear friend as well as my servant. I wouldn't have stayed for so long without her. And then Hugh comes and stays for a few months in the summer and the time passes quickly.' She sat on a large flat rock.

'What do you do together?'

Picking at the moss by her feet, she told him of the uncomplicated days they shared. 'The first week he is here I simply read all the newspapers he brings for me, a great many of them so I can catch up on all the world events. It's too hard to get a regular newspaper up here to the cottage. Hugh and I have wonderful discussions about what we read. He tells me all about the events he has attended in London, the plays and operas.'

'What else?'

'We read books, go on picnics. Hugh is an enthusiastic painter. When the weather is fine we spend days outdoors while he paints, and I read. We grow vegetables and harvest them. Last summer we made jam and conserved the fruits we picked. We walk. Sometimes we fish in the river down there.' She stood and pointed to the streak of silver glittering in the sun far below. 'Though not so much last summer, as the rough terrain was difficult for Hugh. His age and health restricts him now. Mainly we talk. We talk for hours about everything and anything.'

She walked on over the summit and, holding her skirts high, headed down the narrow sheep rut. The blurred grey-green view of the seemingly never-ending distant highlands and the dark North Sea didn't hold appeal for her today. She'd seen it all before, many times, and with Travis here, her mind was annoyingly distracted by his close proximity. Her emotions swung in every direction with him near.

Travis followed her, their aim a wooded area much further down the incline. 'And at night?'

'We dine and play cards or chess. That is all.' She huffed and shook her head. 'You still don't believe me, do you?'

'Yes, I do. I'm sorry. I'm behaving badly again.' He dipped his chin and looked at her from under his lashes.

'Indeed.'

'Perhaps tomorrow we could go into one of the towns and have some tea.'

'I don't think so.' She quickened her steps despite the hazardous descent.

'Why not?'

She rounded a rocky outcrop and kept going, the edge of the thick woodland looming closer. 'I don't go to any of the towns or villages.'

'Surely you must have at some point?'

'Rarely ever,' she snapped then wondered why she was irritated. It wasn't his fault she lived like a hermit. Often Hugh had suggested they go to Inverness or some other town, but she declined each time. It was easier to hide from the world.

'Well, we'll change that I think. I fancy taking you out. I want to buy you things.'

'Don't be absurd!' She glanced over her shoulder and gave him a quelling glare. 'I'm not your plaything, something for you to bring out and show off and then hide away again. I didn't let Hugh do it and I certainly won't let you!'

'Catrina!'

Once in the shaded shelter of the trees, she darted along faster, putting distance between them. Why did he have to come and change her world - again! Tears rose, blinding her to the pitfalls of the forest floor. She tripped over a tree root, but steadied herself.

'Catrina, stop for God's sake, will you? You'll twist an ankle or worse.'

She skidded to a halt and turned back to him. 'Yes, we should go back. This was a terrible idea.' As she went to pass him he grabbed her arm in a crushing grip, stopping her.

'Now.' He peered down into her face, his eyes narrowing with impatience. 'What's this game you're playing?'

'Game I'm playing?' Wide-eyed and confused, she stared at him.

'Yes. A simple stroll has turned into some mad race with

you snapping and snarling at me.' His fingers lessened their powerful hold. 'Do you want to explain why you're behaving this way and saying those outlandish things to me?'

'Why have you stayed?' She asked a question of her own, pulling her arm out of his grasp.

'To spend time with you. Isn't that self-explanatory?'

'To what end, though?' She persisted, angry at the tears burning her eyes. She hated to show such weakness. If only he hadn't come and reminded her of all that she had lost.

'I want to get to know you again.' Travis frowned, the expression on his handsome face showing the uncertainty he felt.

'What good will it do?' She pushed past him and headed back up the incline.

The effort it took for them to climb back up robbed them of breath and the ability to talk easily. At the top, she paused to suck in air and rest her burning legs. But before Travis had the chance to speak, she strode off once more, back to the cottage.

Once inside she fretted, knowing that any moment he'd join her and want to talk. She was tired of talking. Tired of dragging up the past. The past was dead, and her future wasn't too bright either.

Why couldn't he just leave her alone and let her get on with it?

The room grew dark as clouds skittered across the sun and she shivered. Tiredness plagued her eyes. All this emotion wore her out. And for what outcome? He'd leave, and she'd be forever tied to this cottage, living quietly until she grew old and died.

Was it enough?

Suddenly, the thought of the lonely years stretching out before her was so distressing she couldn't breathe.

She bowed her head, hating herself for allowing her life to go down this forlorn path.

Was it too late to start again? She'd be twenty-six years old on her next birthday. Was it too much to ask for a little bit of happiness or contentment?

Did one awful incident, years ago, need to be repaid by a lifetime of nothing? None of it had been her fault, she knew that. And if she was honest with herself, she knew she had made a huge error in leaving home and not facing her brother and his friend. But she had been so ashamed, so frightened of what the consequences would be that fleeing into the night had seemed the best alternative.

So, hadn't she suffered enough?

Wasn't it time to strike out on her own again. Travel the continent perhaps, as she longed to do once before. Hugh would not deny her the expense of it. He often encouraged her to do something similar. But she'd been a coward and remained in the cottage, afraid to let the world in. However, Travis's arrival heralded a change, a chance once more to live.

Her mind swirled with ideas until she felt sick. Travel. Independence. Adventure. Striking out. Exploring beyond this cottage. Making larger decisions than just the small everyday concerns here. Could she do it?

She bit her thumbnail and thought of the intrepid female travellers that criss-crossed the globe, never caring of opinion, of society or that standards of class that relegated them as oddities for daring to step outside the role of wife and mother.

How brave they were...

'You are lost in thought.' Travis stood in the doorway.

'Yes. Your appearance here has shown me that I'm wasting my life in these mountains.'

'Then some good has come of my actions then.' He gave her a half smile.

'More than you know. I plan to travel. Hugh will finance me, I'm certain.'

His face tightened. 'I hardly think he should be made to. Write to your father, perhaps?'

Catrina shook her head, suddenly impatient to start living again. She held her hands out to the fire and he came to stand beside her. Her stomach clench at his nearness. Her sense sprang alert, hungry for him, as if they had laid dormant like a bear in winter, and who was suddenly in need of a feed.

As far as the hamlet believed she was a fallen woman living here with Hugh. She had no reputation to uphold. If so, then she might as well make the most of it and be doubly damned.

Half formed ideas whirled.

Could she do it?

Was she bold enough?

Independence. Adventure. The words filled her head like a chant. Catrina straightened her spine, finding courage.

Could she have one night with Travis – one night to last a lifetime? A night that would erase the sordid, humiliating and hurtful attack she endured at Phillip's friend's hands?

One night to be loved properly by a good man, then putting the past behind for once and for all, she could leave England.

Catrina stared at Travis, who was watching her. The only time she'd felt alive was when she'd been in his arms. For one hot summer she'd laughed, loved and been reckless and free.

Could she do it again?

Could she seduce him as easily as she had a few years ago? Would he go further than just a kiss?

Would he agree? Yes, he would. She'd seen the way he'd

looked at her, touched her. His eyes spoke to her a language of their own.

What did it matter that he didn't love her. This could be a fitting farewell. A goodbye.

One night…

As if he sensed it, Travis took a step closer. 'What are you thinking?'

'It's getting late. Would you care to stay for dinner?' She held her breath, waiting for his answer.

His gaze didn't falter. 'I'll not make it back down the valley once it's dark.'

'Then perhaps it would be wise to stay the night here.'

'But *would* it be wise, Catrina?' His wry smile made her stomach clench.

'Maybe not, but I have nothing to lose.' She raised her chin in challenge, ignoring the way his eyes darkened with some inner desire. She was insane to do this, had completely lost her wits. Yet, she wanted him, nothing had changed on that score. At twenty-two she had laid down on the sweet lush grass in the wood and wallowed in the sensuous glory of being kissed by Travis Millard. The memory of their affection lingered to this day. Could she do it again? What harm would it do to sample such heaven again?

The sun of the morning gave way to typical Highland weather of low grey clouds and mist covering the peaks. Sudden rain beat a steady tattoo on the window, as though playing a musical solo just for them.

Catrina lit another lamp on the sideboard while Travis added more logs onto the fire. The crackly noise of the sparks going up the chimney became a duet with the rain.

She set out the chess board for them to while the hours away until night descended.

Later, in the middle of the sitting room, Lettie set the table for their simple meal before leaving them to return to the kitchen. Sitting down, Catrina glanced around, hoping all was perfect. She expected to be nervous, but instead was rather numb… or accepting, and that worried her more than anything.

Was this always meant to be? Had fate destined Travis to come here and for her to spend this night with him?

Travis sat down opposite her and poured them some wine she had brought out from her meagre supply. Hugh always came with fresh supplies from town, wine being amongst them.

'I hope you like chicken soup?' She ladled a good portion into his bowl and then her own.

'Indeed, I do.' He picked up his spoon, a smile playing around his lips.

'What is it?' She paused in taking the first sip from her spoon.

'I never thought this day would end with us having a meal together.'

'What did you expect?'

'I don't know.' His smile faltered. 'I didn't stop to think about any of this. I just wanted to be with you. I am filled with questions.'

'Still? Haven't I answered enough of them?'

He ate some of his soup and then leaned back in the chair. 'You've changed, Catrina.'

'Naturally.'

'I think I expected to see the young woman I once knew.'

'That would be impossible.'

He reached across and took her hand and her spoon splashed into her bowl. 'In the last few hours since inviting me to stay you've changed again, grown hard and appear uncaring, but I'm hoping it's just to protect yourself, which I fully understand.' He brought her fingers to his lips and kissed them. 'Talk to me.'

She tingled at his touch. 'There's nothing more to talk about. I've told you so much already.'

'I want to get to know you again, but if you'd rather not, then I can leave this minute if you wish it.'

'Do *you* wish to go?'

'No.'

'Nor do I want you to leave.' She slipped her hand away from his and lifted the spoon to her mouth, although she wasn't hungry. 'Eat before it gets cold, Travis.'

He did as she asked, but she could tell his mind wasn't on the food before him. They finished the soup and Lettie carried in plates of fish and vegetables.

'Tell me about Hugh Henley,' Travis asked, sipping his wine leisurely.

'What more do you wish to know?'

'Tell me of the first time you met him.'

Swallowing a mouthful of fish, Catrina wiped her lips with the napkin. 'He found me in a wretched state at a train station. I cannot even remember where, but Hugh tells me it was in Stirling. I have no clear memory of it really. I had a terrible cold and I'd been robbed by a group of boys that morning. They seemed to be barely ten years old, I felt so stupid and useless that I could let children do that to me. I had nothing but the clothes I wore.' She played with the stem of her wine glass, replaying the horror she felt at being robbed, of being sick, the despair. 'Hugh says that as soon as I spoke he knew I wasn't from the working class and this interested him. He wondered how I had got into such a state with no family to protect me. His kind heart did the rest.'

'Where did he take you?'

'To a hotel at first. He came back the next morning and we talked. I told him my sorry tale and he mentioned he had a hunting lodge in Scotland. Naturally, I accepted. I'd have done anything to have a safe roof over my head after days of moving around the country wondering what I'd do. I'd acted irrationally in trying to find my mother's family without a proper address. They may not have even wanted to know me anyway, least of all take me in. It's been years since my mother died and even when she was alive we had little contact with them.'

'What did Henley ask for in return for his help?'

'Nothing. What could I give him at that time? I was sick and became sicker. The cold turned into pneumonia. He brought me here, hired Lettie and helped nurse me back to full health. A few weeks later he had to leave before the first snows trapped him here.' She took a gulp of the tart wine. 'Once the snow falls we are cut off for months. After his wife died that winter, Hugh divided his time between London, his home in Gloucestershire, and the odd visit here in the warmer months. I saw him only twice in those first eight months. He kept supplies coming so I or Lettie wouldn't have to venture out to the nearest town.'

'Didn't he think it was odd? What of your family?'

'He understood my need to simply hide for a while. I wrote to my father and assured him I was well and comfortable. Hugh was the perfect gentleman. He saved me, and I will always be grateful to him for that. I love him for that. Hugh wrote every week, he sent books and newspapers and I had Lettie to talk to. I was quite content.'

'Are you still content?'

'I was...' She took a deep breath. 'If this is how my life is to be, being alone, I will not argue. It could be a lot worse.'

'But don't you want more? A husband, children?'

'I plan to make changes to my life. It may not involve those particular issues, but I —'

'What about going home?'

She shook her head. 'It's too late for that now. My family has weathered the storm about me without too much suffering. I shan't re-enter their lives to cause problems again. After my mother died, my father withdrew into himself and I've never been close to Phillip. Hugh tells me my brother is married now, so Davmoor has a new mistress.'

'I know that. I went to the wedding.' He looked apologetic.

'Oh, yes, of course.' She blinked and glanced away. Travis would likely know more about her family now then she did.

'Why haven't you asked me about them?'

'Hugh writes and lets me know if he's seen or heard anything regarding my father. He kind of spies on him from a distance. As for Phillip, I care nothing for him at all.'

'He does make it difficult for people to like him.'

'He is an ogre and much more.'

'You don't miss him then?' Travis laughed.

'Not at all. But I do miss my father and the estate.'

'I believe he misses you, too, most dreadfully.'

She smiled, thinking how kind he was to say that, then she sighed deeply. 'You must understand, Travis, for me to live here I have to forget my old life. It's the only way I can survive.'

'Have you thought of moving away, to one of the cities and perhaps get work as a teacher or governess or something?'

'No, I hadn't thought of doing that. Not teaching.'

'Why? It a noble profession.'

'Because I couldn't think of nothing worse than looking after someone else's children when I cannot have my own. Because living in a large house as a *staff member* when I have been brought up to be a mistress of one, is beyond endurance. If I rejoin society in any capacity, I will want all that I cannot have – a lovely home, children, a man who loves me.'

'It is not beyond hope, Catrina.'

She played with the edge of the starched white tablecloth. 'I'll be twenty-six soon. I have no way of obtaining any of that now due to my actions, and it hurts too much to pretend otherwise. I lost my chance to marry. And I cannot live at Davmoor and be content with becoming an old spinster, pitied by my family. It would kill me.'

'And existing here is better?'

'I am my own person here, and I am not faced with friends becoming married, having children, experiencing things denied to me.' Sadness overwhelmed her.

'They are only denied to you if you allow it.'

'It's not so simple. I am attached to scandal, who would want me now?'

'You are beautiful, many a man would want you, believe me.'

Her heart fluttered at his words. How easy it would be to believe what he said, but she knew her father's society and how they would talk about her. 'I am no longer a young girl who has beaus wanting my hand in marriage.'

'People get married at any age, Catrina. You're not even thirty yet.' Travis scoffed. 'Your excuses are very weak, my dear.'

'You don't understand!'

He raised his eyebrows mockingly. 'I never expected you to be a coward.'

'That's not fair!' She gripped her napkin.

'The girl I knew thrived on challenges.'

'That girl is dead.' Picking up the napkin, she straightened it out again.

'No, you're alive, but living like the dead by being buried *here*.' He shot up from his chair, throwing his napkin on the table in disgust. 'I never had you down as someone who'd just exist, Catrina. You of all people I thought would grab life with both hands and do with it what you will.'

'Well, that shows how little you knew me.'

'The girl I used to know was strong and fearless. She would light up a room the minute she entered it with her beautiful smile and happy laughter, so vibrant. Men would follow her about the room, hanging on to her every word. Women envied her, wanted to be her.'

She laughed derisively. 'I doubt that is the case now.' She fiddled with her fork. 'For some reason since coming here I lost the urge to...' She rubbed her forehead. 'Oh, I don't know. I just changed, that's all. It seemed too hard to leave. Perhaps I am a coward.'

'You don't have to live this way anymore.' He stormed over to the fireplace and savagely kicked a log into place. 'You can have all that you wish for.'

Catrina pushed back her chair, the food forgotten. It seemed like forever since she'd been confronted with such masculinity. She found she liked it and had missed being with the opposite sex. Hugh, an old man, never stirred anything fierce within her when he was here. They would sit and talk, go for walks, or eat their meals all in a genteel atmosphere of friendship and devotion.

The tension became thick in the small sitting room, full of suppressed anger and something else simmering under the surface. Catrina smiled, enjoying the confusion on Travis's face. She had the urge to upset him some more, to make him feral with rage. She wanted to see his emotions, hear the sounds of a real man. The cottage needed to be filled with the essence of a man in his prime.

He turned to face her, his gaze stripping her with its naked longing. 'Catrina...'

Her skin tingled with anticipation. Was it something primeval within her that wanted this? Or was she really a despicable wanton?

She held out her hands.

Travis flung himself at her, clutching her to him like a drowning man. 'Lord, I've missed you.'

'And I've missed you.' She couldn't fight what she felt for him. She closed her eyes as his head lowered, and when his lips barely touched hers, she sighed thankfully. Digging her fingers into his hair, she pulled his head closer and captured his lips.

As though drugged, she arched into him as he sought the soft skin beneath her ear. His hands gripped her hips bending her into his frame, moulding her against him.

'I've dreamed of you...' she whispered.

'Sweetheart, you've never been out of my mind.'

'Upstairs...' The words whispered over her lips as she kissed him with abandonment, holding him tight.

He leaned back to stare at her. 'What? Are you sure?'

'Absolutely. I have nothing to lose now.' She swallowed, slightly frightened of the act to come, but instinct over-rode her brain. Her body melted for him, knowing impulsively that Travis wouldn't hurt her - that what she experienced that night long ago was not normal, not how it could be.

'No, Catrina, I—'

'Don't talk.' She placed her fingertips over his lips, silencing him. 'We can do that later.' She smiled, taking his hand.

'But.'

'I want this, Travis.' And she did. With complete surety she needed to erase a brutal attack with one of tenderness and caring.

'Are you completely certain?'

'Yes. I know my own mind. Please don't deny me.'

'I could never deny you.' Travis shook his head, and with a grin, left her to lock the door. From the back of the chair he took the blanket that she used on cold winter nights and laid it down over the rug before the hearth. On his knees, he beckoned her.

She didn't hesitate to join him, but walked leisurely towards him, soaking in the scene before her. She would make this one night last a lifetime and in the end she would know what it was to be loved properly.

Joining him on the floor, she reached out and undid the knot of his tie, then next she unbuttoned his collar and tossed it aside, too. With deliberate slowness she concentrated on one button at a time on his shirt, gradually revealing the smooth skin beneath that held a smattering of dark hair. One-handed, she slipped the shirt over one powerful shoulder and then the other, kissing the exposed skin. His harsh intake of breath made her smile. Did he think she'd forgotten what he'd taught her that summer three years ago? Skills that she had perfected in her dreams ever since.

Tugging the shirt free of his trousers, she ran her fingertips over his ribs and downwards towards the ultimate prize. Her heart skidded in her tight chest, making her breathing shallow and rapid.

'Now my turn, beautiful,' he murmured, kissing her throat.

With the same slow pace she had used, he undressed her. Her dress followed his shirt onto the floor and her corset proved no match to his nimble fingers. Within minutes he had her freed from its constraints and her breasts spilled out into his hands.

It was her turn to suck in a breath as he licked and teased her nipples through her cotton chemise. Heat invaded her, spiralling from deep inside, urgent and needy. She grasped his shoulders, tilting her head back, allowing him access to whatever he wanted. This was right and true. With every kiss, her fears and nightmares receded.

He stripped her of her chemise and laid her down on the

blanket, the only sounds were the shifting logs in the grate and their own breathing. His hands roamed her body, seeking all her dips and curves. Where his fingers led, his mouth followed, sucking and licking, kissing and savouring every inch of her.

Her pulse pounded loud in her ears, her skin felt on fire and inside she was a pool of melted sensations.

'Catrina...' Travis murmured, his lips pulling on her nipple, first one side and then the other.

She clutched at his hair, arching up to him, eager to be fulfilled and satisfied. She felt like she had waited her whole life for this one moment, for him. 'Travis, oh...' Her voice came out on a low moan as his fingers stroked her most private place.

'Are you sure?'

'Definitely. I've dreamed of this, of you.' She knew it could be beautiful with him.

'You're so ready for me, darling...' He left her for a moment to rid the last of his clothes and she urgently reached for him.

With deliberate slowness, Travis slid one hand behind her head to kiss her thoroughly. She responded eagerly, clutching his back and buttocks. When he entered her, she gasped. He filled her so completely.

For a second, they lay still, savouring the moment as one. Then Travis moved gently. He set the rhythm and she was a willing participate in the dance. As his thrusts became more urgent, Catrina felt herself rise again. Pinpoints of explosive sensations burst in her body, spiralling up until with one final lunge, Travis pushed her over the edge of reason and she was soaring with him on a sensual journey made for two.

CHAPTER 5

*C*atrina turned her head and gazed at Travis's profile. His hair seemed so dark against the snow-white linen of the pillow. In sleep, the hard planes of his handsome face seemed more gentle. His eyelids moved and she wondered what went on in his head right now. Was he dreaming? She stretched slowly, careful not to wake him. She was a little tender in a few intimate areas, but couldn't help smiling as the sun streamed through the curtains they didn't close last night.

Last night...

Her smile became a contented grin as she thought of the passion, the sheer pleasure of what they shared. The first time she had kissed Travis, all those years ago, had been lovely, yet she'd been an innocent. Then, Phillip's friend had abused her and her world had shattered. However, last night had been a completely different experience, as she knew it would be. Travis's gentle loving had wiped away the brutal assault of the man in the dark, the man who'd been an animal, goaded beyond his sensibilities by a braying, drunken crowd.

She shook away the memory and concentrated on watching Travis sleep. After hours of loving in front of the fire, they'd retired upstairs to begin again. In the quietness of the midnight hours, she had delighted in exploring Travis's hard male body, and in turn had marvelled in the way he studied hers. His hands and mouth had discovered every secret, every hollow and inch of her body. Time and again they had brought each other to the height of excitement, and afterwards, luxuriated in being close. They reaffirmed the link, the affection they once shared.

Not once had she felt guilty. What purpose would that serve? She was already ruined for any man and would continue to suffer her self-imposed isolation. Therefore, free from social restrictions and her own conscience, she had abandoned herself to Travis and the illicit gratification a man can give a woman. During the night hours she gave no thought to the past or to the future. Probably that was naive of her, but so be it. With a future as dim as hers, she needed some memories to take with her into old age.

'What thoughts run through your pretty head, I wonder?' Travis rolled onto his side, facing her, and kissed the tip of her nose.

She refused to answer that question. Sharing her body was different than sharing her mind. In the night hours they had made no promises to each other, and so she would guard her heart. 'Good morning.'

'Indeed, it is a good morning, my sweet.' Under the sheet, he found her breast and fondled her. He gently pushed her back, so he could kiss her.

She squirmed, giggling like a girl as heat invaded her again. She could never have enough of him. Catrina ran her foot up his leg and inched closer, welcoming the carnal hunger that once more built within her. 'What would you like for breakfast?' She nibbled his ear, enjoying the chance to touch and feel him in the lightness of day.

'Can you not guess?' His hand slipped over her hip and he pulled her firmly against him, letting her know just how aroused he was. 'I'm hungry as a horse.'

'Then I'll get you some hay.' She wiggled against him, chuckling.

Travis laughed, rolling onto his back and taking her with him so she lay on his chest. 'Is that the best you can offer me?'

Catrina nipped his bottom lip with her teeth. 'Give me a minute or two and I may come up with something else.'

'Well, while you think about it, I'll play,' he murmured, running his hands over her bottom. 'And perhaps I'll provide you with some inspiration.'

'Yes…' she whispered, kissing him, liking the raspy feel of his unshaven jaw. 'Yes, perhaps you will…'

'Sweetheart…' He closed his eyes and she smiled at the pleasure she gave him.

Much later, wrapped only in a sheet, Catrina sat on the chair by the window and nibbled on the toast Lettie had brought up for them. Far from embarrassed, Lettie had breezed into the bedroom with the breakfast tray, despite it being after midday, and left it on the small table before tidying up the tossed clothes and straightening the curtains to let more sunshine into the room.

'What shall we do today?' Travis asked, sipping tea while reclining on the bed, the blanket barely covering his groin.

'Do?' Catrina stared at him. 'Aren't you returning home?' She tried to keep her voice neutral sounding, not wanting to dwell on the moment when she'd have to say goodbye to him.

'No, I hadn't thought to go today.' Travis frowned and sat

straighter. 'I thought I could stay here a while longer. We have much to discuss.'

'Oh?' She blinked in surprise.

'You wish me to go?'

'I simply expected it, that's all.'

'Can I stay?'

She smiled, ignoring the way her stupid heart thumped in response to his plea. 'Of course, you may stay.'

'Good.' Travis grinned, and she glimpsed the cheeky younger man she once knew who had swept her off her feet. He placed his teacup down. 'Let's take a hamper and go for a walk. The weather looks fine.'

'Yes, I'd like that.' Catrina stood and tucked the sheet more securely around her. 'We can walk to the next peak or find a spot by the river. Very few people come up this way until it becomes warmer.'

Travis left the bed and, unashamed of his nakedness, walked over to her and wrapped his arms around her waist. 'As I said, we have much to discuss.'

Her smile faltered, and she moved out of his arms to start dressing. What did they have to discuss? She could think of nothing that would cause that statement. She had given him all that she had. Did he wish to continue their relationship? Did he want her for his mistress? And what of Hugh? He was due to arrive any day now and he cared deeply for her. What would his reaction be to Travis? After all, this was Hugh's cottage.

With these tortuous thoughts whirling around in her head, she hardly listened to Travis's light chatter while they dressed. She paused as she pulled on her stockings and watched him button his shirt. Why didn't it feel odd to have him in her bedroom? The feeling of him walking around such a feminine room should be foreign; her personal effects were all open to his gaze, yet she felt nothing out of the ordinary. Was she now so completely opposite to everything she'd been taught as the daughter of a respectable family?

As each minute ticked by, the original idea she had planned of spending one thoughtless night with an old love was slowly unravelling. The last thing she expected was Travis staying beyond the morning.

An hour later, the hamper in his one hand and his other holding her elbow, Travis guided her to a delightful spot by the river. A slight breeze blew his hair and Catrina fought the urge to reach up and touch it. Their passion and loving indoors only an hour ago now seemed distant and she didn't know why. It was as though the world outside had calmed their heated blood and brought them to their senses.

After laying the red plaid blanket on the lush grass, Travis opened the hamper and together they brought out the food and drink. 'Lettie has done herself proud.' He grinned, uncorking a bottle of cider and pouring out two glasses. 'Which do you want? Chicken or ham?' He held out the plates for her to choose from.

'A little of both, I think.' She filled her plate and ate, savouring the tenderness of the chicken leg.

'Cheese, or onion?'

'Cheese, please.'

He loaded two small chunks onto her plate and then held up the loaf. 'Bread?'

'No, thank you.' She leant against a tree trunk and cradled the plate in her lap as she sipped her cider. Birds twittered high in the branches and the rush of water flowing down from the melting snow created a symphony of nature music that was soothing and pleasant. For a while they ate in peace, content with their own thoughts and the scenery around them. Every now and then, a fish leapt from the water, making them jump at the sound and they would smile at each other.

Crunching on an apple for dessert, Catrina finally broke the quiet. 'Tell me about yourself. Why did you leave my father's employ? What have you been doing since?'

Tossing away his apple core, Travis laid down on his side, propped up by his elbow and faced her. 'A year after you left, I turned thirty and came into my inheritance. My grandfather was a fickle man, studious and clever. He believed men didn't become men, or gained suitable knowledge, until they gained the age of thirty. So, my inheritance had languished in a bank account. I always slightly resented the fact, because since Grandfather's death, when I was two and twenty, I had the sole responsibility of Grandmother and Estella. In my eyes I was not only a man, but head of the family. Yet, Grandmother handled the finances left to her, and with mine unattainable, I needed to work, or find an income in some way.' He paused for a moment, as if thinking of that time again. 'At school I had studied hard and then afterward, worked for various people in a variety of jobs to prove myself.' He plucked at a loose strand of wool from the blanket. 'I didn't know what I wanted to do in regards to my future. I knew my inheritance wouldn't be enough to allow me to become a man of leisure, but nor would I be happy with some menial employment.'

'I remember you once telling me that you worked in a bank because you didn't want to study to be a doctor, or lawyer, or join Her Majesty's services.'

'Yes, that's true. Only, I hated the whole environment of the bank. I need to be outside, feel the sun on my face. I had studied agriculture at school and felt that was where I should be. My dream was to buy land in another country. Only, profitable farms, in my reduced circumstances are hard to find. In the meantime, I knew I'd have to learn about farm management. It seemed the sensible thing to do was to become an estate manager. However, those positions rare.

Plus, I didn't want to move away from grandmother as she is feeling her age.' He wound the wool thread around his finger, pulled it off and wound it again. 'Your father is a friend of the bank manager. One day he came in and we started talking. An hour later I had an invitation from your father to visit Davmoor Court and see what I thought about managing the estate.'

'Our former manager had died.' She recalled the older man, who died of a stomach complaint.

'Yes, and I replaced him.'

'From what I remember, your Grandmother wasn't very happy about it.'

'She was extremely upset. Felt it was beneath me to work for another man. She wanted me to follow Grandfather and become a doctor, or at least go on to Oxford and continue to study. And maybe mix is higher circles, so I would meet an heiress. But it wasn't for me.' He smiled, reaching out to pluck a grass stem from the edge of the blanket. 'Do you know my Grandmother's father was a wool trader? Her family believed she had *married up,* by becoming a doctor's wife. In her eyes, I was going down. She wanted me to go on to Oxford. Sadly, I'm not that much of a scholar.'

'An estate manager isn't the bottom of the scrap heap,' Catrina said, indignant. She'd never liked his grandmother.

'No, but nor was I my own boss. Also, I didn't gain the respect my grandfather had.' He shrugged. 'She was right in many ways. I wasn't happy working for another man, any man.'

'My father treated you well.'

'But I was still a staff member, not an equal, Catrina. You don't know what that is like.'

Bowing her head, she stared at her half-eaten apple. 'No, I don't know what it is like. I'm sorry.'

'I stayed with your father longer than I wanted to, only

because I thought I would hear of you through them. After two years though, I knew it wasn't going to be. Your father never once mentioned your name.'

His words brought her pain, but then, she deserved it, for hadn't she given her father pain too? 'Was my father unhappy about you leaving?'

'Yes, but he understood. He is a good man. A true gentleman.' Sitting up, Travis rested his arms on his bent knees and stared out over the river. 'I had invested a good portion of my inheritance on your father's advice. The returns were better than I ever dreamed of. His guidance allowed me to buy a place of my own.' He gave her a sideways glance. 'I always wanted to be a land owner and suddenly I had the chance to purchase well.'

'I am pleased for you.' She smiled warmly, happy that he'd got what he wanted. 'Where is this land?'

'Davmoor.'

The blood drained from her face. 'What did you say?'

CHAPTER 6

*D*avmoor Court? How is that possible?' she whispered, both puzzled and shocked. 'How did father allow it? I mean...how did you buy the estate?'

'I didn't buy the entire estate, just one of the smaller farms.'

She stared at him unable to comprehend it. Travis now owned part of the estate?

'Your father is ill, Catrina. He has been for the last two years.'

This extra news hit her harder. 'Hugh told me in a letter that he'd heard about Father being sick during the winter, but he said it wasn't serious.'

'Not many people have known the extent of it, but he's been laid low for months at a time. While he is incapacitated, Phillip is in control.'

She leaned closer, peering at him. His evasive gaze and the tone of his voice alerted her to something more. 'Tell me everything.'

Travis turned and cupped her cheek. 'Sweetheart—'

'Tell me.' She jerked away, sensing bad news.

'Phillip has money problems.'

'Are you certain? My father is a wealthy man, you know that.'

'But your brother has been in a position of power...' A nerve twitched in his jaw. 'He gambles.'

'Gambles?' Her eyebrows shot up. 'So? All men gamble in one way or another.'

'Not just at cards or dice, like a normal man, but on wild investments, both here and in other countries. Also, he wagers huge sums on the racehorses and the like. He spends more money than is earned.'

He wasn't serious, surely? She closed her eyes momentarily. 'And?'

'It's become common knowledge, especially now that he is selling so much.'

'Selling?' Why did she keep repeating him like some village idiot? Saying it a second time didn't make it sound any better.

'To recoup his losses, he sold off some of the estate. Last autumn, I bought eighty acres and Bottom End Farm from him.'

Catrina stared at him. 'That's the whole southern end of the estate!'

'The eastern boundary is shorter too. Fred Carstairs bought sixty acres that borders his property.'

'Why did Father allow Phillip to do such a thing?'

'I have a feeling your father isn't in any state to know.'

Her heart skipped a beat and she read in his eyes what he didn't say. 'Is my father dying?'

He took her hand and nodded. 'Yes. I believe he is.'

Scrambling to her feet, she yanked at her skirts, freeing them from the remains of the picnic. The blood roaring in her ears seemed as loud as the white water of the river. Her father dying? Oh God! Tears pricked behind her eyes and she hurried along the length of the riverbank. Her father dreadfully ill and Phillip gambling away the family money. Could it be any worse?

'Catrina!' Travis rushed after her but didn't speak as she stopped and covered her face with her hands. Pulling her against him, he let her cry out her deep sadness.

A little while later, he tilted her head back and kissed away the dampness of her tears and then held her tight once more. 'I'm sorry I had to tell you such news. I will take you home.'

She nodded into his shirt. 'Lettie will be wondering where we are.'

'No, I mean home to Davmoor.'

'Davmoor?' She reared back out of his arms. 'I can't go back.'

'You must want to see your father?'

'Of course, I do, but it's not possible.'

'Why ever not?'

'Because it's been too long. How will they receive me? He will be hurt by my behaviour. He might have cut me from his life altogether when I left.'

'They are your family. They love you. I'm sure of it.'

Her mind whirled. Could she go home? She ached to see her father again, but what of Phillip? The thought of being in his presence sent shivers down her spine. 'I don't know...'

'Could you live with yourself if you never spoke to your father again?'

'You don't understand.'

'Then allow me to understand by telling me what keeps you from your family and home.'

A silver fish jumped clear of the water, showering droplets of water on the river's surface. Catrina took a deep breath. 'There is no sibling affection between Phillip and I. We barely tolerated each other.' An understatement if ever there was. 'That's why I didn't want to stay and be dependent on him for the rest of my life if I didn't marry. But I couldn't marry the eligible men who came calling. I didn't like them, never mind love them. Father allowed me to follow my instincts, but Phillip became pugnacious. I rejected too many suitors, many of them his friends... We, Phillip and I, argued all the time. Father didn't care about my future...' She knew she was rambling but couldn't stop. 'To go back to them, to their match-making. To all the dinner parties listening to the overbearing, preening assortment of gentlemen who bored or disgusted me...'

'That's the reason? But I won't—"

'I haven't finished.' She bowed her head. 'The night I ran from Estelle's wedding I arrived home to find Phillip and some of his worst friends were having a party. They were wild and disgusting as always. I tried to make it to my room unobserved...' She lifted her head to stare out unseeingly across the water. 'Phillip was drunk, as they all were, and he saw me. He alerted his friends to my presence, jested that the virgin ice queen was home. He told them I was frigid with gentleman, but I panted after the working class.' She gave Travis a sideways glance when he stiffened and swore.

Focusing on the dazzling, rushing river, she continued, 'Phillip had a hunting horn in his hand and blew it. He said I was a fox that needing catching and that I must be taught how to behave towards gentlemen or I'd never be married. He spurred the men on, wagering that none of them could tame me. As I ran upstairs, he blew the horn again and they all chased me. I didn't go to my room, knowing that Phillip would think of there first, so I went up the staircase to the nursery above and then up again to the attics. I didn't have a lamp with me. It was so dark. I fell over some furniture and they heard. Braying like dogs at one of my father's hunts, they came after me. A man, I don't even know his name, grabbed me from behind. They all started chanting and laughing, drinking and clapping as he...he...'

Travis rubbed his hands up and down her arms. His hard expression tightened the skin across his cheekbones. 'Enough, darling, you don't need to go on.'

'You need to know.' She stared into the distance, her ears throbbing with the sounds of that night. 'From behind the man lifted my skirts and... violated me while Phillip and his friends watched on.'

'Where was your father?' Travis grunted, emotion making his voice catch.

'Away in York.'

'And that's why you ran away?'

'Yes. I couldn't look at Phillip. I wanted to kill him, but I was so humiliated that all I could do was run. I couldn't face anyone. I was worried I might be with child and I didn't want to marry the man who...who did that to me.'

'I will *kill* him and the bastard who did that to you!' Anger gave his words a clear and lethal tone.

She spun around to face him fully. 'No. I'll not see you hang for him. He's not worth it, none of them are! I've done enough penance. I won't suffer again because of Phillip, not ever.'

'He must pay for such brutality. You're his sister for Christ's sake. He's an animal.' Travis whirled away from her, swearing. Picking up a stone, he flung it across the river, where it landed with a thud on the bank on the other side.

'Phillip has hated me ever since I was born. He resented Father marrying my mother when he was a boy. That hatred intensified towards me as Father and Mother were devoted to me, not that they didn't try to love Phillip, but he was such a difficult person to give affection to.' She sighed to herself. 'The years spent here with my own thoughts have allowed me to realise all this, if nothing else.'

'I am amazed at your acceptance.'

'I've had time to heal. It wasn't easy, believe that.'

'He'll never be allowed to hurt you again. I promise you.'

'What happened to me...well, nothing can be worse than that, can it?' She stepped towards him, aware he only just kept his rage in check. 'He doesn't have the power to hurt me anymore.'

Travis's gaze held hers. 'Then you can go home.'

'I suppose so.' She put on a brave face, though inside she quavered. He didn't know what he was asking.

'Catrina, you won't be alone. I will be with you.'

'Don't be foolish. How can you possibly be with me?' She frowned. 'I won't be your mistress, despite last night.'

He jerked as though she'd slapped him. 'You do not think very highly of me if you believe I would reduce you to that, my dear.'

'Then what?'

'Surely last night—'

'Last night was meant to be one night only. A memory for me...'

'I don't comprehend your meaning.' He stepped back, his expression cold. 'You planned for it?'

'I never expected you to come here, to find me.'

'I know it shocked you, but I meant no harm to you.'

'Harm?' Catrina huffed. 'You have no notion of what you've done coming here. You've invaded the one place I was safe, the place I now call home.' She clenched her fists into the folds of her skirt. 'You've turned my life upside down. Again!'

Travis went white around the lips. 'Then why ask me to stay? Why invite me into your *bed*?' he scorned.

'Because I wanted something to remember you by once you had gone.' Her bottom lip wobbled, and she bit it. What a fool she was, allowing her simple heart to thaw and feel again. 'I have nothing, Travis, and you coming back into my life only reminds me just how much I left behind. Whatever reason made you come here, it wasn't for my benefit, but yours. You will leave here, and I shall remain.'

'No, you won't.' He shook his head, puzzlement in his eyes. 'Do you honestly believe I would leave you now? Do you think me such a cad as to do that?'

'But you must. There is no alternative.'

'Nonsense. Stop being a coward and face things.' He took a step closer, speaking urgently, but she backed away. 'Catrina, I may have only been here for three days, but I knew within one minute of stepping through the front door that I would never leave you, that I would never give you cause to be alone for another day.'

She put her hands up, as though to warn him off, to protect her heart from any possible glimpse of happiness. 'We cannot.' She wanted to slap him silly for giving her hope. 'You are cruel to do this.'

'Catrina,' his earnest look made her catch her breath, 'I love you. I always have. Why do you think I asked to stay and wanted to get to know you again?'

'It's-it's impossible,' she murmured, though the cracks of hope were growing larger and shattering her reservations.

'By what law? I am unmarried, as are you.' Travis took her hands and kissed them in turn. 'If you'd not run away that night, we would have been married these last years.'

'But would we have been happy?' She dragged her hands out of his hold and walked away.

'Do you honestly think we wouldn't have been?'

She looked back at him. He was so handsome, so very male. 'I would have, but you might not. You weren't ready for marriage back then. I have figured that out if nothing else.'

'I am ready now.'

She smiled at his words and the honesty in which he said

them. She had adored this man so intensely, but could they recapture what they once had? Could it be more than just a physical attachment? 'And what of your family, your friends and acquaintances? What would they say about you marrying me?' Why was he doing this to her? 'The same problems we had then are still there. If I return, there will be scandal attached to me. Can you live with the talk?'

'I'm not saying it will be easy, Catrina, all I'm saying is that I care for you and want to be with you.'

'You are not a fool, Travis. There will be gossip, I can't re-enter society again. That alone would put strain on a stable marriage, let alone one with the history we have.'

'I don't care about your family's society. We don't need them, do we?'

'No.'

He leant against a tree trunk, crossing his feet at the ankles. 'I have thought about this.'

'Really? When?'

'Since the moment I saw you again.' He pushed away from the tree and walked towards her. 'Yet before that, I always knew that if I found you, and you were unmarried, then I'd marry you.'

Taking a deep breath, she stared down at the ground. 'I have schooled myself to not wish or hope...I've had to be satisfied with what I have now.' She gazed at him. 'It is hard to be offered something so wonderful...'

'Catrina, listen to me. We will be married.'

'Can we be happy?' She thought of his grandmother and shivered. The woman's sour face and barbed comments would likely be a thorn in her life should she return home. And she dare not think about Phillip's reaction.

'I don't doubt it, my love. We'll get married, have children and be together. I predict we will be very happy indeed.'

'I'm scared. It's all happened so fast.'

'No, we've had years to prepare, only we didn't know it at the time.'

'I can't help being frightened, Travis.'

'I know, sweetheart. Come here.' He gathered her into his arms, crushing her in his effort to show his affections. 'We'll be blissfully content I promise.'

Catrina laid her cheek against his chest, breathing in the scent of him, a mixture of soap and the fine wool of his jacket. Could she risk leaving the safety of the cottage to be with this man?

Travis tilted her face up and kissed her softly, reverently. Then, releasing her, he knelt onto one knee and from his waistcoat pocket brought out a small box. 'Will you marry me, Catrina?'

Her breath caught in her throat as he opened the box and a small diamond on a thin gold band sat nestled in a bed of blue satin. 'Oh, Travis. A ring?'

'I know it isn't terribly grand...' He slowly rose, his blue eyes unsure.

'It's beautiful.' She gently touched the box, awed by the gift. 'I never expected this.'

'It is the reason why I kept you waiting yesterday. I had to go into Inverness to buy it and the supply wasn't ideal.' He flushed a little. 'And my funds at present aren't as I would like.'

She silenced him with a kiss. 'You didn't have to buy this. A plain gold band is all that matters.'

'I'll get you one of those too.' His eyes shone with the love he held for her. 'Is that a yes, then?'

'Yes.' The intense power of emotion that only this man could evoke within her, rose again, squashing her doubts. Yes, the time had come to take a chance on life again, to take a chance on him once more. He had offered marriage and she would take it gladly, and make of it what she could.

'Catrina…' The huskiness of his voice cut through her thoughts and she sank to her knees and joined him on the carpet of new spring grass.

'Love me, Travis, please.' She held him tight and pushed away the shadows of those who wouldn't be happy to see her again.

'I do, darling. I will forever.' He shrugged off his coat and laid it out for her before quickly joining her. 'I'll keep you safe, I promise.' He kissed deeply, letting his lips and hands show how much he could love her.

Unlike the love making of last night, which had been slow and sensual, this time they came together fast and urgently. Removing only the parts of their clothes necessary, Catrina welcome Travis's strength as he nipped and sucked at her. In one deft move, he nudged her knees apart and entered her, holding her against him in a fierce embrace.

'I'll love you till I die…' His agonised whisper filled her ear as he thrust deep inside.

'And I you, my love.' She raised her hips, urging him in deeper, needing him to fill her.

'Catrina.' His cry echoed throughout the trees and she grinned, enjoying the power she had, the way she could make him lose himself. She gripped his buttocks and rode the wave of magic until she forgot the past and believed only in a bright future.

CHAPTER 7

*H*and in hand, talking quietly, they strolled back to the cottage as the sun slipped down, heading for the horizon.

Catrina smelled the small wildflower bouquet she held, one that Travis had picked for her as they ambled through the woodlands and along by the river. 'A perfect day.' She held out her hand and gazed at the ring on her finger.

'The best day ever.' Travis grinned, kissing her hand he held. 'It is a promise of what our future holds.'

She smiled, feeling a range of emotions flow through her. She was excited and relieved to be loved by Travis, but also sad and frightened by her father's illness and the changes ahead. Returning meant being near Phillip, which filled her with dread, but at least she wouldn't be living with him, having to put up with his spitefulness. Instead, she'd be married to Travis and have a new home with him. 'I cannot believe I'm going home, at long last.'

'I can't promise that our future will be perfect every day, but,' Travis swung her hand high, a mischievous smile playing on his lips, 'I'll work hard to make it so. Naturally there will be some small differences of opinion at times. And we'll have children to share our time with. Lots of children.'

'Really?' Her eyebrows rose, and her stomach fluttered. How she had dreamed of babies and children. 'Lots?'

'Dozens?'

'I hope not dozens, though perhaps three or four. I don't want to be fat for the rest of my life.'

He pulled her to his side. 'You'll still be beautiful to me, fat or thin.'

'Get away with you!' She jumped away, chuckling. 'Tell me again of the travelling we'll do.'

He swung her around, kissing her and laughing. 'We'll go everywhere, Africa, India—'

'And America!'

He kissed her again. 'Yes, we'll see the whole world if we can. I have such plans, Catrina. The farm is only the start...' Travis paused as the cottage came into view. 'Your maid is at the gate. Did she think I had kidnapped you?'

Catrina looked up to see Lettie waving at them.

'I'm starving.' Travis adjusted the empty hamper in his hand. 'I hope Lettie has cooked a fine meal.'

'I believe food is all you think about, Mr Millard,' she said saucily.

'I believe it is. Well, that and you.'

Amused, she shook her head and smiled at Lettie as they reached her. 'Have you cooked a large meal, Lettie? Mr Millard is a hungry man.'

'Indeed, I have, Miss.' Lettie grimaced. 'And it's a good job too, for Mr Henley arrived only ten minutes after you left.'

Shocked, Catrina hesitated. 'Why didn't you come and find me?'

'Mr Henley bade me not to.'

Some of the joy left Catrina. How had she managed to forget that dear man and his imminent arrival? Searching the cottage windows, she could see no evidence of her friend and champion, but beyond those walls he waited and no doubt wanted an explanation.

Travis gripped her elbow, all laughter gone from his face. 'Whatever he says or does, makes no difference.' His gaze locked with hers. 'You're mine, and I am yours. We'll be married and be happy.'

'I know.' She ducked her head, knowing that while happiness beckoned sadness would also come. 'Yet, I owe him everything, Travis. You need to understand that.'

He frowned. 'Will he be violent?'

'No, of course not. He's over sixty.' Catrina placed her palm against Travis's chest where his heart lay. 'He's a good man. Like a grandfather to me. Let me talk to him first. You stay in the kitchen.'

Travis bristled at the request. 'You want me to stay in the kitchen? Why? We should face him together. Are you ashamed of me? Do you think—'

'Shh!' She placed her finger on his lips, his male pride making her shake her head. 'Please, Travis. Let me talk to him first.'

He ran his hand through his hair, but nodded. They carried on through the gate and vegetable garden. Once inside, Catrina washed her hands and tidied her wayward hair. With a fleeting smile at Travis, she left and walked to the sitting room. After a calming deep breath, she opened the door.

Hugh, seated in the chair opposite the one she always used, lowered his newspaper and smiled at her. 'Dearest girl.'

'Hugh. Lovely to see you.' She hurried across to him and kissed him as he rose to his feet. Their embrace was heartfelt and strong.

'You look magnificent as always, my dear.' He lifted her

chin high to study her face. 'Have you been spending time in the sun again? There are more freckles I fear.'

'Who cares about freckles when there is warmth in the air? Winter was too long and too cold this year.' She took his hand and sat on the stool at his feet. He looked tired and his skin a little grey. His sparse hair, now all white, had been combed, but his suit held creases and his blue eyes, usually so sharp, seemed dull. 'Did you have a good journey?'

'The journey was tolerable.' He shrugged, scratching his side whiskers. 'But I'm getting too old for it, I fear.'

She blinked, wondering at his meaning. He'd lost weight and his age showed more today than at any other time she'd known him. 'Shall I get you some tea?'

'No, my girl, for Lettie has plied me with enough tea to fill a bucket.'

'I'm sorry I've kept you waiting.'

'Nonsense. You didn't know I'd arrive today. I decided to arrive a day or two early.' He smiled tiredly. 'In fact, I think my letter only mentioned sometime this week, is that not so?'

'Yes.' She lowered her lashes, feeling the unease between them, or was it just her imagination?

'Now, tell me about your young man.'

Her head shot up and she stared at him. 'My-my—'

'Lovely girl, I saw you from the kitchen window.' He patted her hand and brought her ring closer to inspect. 'Do not be alarmed. Nor must you feel guilty. I won't have that at all.'

'Hugh, I—'

He held up his hand, silencing her. 'I have been a selfish man, Catrina,' he paused and sighed, 'such a silly old man.'

'No!'

'Hush, hear me out.' He looked out the window, his gaze softening. 'The day I brought you here...it seems so long ago, doesn't it? I feel like you've always been in my life, always brought joy to my heart just by thinking of you. However, I cannot, *will not*, keep you any longer.'

'You saved me.' Tears filled her eyes. 'Without you, I shudder to think what might have become of me.'

'The same could be said for me too, you know.' He gave her a wry smile. 'I was a man drowning in the last years of his life, hating and denying the fact I was growing old, am old.' He shook his head, the light leaving his eyes. 'I refused to accept that my wonderful wife was leaving this earth, leaving me. So, I clutched at you to save me from loneliness. For a while I felt beyond death, having you was like having the daughter I never had. You gave me a few years of happiness that I otherwise would have been denied.'

She nodded, wiping away the single tear that trickled down her cheek. 'Happen we saved each other then.'

'It's a certainty, my dear.' He cleared his throat and sat straighter in the chair. 'Only now...now I believe the time has come to part ways. We no longer need each other.'

'We don't?' The thought scared her for a moment.

'You need to leave here and find a new life. There's so much you have to live for, Catrina. From what I saw, that fellow seemed very enamoured by you. I take it he's the one from your past? What is his name...Milton?'

'Travis Millard.'

'Millard. Yes. And are you pleased he's come here.'

'Very much so.' She smiled and squeezed his hand, hoping to reassure him. 'I still love him, Hugh, I never stopped.'

'Hopefully he will love you just as much in return then, as you deserve.'

'He says he does, and I believe him.'

'Good.' He patted her hand. 'That delights me greatly.'

'What about you though?'

'Me?' He settled back in the chair, relaxing his shoulders. 'I'm going home to Gloucestershire for good. My health isn't great and I'm tired, so very tired. I'm selling my London home.' He smiled lovingly. 'Knowing you are taken care of will comfort me in the time I have left.'

'Don't talk of that.'

Frowning, he shook his head. 'Death comes to us all, my dear. I've no regrets. I've lived a good life and I believe I have been a good person, on the whole.'

'Of course, you have,' she chided. 'You're a wonderful man.'

'Enough of me for the moment. Tell me what Lettie doesn't know. How did Millard find you?'

'Travis overheard you talking about me. He heard you speak my name to Mr Digby.'

His face lost what little colour it held. 'Oh lass, I'm sorry.'

'No, don't be. Please, don't give it another thought, for he has come and asked me to marry him.'

'And it is what you want?'

'Indeed. Absolutely. I have dreamed of such a thing happening for so long. I can't believe it will come true.'

'And are you sure he truly loves you?'

'Yes, I'm sure.'

'Good. This world is a hard place and being loved makes living easier.'

'Hugh?'

'Yes?'

'Do you know the news about my Father? He is ill, Travis tells me.'

'Yes. I heard some gossip, which is why I came straight here instead of staying a few days with friends in Whitby as I had arranged.'

The happiness drained out of her. 'I'm sorry you had to change your plans.'

'I am not. Especially now you are leaving, and our time together is so short.' He rubbed his knuckles with his other hand as if in pain. 'You must see him, your father. I'm not sure how long he has.'

'Yes. Travis is taking me home.'

He gave her hand a final pat and then waved towards the door. 'Send him in, will you? I wish to speak to him.'

'You do?' His stern look made her rise. 'There is nothing—'

'Ah!' He held up his hand. 'Please do as I ask, dearest. Also have my man bring the trap around.'

'The trap? Why? Do you need something from the village?'

'No, I'm going home.'

'Oh no, Hugh. Stay. It'll be dusk in an hour or two.'

'There is enough light for us to get safely down the mountain to the next village. I'll sleep the night at the inn along the way.'

'There is no need.' Distraught, she clutched his arm. 'I'll not have you out in the night air. Your bed is here. There is no reason for you to leave. I don't want you to.'

'Catrina.' He looked deeply into her eyes. 'I wish to go home. I can sleep at the inn tonight and leave early for the train. I only came to see you to persuade you to go home. Now that I know you are, and more importantly, I know you will be cared for, then I can rest easy and return to my own fireside. I have much to do this summer...'

'Surely you can wait until tomorrow?'

'I think not. I'm eager to get started.'

'What can be so important that makes you risk such a journey at dusk?'

'Personal affairs, my dear. Now send young Mr Millard in, if you please.'

She straightened and edged to the door, emotion clogging her throat.

He waved her on. 'Hurry, please, I don't want to lose all the light.'

She sped into the kitchen and gabbled to Travis that Hugh wished to speak to him.

Lettie hovered, her anxious gaze darting between them. 'Is everything all right, Miss?'

Travis put down his teacup, stood and jerked his jacket straight. The distress in Catrina's eyes made his chest ache, but her watery smile helped ease the constraint. 'Lettie, make Miss Catrina some tea.' With a gentle touch to his darling's soft cheek, he left the kitchen and walked through to the front room. The door was open and he walked in.

'Mr Millard?' Hugh creaked to his feet and held out his hand, which Travis shook.

'Yes, and I believe it's Mr Henley?'

'Indeed. Please, join me.' Hugh waved to Catrina's chair.

Once seated, Travis leaned forward, his hands clenched on his knees. 'I am sure you have many questions.'

'Not really. I have gained a great deal of knowledge about you over the years from Catrina.'

Nodding, Travis took a deep breath. 'I've been searching for her.'

'I see.'

'Her disappearance was a profound loss to me. I didn't realise how much so until I saw her three days ago.'

'So, you will marry?'

'Absolutely.' Travis uttered a sardonic laugh. 'You may not believe me, but my intentions are honourable, I assure you.'

'Unlike mine have been, you mean.'

Travis stood and walked to the window. 'No. I know the truth. At first, I presumed Catrina was your mistress, mainly because of Digby's words. I didn't want to believe it. However, knowing the truth, I can never condemn you for looking after Catrina in the way you did.'

'She means the world to me, Mr Millard. I have had no one important in my life, but her, since my wife died. Sadly, we had no children.'

'And I love her.'

'I'm glad. She deserves to be loved properly. Can you provide for her though?'

'Yes. I have a small farm, which is more mine than the banks. I have some investments...' He stopped, wondering why he was explaining himself to this man.

'Good. I'm pleased to hear it.' Hugh's knees creaked again as he rose. 'I'm a sick old man, Mr Millard, and I will tell you now that everything I own will go to Catrina.'

Travis stared, surprised, but remained silent, knowing the old man hadn't finished.

'My entire estate will be put into her name with the hope that it'll be passed on to her children.'

'I see.'

'I hope you do.' Hugh nodded. 'I want to make sure that should she ever be left alone again, she'll find herself in a far more suitable position to take care of herself.'

'Only my death will allow her to be alone again. The moment I return home I'll make arrangements so that she will always have some security should I die before or after we marry. I learn from my mistakes.'

'Admirable. Good.' Hugh selected a pipe from the small pipe stand on the mantelpiece. 'Phillip, her brother, is a blackguard. You know this?'

'Yes, I do.' His guts clenched again at the thought of what that bastard had allowed to happen to Catrina.

'I wouldn't trust him in any way.' The older man took a tobacco pouch from out of an inner pocket in his jacket.

'Nor I.'

'Then you'll know that he needs careful watching?' Stuffing the tobacco into the pipe's bowl, he gazed at Travis.

'Don't tarry in getting married, Millard. I don't like the thought of her being anywhere near that beast.'

'I agree with you. I'll speak to the vicar the same day we arrive home.'

Hugh struck a match and smiled. 'Well then, I hope you both live a long and wonderful life.' He turned at the sound of the trap on the track outside. 'Because we don't move within the same society, I am unaware of your family and their position, but Catrina assures me you are worthy of her. I hope that remains so.'

'It will be my life's work. You have nothing to fear about my ability to provide for Catrina, or that I might live off your estate when it is hers.'

'So, all will be set once you are married?' Hugh puffed on the pipe stem.

'I foresee no financial problems.'

'And what of her family's acceptance, or yours for that matter?'

'We hope they will be happy to have her in their lives again, but if they don't, so be it. We will make our own family, have our own happiness.'

Hugh let out a breath of smoke and smiled with genuine pleasure. 'Catrina needs to travel. She needs to see everything there is to see. If you have the will, show her places and people.'

'I shall make sure she does.' Travis relaxed, liking the man, and starting to understand why Catrina loved him.

Hugh's eyes softened. 'She sees this place as a sanctuary, but soon it would have grown to be a prison. If it hasn't done so already. You've come at the right time. The past weighs heavy on her. It has to be put right.'

'It will be. I pledge you that.'

'That's all I needed to know.' From the table, Hugh picked up his hat and cane, the pipe sticking out of his mouth. In the hall, he called for Catrina, who came running with Lettie behind her.

'You are determined to leave this evening?' Catrina cried, holding his arm as they walked outside. 'I wish you would stay.'

Hugh kissed her forehead. 'I have things to do and so do you.' He glanced back at Lettie. 'Take care of your mistress, Lettie, and close up the house properly. Have all my personal effects sent on, you know where.'

'Yes, sir.' Lettie answered, bobbing her head. 'Thank you for your kindness, sir.'

'And thank you, Lettie, girl.' Hugh placed his hand over Catrina's. 'Keep the keys. This lodge is yours, my dear. I'll have my solicitor change the titles, but there are other things I need to discuss with you about all that. However, it will wait for another day.'

'Thank you, Hugh.' She kissed his cheek.

'You'll come to our wedding, sir?' Travis grinned.

'Would like nothing better, nothing at all, but well… we'll just see, yes?' Hugh hugged Catrina to his side. 'Later, you both must come to visit me when you have the chance.'

She nodded and kissed his cheek. Amazed at the swiftness at how her life had changed again. 'Yes, I'd like that.'

Travis stepped forward and shook Hugh's hand. 'We'll see you at the wedding, sir.'

'Excellent.' Hugh looked up at the cottage and silence stretched between them. 'Make sure you bring your children here during the summers, Catrina. I always thought it'd be a great place for children.'

'I promise.'

With help from his driver, Hugh climbed into the trap. Once settled, he reached out and clasped Catrina's hand. 'Look to the future, my girl, it is bright.'

'I will.' A cloud passed over her at the idea of seeing her

father dying, but she pushed it away. Whatever happens, she had Travis and he would help her, and that's all that mattered to her.

Travis moved closer and wrapped his arm around her shoulders in support. After watching the trap disappear down the winding track, Catrina snuggled more into Travis's arms. 'I still can't grasp how quickly all this has happened.'

He twisted her around to face him, his arms snaking around her waist, holding her tight. 'You've had Hugh to look after you, but it's my turn now.'

'But are you sure you want to for the rest of your life?'

'Utterly and completely sure. I promise you that you'll never have a moment to regret marrying me.' He kissed her and then smiled down into her face. 'Now, let's go and pack. Tomorrow, we go home.'

Her hesitation was only slight as she smiled up at him. Yes, tomorrow would be the start of the rest of her life. It also meant she'd have to face her father's fragility and her brother's hatred. Would she be strong enough?

CHAPTER 8

*T*wo days later, Catrina, Travis and Lettie were stepping down onto the crowded platform at York's impressive train station. The previous forty-eight hours has passed by in a blur for Catrina as they packed up the lodge and travelled to Inverness to catch the train. Saying goodbye to the mountains had drawn a few tears, but she knew that it wasn't a forever goodbye. She would bring her children to the lodge one day.

Her nervous excitement grew as the rumbling train ate each mile towards York. She hardly believed her eyes as she watched the passing scenery change from rugged Scottish mountains down through the lowlands and then into cultivated English countryside. The hectic noise of the stations where they changed trains or had refreshments shocked her. After the solitude of the lodge and mountains, it was hard to reacquaint herself with the mass of people again.

Now, as they manoeuvred through the piles of luggage and milling passengers, Catrina's head pounded. She tried to look everywhere, to see everything. It was like emerging out of a fog, or learning a new skill. She felt disorientated and had to readjust her senses to her surroundings. The noise, colours and smells of the city's large railway station bombarded her.

Travis leaned close. 'Don't look so frightened, darling. All will be well, I promise.'

Catrina smiled to reassure him she was all right and then peeked at Lettie to see if the girl appeared as tense as she was, but Lettie was counting the smaller baggage, her mind purposely occupied.

A black clad porter blew his tin whistle directly behind Catrina and she jumped. Crowds pressed her as they rushed to board the train. Some women wore beautiful clothes and ordered servants, while others, the lower classes, wore old coats and battered hats, held tightly to little children and baskets, their eyes wary and expressions resigned. Catrina held onto Travis's arm as he guided them through the people towards their trunks waiting at the end of the platform.

'We'll hire transport.' Travis signalled to a young porter to follow them with their luggage and took Catrina's elbow. 'Do you wish to go to *Davmoor* immediately, despite the late hour? If you are tired you can sleep the night at the farm and go there fresh in the morning.'

'As much as I don't wish to meet with Phillip, I must see my father straight away. I don't know how much time he has,' she said, climbing up into the first carriage lining the street. The setting sun threw long shadows. 'I just hope I'm not too late.'

After days of talking, they rode in silence through the dirty, congested city streets. People rushed home from an exhausting day's work, while shopkeepers began to bring goods inside off the pavements. The market stalls stood empty, fallen produce staining the cobbles. Turning away from the streets, the driver hurried the horses out towards the soft green countryside where the Davies estate lay. With bittersweet memories, Catrina stared out of the carriage at the passing familiar landmarks. Her stomach churned, and her throat grew dry the nearer they came to her old home.

Within twenty minutes, they were trundling through the old local village, bordering her father's estate. She was surprised that it hadn't changed, except perhaps it looked more worn. Ancient shop frontages remained the same with dark painted colours on their window frames and doors. The only brightness was in Mrs Hoddlesworth flower boxes in front of her haberdashery shop. Every spring Mrs Hoddlesworth planted blood red geraniums. The wide high street was nearly deserted apart from a couple of men sitting outside of the Blue Boar Inn, sipping pints of ale. They stared at the passing carriage and Catrina wondered if they recognised her. She remembered them. Sam Kilmister and Barney Poppleton both worked at the flour mill a few miles away. Sam's sister had once worked in Davmoor's laundry and Barney's mother had grown the best cabbages in the area, often winning prizes at the local fairs.

Catrina smiled to herself, remembering such small things before her gaze caught a scruffy black dog cocking his leg on a lamppost and, further on, a woman walked carrying a basket over her arm. Catrina didn't know her and thought it strange. Once, she'd known every person in the village and most in the district. Travelling beyond the green, which spread out at the end of the street and was boarded by mature fir trees, they veered right and headed for the estate driveway. Alongside the road, a young girl was shepherding a flock of squawking geese with a long stick. Again, Catrina didn't know her. Melancholy dampened her spirits. She was foolish to think things hadn't changed. Time didn't stand still.

She frowned passing through the opened iron gates. The

little gatehouse looked neglected and abandoned. Why weren't the gates closed and where was Bunton, the gate-keeper? She glanced at Travis, but he shook his head sadly. Rounding the bend in the drive, Davmoor Court loomed between the trees and her eyes filled with tears. The soft sandstone house, sitting directly behind a circular fountain, hadn't changed. For generations the manor had cradled the descendants of the Davies family and seeing it again after so long, Catrina's heart squeezed with love for it.

The driver slowed the horses and the carriage came to a stop in front of the steps. Travis helped her and Lettie down, but no staff opened the front doors. Catrina gazed around. The grounds showed the same neglect as the gatehouse. The lawn wasn't cut, overblown spring flowers drooped, their petals scattered on the drive. Weeds grew between the plants. Turning and walking up the steps, she noticed leaves and dust accumulated in the corners of the steps and by the doors.

Suddenly, one of the doors opened and Mrs O'Toole, the housekeeper Catrina had known all her life came out, her eyes wide with shock. 'Nay, it isn't Miss Catrina.'

Laughing, Catrina held out her hands and took those of Mrs O'Toole. 'It is me. I've come home.'

'Oh, child!' Mrs O'Toole forgot all etiquette and hugged Catrina to her ample bosom. 'Oh, dear girl, my dear girl. You're home. I never thought I'd see the day, truly I didn't.' She ushered Catrina into the house, talking excitedly.

At once the old smells of beeswax and lavender filled Catrina's nose as she stood in the hall and unpinned her hat. The house was exactly the same. Not a piece of furniture had been changed in the years she'd been gone. It was as though she had left only the day before.

'Your father will be overjoyed to see you.' Mrs O'Toole

took her hat and gloves. 'This is just what he needs. How have you been, my pet? Are you home for good? I'll have your room prepared. Nothing has been touched, only cleaned. The master has kept all your things.' The older woman turned and peered down the hall. 'Where is Ida? I'll have some tea brought in. Are you hungry?'

'First, I'd like to see Father.'

'Of course, of course. Silly me.'

'How is he?'

'Better today. He rallies a bit, and then will have a bad day.' Mrs O'Toole looked past Catrina at Travis. 'Oh, Mr Millard.'

'Good day, Mrs O'Toole.' He bowed his head and smiled. 'Can I leave Miss Catrina in your safe hands for an hour or two?'

'Need you ask?' She tutted.

Catrina turned to him. 'Aren't you staying?'

'No, darling.' He took her hand and kissed it. 'I'll go home and see how things are. You need time with your father. But I'll be back later this evening.'

'No, don't come back. You'll be tired. I'll see you in the morning.'

'Are you sure? I don't mind.' His eyes sent a clear message that he was at her disposal if she needed him.

'No doubt you have much waiting for you at home, including your grandmother.'

'Well, if you're certain, then I'll see you in the morning.' He kissed her cheek.

She watched him go back outside, sidestepping the piled luggage.

'Miss?' Lettie whispered, her expression anxious.

'Oh, Mrs O'Toole, will you show Lettie to the kitchen? I'm sure she is eager for a cup of tea and something decent to eat. It's been a long day. And then afterwards she can unpack in my room.' She touched Lettie's arm in reassurance. 'Mrs O'Toole will take care of you.'

'Come this way, lass.' The housekeeper guided Lettie down the hall and into the gloom of the back service corridors.

For a moment Catrina stood and soaked in the essence of the house with its thick dark wood furniture, the oriental carpets, the gold-framed portraits on the damask papered walls. Despite it all being the same as when she left, something alerted her to the fact that in some ways it wasn't. She couldn't put her finger on what it was though. She had missed the house, perhaps more than the people in it.

Taking a deep breath, she summoned the courage to go upstairs. Her hand slid up the smooth banister, her footsteps silent on the red carpet. On the landing, the only sound was the ticking of the long case cloak near the window. Shadows hugged the far end of the corridor, the east wing she'd never seen completed.

Turning right, she stole along towards her father's bedroom, feeling like an intruder. Her heart banged in her chest and she felt sick. Taking a deep breath, she steadied her nerves and pulled down her cuffs. After a soft knock, she opened the door and stepped into the quiet room. Her father lay in the middle of the large four-poster bed. She inched closer and found him asleep and looking older than she thought imaginable. Her father was a tall man, but always lean with it. Now he seemed skeletal, his skin stretched tight over his bones. His thinning hair was completely white, as pale as the pillow beneath his head.

Pulling a gold velvet-padded chair closer to the bed, Catrina sat down and took his dry warm hand in hers. 'I'm home, father,' she whispered, but received no response.

Looking around, she saw that the room was neat and dusted, a fresh vase of primroses stood on the mantelpiece. A small fire burned in the grate. The half-closed curtains kept out most of the evening sunlight, giving the room a golden gloom.

Her father stirred, his eyelids flickered and then opened. He stared straight ahead for a second and then slowly turned his head. He frowned. 'Catrina?'

'Yes, Father. I have come home.'

'Daughter.' His lips lifted slightly. 'So glad.'

She rose and kissed his grey-whiskered cheek. 'You must get better now, Father.'

'I'll try.' His eyes closed again. 'You'll stay?'

'Yes.' She sat down once more and let out a breath, relieved she had been given the chance to speak to him.

After a while, Mrs O'Toole quietly bustled in, carrying a tea tray. 'Here, Miss, you must be dry as a desert.'

'Thank you. I am.'

'I've informed Cook to make up a light meal for you.'

'Don't go to too much trouble. I'll just have it on a tray in my room.'

'As you wish, Miss.' The housekeeper gazed at her employer as she set out the cup and saucer. 'It'll do him the power of good to have you home. Has he woken and seen you?'

'Yes, we spoke, but only for a moment.' She accepted the tea and sipped it gratefully. 'Is my brother home?'

'No, Miss.'

Relief washed over Catrina and she relaxed the strain from her shoulders and neck.

'Mrs Davies is though, of course.'

'My sister-in-law.' Catrina felt odd thinking about the woman she didn't know and who was now related to her.

'She was having a rest when you arrived. You should go along and see her. Poor dear is aching for company...' Mrs O'Toole pressed her lips together as though to prevent herself from saying another word.

'I'll find her after I've drunk my tea. Unless Father wakes.'

'He'll sleep until morning. I've already given him his medicine. She, Mrs Davies, will be in her rooms, as always, Miss.'

'Is my sister-in-law, Aveline, is her name isn't it? Is she a nice woman?'

'Nay, it's not my place to say, Miss.' Mrs O'Toole avoided her gaze.

'That has never stopped you before if I remember correctly.' Catrina grinned.

'Aye, well...I best get back downstairs.' Mrs O'Toole bustled back out again and closed the door.

Her curiosity pricked, Catrina replaced the tea back on the tray and checked her father before leaving the bedroom. In the corridor, she turned and headed for the east wing. Recalling the original plans for the layout of the rooms, plans she had once pored over with Travis, she tapped on the last door and went in. The private sitting room was empty. 'Aveline? It is Catrina, Phillip's sister,' she called towards the bedroom. She gazed about in wonder at the room richly decorated in deep red, gold and coffee colours. The furniture was heavy and ornate. Large frames hung on the walls, all the paintings showed various naked female forms. It wasn't to her taste, but she couldn't help staring. She crept closer to the bedroom door, which stood open. 'Aveline?'

In the middle of the bedroom a wide bed dominated the space. In it, lay a petite young woman, her stomach large with pregnancy. She looked up and brushed away creamy-blonde curls from her pretty delicate face. 'Oh, a visitor?'

Catrina stepped forward into the room. 'I'm not disturbing you, am I? I'm Catrina, Phillip's sister.'

The green angelic eyes widened, and she clapped. 'A visitor! How delightful.' She clapped again. 'Would you like a chocolate?' Aveline held out a red box. 'I have them sent to me every week. Do have one.'

'Thank you.' Catrina picked a chocolate at random and popped it into her mouth, savouring the sweetness. 'May I sit down?'

'Oh, where have my manners gone.' The wide-eye stare returned as though the question was a serious one. 'Please sit and stay for a little while.' Aveline selected another chocolate. 'You are truly Catrina, my sister-in-law? Phillip never speaks of you.'

'Yes, well, I've been gone a good while.'

'Phillip said you consorted with an unsuitable, whatever that means.' She waved a dainty hand in the air. 'I am fat.' She patted her rotund stomach beneath the white bedspread. 'It's a baby, you know.'

'Yes, I know. When is it due to be born?'

Aveline frowned. 'The doctor says soon, but not today.'

Catrina stared at her, alarmed. 'Your baby is to be born very soon then, this week?'

'Is it?' The green eyes returned the stare, as equally surprised. 'How exciting.'

'No, well, I mean, I don't know. What did the doctor say exactly?'

Aveline ate another chocolate. 'Soon. Though what do doctors know? They know nothing. I'm so tired of them.'

'Them? You have more than one doctor?'

'Oh indeed. A great many.' She glanced at Catrina, her delicate features screwed up in confusion. 'But how does it happen?'

'How does what happen?'

'The baby. How does it get out?'

Catrina's jaw dropped open and a sense of unease filtered through her shock. 'You don't know?'

'Know what?' Aveline smiled sweetly. 'I would like a puppy. Phillip says no though. Too much of a nuisance. It would piddle everywhere. But Papa George said I could, before he became sick.' She bit into another chocolate and frowned at the half-eaten confection. 'I don't like that one.' She dropped it back into the box. 'Do you know Papa George?'

Desperately puzzled and at a loss as to what she was facing, Catrina nodded. 'Papa George is Phillip's father, yes?'

'That's right. You are clever.'

'He's my father too.'

'Who, Phillip?' Aveline's expression changed to surprise.

'No, George...' Standing, her heart racing, Catrina gave a gentle smile. 'I must go now.'

'Oh, no, really? Must you? I get so lonely. Phillip won't be home for hours yet, or maybe not at all. He's very busy, you know.'

'I promise to come and see you tomorrow.'

'You will?' Aveline grasped Catrina's hand and kissed it. 'You can be my special friend.'

'That would be nice. Rest now.' Catrina fled the bedroom, out through the sitting room and into the corridor. Resting against the closed door, she took a deep calming breath. 'Good God,' she whispered.

'Miss?' A young maid Catrina didn't know stood near the linen pantry, folded white sheets in her arms.

'Where is Mrs O'Toole?'

'In her rooms, I think, Miss.'

Catrina hurried down the corridor to the servants' staircase, knowing this would be a quicker route than the main staircase. At the bottom she turned right and headed past the service rooms, turned right again up three steps and into a narrow hallway that was the higher staffs' quarters. Here, was the butler's pantry and housekeeper's room, plus the servants' dining room. After a brief knock, Catrina opened the door to the housekeeper's small sitting room. 'Mrs O'Toole?'

'Come in, Miss,' Mrs O'Toole's weary tone beckoned as she came out of her bedroom, adjusting her lace cap. 'Sit down, Miss.' She waved her to the small wooden chair and table by the fire. 'You saw the young mistress?'

'Yes.' Not sure if her legs would hold her, Catrina sat on the straight-backed chair. 'She is…That is, I believe…' The words wouldn't form, her brain refused to recognise what she had seen.

'Aye, Miss, I know.'

'Why did he marry her?'

Sighing, Mrs O'Toole took the opposite chair. 'Can I be blunt, Miss?'

'I insist.'

'Your brother married her because she was rich.'

'Surely he could have found other rich women with sound minds to court?'

The older woman shrugged and smoothed down the black skirt she wore, before fondling the bunch of keys at her waist, her symbol of office. 'She wasn't so bad at the start, but within the first few months of marriage she grew worse.'

'What did my father say?'

'To be honest, Miss, I don't think he realised. As I said, when your brother brought Miss Aveline home, she was better than she is now. She was a delightful creature, with child-like ways and I think she filled a small hole in the master, created by your leaving. But not long after they returned home from their long honeymoon, she grew quiet and withdrawn. The master became ill and the young mistress started to become different in her manner.'

'Didn't Phillip say anything?'

Mrs O'Toole looked incredulous. 'To me? Why would he?'

'Yes, of course. I'm sorry. But he must have confided in someone. Did he know she was like that before they married?'

'I don't think he really cared, Miss, if you don't mind me saying so...' The housekeeper's gaze drifted away.

Anger filled Catrina. Phillip had a selfish streak in him, and was a mean beast to be certain, so why did she think he wouldn't go to such lengths just for money? 'When is my brother due home?'

'That I cannot say, Miss.'

'Aveline said it could be hours or not at all.'

'The hours have no meaning for her, Miss, not really. He comes and goes without any advance warning. He stays away for days and weeks.' Again, she fiddled with her bunch of keys, the only sound in the sparse room.

'There is more, Mrs O'Toole, so you might as well tell me.'

'I'm sorry, Miss. You shouldn't have this burden on your first day home.'

'Who else is to suffer it? My Father, Aveline?' She raised her chin, ready to accept whatever else she had to hear.

'There are the debts, Miss.' Mrs O'Toole bowed her head. 'The Master would already be dead if he knew of them. I thank the Lord every day that he is too ill to know what is happening.'

'I understand that Phillip has sold off estate land in the last two years.'

'Yes. I heard gossip from the village that another twenty acres is to go next month. Then there are the paintings, furniture, silver... your mother's jewels.'

'Mama's jewels? They were mine!' Rage built. How dare he do this.

Mrs O'Toole sighed and looked dreadfully tired. 'He's cut staff both inside and out. The worst of it was that Mr Whetherby received no pension when he retired last year.'

Catrina stiffened. The beloved old butler who'd served not only her father, but her grandparents too, had no pension. That wasn't to be borne. 'Where is Mr Whetherby living now? I shall visit him and sort something out.'

'He died three months ago, Miss.' Mrs O'Toole seemed to grow older by the minute. 'He was a good man, decent, loyal. He didn't deserve to die in some strange lodgings alone and with no money for burial. Master Phillip said he'd take care of him, but the savings Mr Whetherby had was all he had to live on. He lost the will to live once he left here. He could have stayed, you know, Miss. We'd have managed to see to him. He only had a cough. Master Phillip said retiring him was the best thing, that Mr Whetherby could rest. Instead he died in a rented room amongst strangers, not us who were his family.'

Unable to sit still another minute, Catrina jerked to her feet and paced the small room. The anger towards her brother simmered in her chest like heartburn. 'The accounts for the house, Mrs O'Toole, are they in order?'

'Much behind, Miss. I'm sorry. Wages weren't paid last quarter. We're struggling to keep tradesmen demands at bay, and some of the shops in the village refuse to send a cart out.'

Rubbing the strain in her neck, Catrina thought fast. She had little money of her own, so she was no help there. 'Does my father know any of this?'

'No, Miss. I felt it would be too much for him.'

'He gave financial control to Phillip I take it?'

'Yes, Miss. When he became ill, a solicitor came, and your brother was allowed control of everything. That is what Mr

Whetherby told me before he left us.' Mrs O'Toole sounded as exhausted as Catrina felt.

'Leave it with me. I'll try to sort this mess out.' With a gentle squeeze on the other woman's shoulder, she left the room and made her way to the front of the house. At the bottom of the stairs, she paused, one hand on the banister. An overwhelming sense of hopelessness bowed her shoulders. How on earth was she to make it all right again? What's more, did she have the strength to fight Phillip?

CHAPTER 9

*C*atrina slipped her arm through Travis's as they strolled the gardens. Bees hummed, hovering from flower to flower in their own special dance, while wall and blackthorn butterflies fluttered about. Above their heads the trees were bright green with new foliage and bird fledglings could be heard chirping in their nests.

She'd spent the morning sorting out her old wardrobes with Lettie. The clothes she wore three years ago were out of fashion, but with Lettie's skill with the needle, she'd soon have them altered and Catrina would have a full summer collection of new clothes.

'Are you feeling more rested today?' Travis asked. 'You've had a rough first week at home.'

'I'm not sleeping well, and I'm extremely tired. I should be sleeping like a baby with all I have to do during the day.' She watched a swallow dive between the alder trees lining the end of one walk.

'It's not surprising, considering all you've been doing. What did the doctor say about Aveline when he called yesterday?'

'Doctor Robertson said the baby was probably due in the next three weeks as far as he could judge. He said it was difficult to get a clear answer from Aveline as to when her... her...' She blushed and glanced up at him.

'When it was her last time of the month?'

'Yes.' She grinned at him, then grew serious again. 'He is a nice man, well spoken and—'

'And new to the district. Grandmother isn't happy about that. She was most put out when Doctor Stephens happened to die last winter.'

Catrina rolled her eyes at the mention of his grandmother, Ailsa Millard. The woman was a perfect witch. Catrina bent and snapped off a primrose from the edge of the walkway and twirled it between her fingers. 'Well, I liked him. Anyway, he's keeping a careful eye on Aveline, since her state of mind is fragile.'

'Poor girl.'

'Yes, another thing Phillip should be taken to task about. I have a feeling he makes her worse somehow.'

Travis kissed her cheek as they ambled along the path. 'Let us not speak or think of him. It ruins the day.'

'Then what shall we talk about?'

'You should see my lambs,' Travis said, plucking a hothouse pink rose and de-thorning it before giving it to her. 'They play and jump about. A sight to behold. I know I've seen it before, but this is my first year where the lambs are mine. I'm as proud as if I were the father.'

She laughed quietly and sniffed the fragrant rose scent, holding both it and the primrose – one small and insignificant, the other larger and bold in colour and smell. 'How will you do when they are sent to market?'

'I'm not sure.' He grinned down at her. 'Perhaps I'll keep them all.'

'You'll need more land, Mr Millard.'

'Then I shall buy more land.' He kissed her hand and rested it back on his arm.

'And send yourself bankrupt?'

'You are so pessimistic, Miss Davies.' With a whoop, he twirled her off the lawn and into a secluded corner of the tall yew hedge, there he crushed her into his arms and kissed her deeply, satisfying her need to be held and adored. 'I've missed you, my darling. Now I've tasted the heaven that is your body I want it all the time.'

She linked her hands behind his neck. 'Soon, my love, soon. Only three more weeks and we will be married and then, the nights will be ours.'

'When will you come to the farm? I'm eager for you to see it and make decisions about the house. I want you to be happy there.'

'I know, and I'm sorry, but you do understand how it is here.'

He sighed and kissed the tip of her nose. 'Yes, I know...'

'Try not to be too impatient. I'm doing the best I can.'

'Sorry.' He gave her a half smile and tightened his arms about her. After another lingering kiss, they rejoined the network of pale gravel paths that threaded through the gardens. With less outdoor staff, evidence of neglect was everywhere, but Catrina closed her eyes to it today. For the last week she'd done her best to sort out the mess that was the household accounts. Only, without the power to withdraw funds from her father's bank, she was hard-pressed to find a suitable answer to the problems. Phillip had yet to make an appearance, and most of her time was divided between her father and Aveline, both of whom were becoming more and more dependent on her.

As white throats and the odd thrush twittered in the grove of silver birch trees, she held Travis's hand and they walked in contented silence for a while before Travis spoke. 'Have you heard from Henley?'

'Yes, just this morning. He's in Gloucestershire, home for good, so he says. His letter has his instructions to his solicitors, regarding his will.' She patted her skirt pocket. 'I have it with me, do you wish to read it?'

Travis stopped. 'May I?'

'Of course.' She fished the document out of her pocket, gave it to him and then went to sit on the iron bench under mature Plane tree, which sprouted tiny flowers of yellow high above her head.

Travis read the pages of the letter while sauntering towards her. 'His solicitors are amending his last will. You get it all, held in trust for your children.'

'Our children.' She smiled, but the smile slipped when she saw his tight expression. 'What is it?'

'Nothing.' He handed the letter back to her.

Tucking it into her pocket again, she kept her gaze on him. 'If we are to be married then we must be open and honest, Travis. I will not live my life with you under a cloud of unspoken hurt and hostility. So again, I ask you, what is the matter?'

'Henley.'

Coldness entered her heart. 'Hugh? You still think we were…'

'No. No.' He stared out over the gardens to the distant fields, fields that once were heaving with animal stock, but were now bare.

'Well then?'

'You will be a very rich woman, Catrina, when Henley dies.'

She studied the tautness of his back, the rigid line of his jaw and her heart softened with love. She went and stood behind him, wrapping her arms around his waist. 'Rich or poor, you are all I want.'

'But it won't be poor, will it?'

'What is mine is yours.'

'I want to be the one to buy you things, not Henley.'

She smiled into his back. Men and their pride. 'Do you know how much I will need your guidance and advice when that time comes? Hugh has many interests. His Gloucestershire estate alone is large enough. I cannot do it all by myself.'

'And what of my farm?'

She came around to the front of him and grasped his hands, holding them tight in hers. 'Your farm will always be important, because it is yours.'

'But will you want to live in it after Henley's house?'

'Yes. We will divide our time between the two.'

He gathered her into his arms, but he wasn't completely relaxed. 'I suppose we'll manage somehow.'

She grinned cheekily. 'It seems we'll just have to make sure we have plenty of sons, to divide up our good fortune for.' She rose on tiptoes and kissed him. 'Handsome sons like their father.'

'And a daughter or two?'

'We'll see.' Arms around each other they walked on. Catrina sniffed at the flower, her thoughts wandering. 'Your Grandmother. How has she taken the news of our impending marriage?'

'She's said very little on the subject since the first banns were read last week. The vicar spoke to her about our impending wedding, but she has little time for Mr French, with him also being so new to the village. She doesn't like change.'

They walked along the gravel path in silence for a

moment, each with their own thoughts. Catrina rested her head against Travis's upper arm, feeling guilty for putting off the dreaded visit to see Mrs Millard. 'I should meet her. Was she very annoyed for me not making it to church last Sunday?'

'She understood that you want to spend time with your father.'

Catrina could guess what he didn't say. 'But she's not excusing me entirely.'

'Grandmother is set in her ways. She's old.'

'And she isn't a supporter of me,' she finished for him.

'She will be. Phillip isn't popular in the village, he's done some awful things and so she is wary of me becoming mixed up with your family.'

'I'm nothing like my brother.'

'I know that and soon Grandmother will too. She saw how much I missed you, not that I ever spoke of it to her.'

'Since we are to be related, and living in the same farm-house, we must get along for everyone's sake. I'll work hard to win her over.'

'She's not an ogre, just loyal to me. Now she understands better my love for you, but she doesn't want to see me...hurt again.' He smiled down at her, the sadness of the past darkening the colour of his eyes.

Catrina looked at him expectantly. 'Does she realise the wedding will be small and the celebration nothing but tea and cake?'

He hesitated. 'She was disappointed, of course.'

'It can't be helped, Travis. Father is ill and Aveline—'

'I know. I don't mind.' He kissed her knuckles. 'Grand-mother isn't truly against the match, for all her mutterings. I think she is more put out by the fact that the farmhouse will no longer be hers to control, but yours, once we are married.'

Catrina paused, twirling the rose stem between her fingers. Living with Ailsa Millard would be a bitter pill to swallow. The old woman was sharp-tongued and sharp-eyed. Nothing got past her. 'We could live with Hugh in Gloucestershire. A fresh start for us both.'

'No.' He stepped away, his face closing down. 'I will not live in another man's home. One given to my wife. My farm will be our main home.'

'But—'

He held up his hand. 'No buts, Catrina. It is the farm or nothing.'

'Let me explain.'

'No, let me explain. The farm is my home, my land. It might not be as glorious as Henley's estate, or Davmoor Court, but it's mine. That is where we will live.' He began to walk away.

She stayed where she was. 'Don't I get a say in the matter? The farm might be yours, but I will have property, too, one day. A large house for us all to live in. Is that to be ignored, forgotten until one of our children inherits it? How ridiculous, Travis. Moments ago, you were happy to divide our time between the two.'

He turned around and walked backwards, his face inscrutable. 'Yes, but now I get the distinct feeling that you'd prefer Hugh's house to mine.'

'Nonsense, but you must understand that it will be difficult for me to have your grandmother living with us. She's a strong woman and used to being the mistress.'

'She'll step aside for you.'

'Under sufferance.' Catrina raised an eyebrow at him. 'I just don't comprehend why you are against living in Hugh's house. Your farm, in all honesty, is too close to here, to Phillip.'

'As my wife, Phillip doesn't have any say over you.'

'I know, but his presence will still be there. While at Hugh's estate I will be free of his shadow.'

'But I will live under Hugh's shadow.'

'Twaddle. If you'd just—'

He threw up his hands. 'By all means live there then, but it will be alone, my dear, quite alone.'

She stamped her foot, then threw the rose away. 'You are the most pig-headed man, Travis Millard!' she yelled, but he had rounded the bend in the garden path and was gone from sight. 'Lord, how you frustrate me!'

Later, when the sun had gone down and the moonlight cast silver across the estate, Catrina knocked on Aveline's door and went in. 'Have you finished eating?'

Aveline pushed the meal tray away, her eyes bright, cheeks puffy. 'Oh Kitty-Kat.' Catrina winced at the new name Aveline had christened her. 'Did you have some raspberry fool? It was delicious.' She licked her spoon. 'Come, sit and talk to me.'

Catrina took the chair by the bed, alarmed by how much weight Aveline carried. She seemed to grow larger every day. 'I was thinking we could walk in the gardens tomorrow, would you like that?'

'No, I mustn't do that.'

'Why? It can't be good for you being cooped up in here all the time.'

'Phillip says I shouldn't leave my rooms. It's indecent to be in public when with child.'

'That's not entirely true.' Catrina shook her head. Damn Phillip. He kept his wife shut away up here to avoid anyone knowing her true state of mind. 'How about I walk with you in the knot garden? There's high hedges all around and no one will see us.'

'Oh, yes.' Clapping her hands, Aveline's expression was adoring. 'You make me happy, Kitty-Kat.'

Catrina smiled through clenched teeth. 'Perhaps I could fetch you some books from the library?'

'Books?'

'Yes.' She fought for patience. Aveline's constant repetition of what was said to her got on Catrina's nerves. 'I thought you might want to read. I can bring you newspapers, if you prefer?'

'I don't like reading. It bores me. I never read in India, only had to when I arrived here.'

'You lived in India?' Catrina's eyes widened at this new information.

'I was born there, silly.' Aveline playfully smacked Catrina's hand.

'I didn't know.'

'Mama sent me away to England when I was fourteen, a week before my fifteenth birthday. My papa had died and she remarried to *that man!*' Aveline shuddered. 'I didn't want to leave Mama, but I was happy to get away from *him.*'

'How sad you didn't like your stepfather.'

'No, but he liked me.' She shuddered again, then suddenly brightened. 'I was treated like a princess on the boat. I had a nanny. She was lovely. We ate chocolate every day. She stayed with me until I reached England and then my Aunt and Uncle came for me at the dock. They lived in Norfolk.'

'How did you meet Phillip?'

'At a dinner party in London.' She wiggled down into the pillows and folded the sheets back across her large stomach. 'I'd just returned from school in Switzerland.' She yawned. 'Phillip said we should get married and we did.'

'Why didn't you return to India? Didn't you miss your family?'

'I missed Mama, but not *him*. I wouldn't go back there where *he* is. And Mama is always busy. Being a Colonel's wife is very demanding, don't you know?'

Seeing the tiredness in Aveline's face, Catrina rose. 'I'll say good night.'

'Can you stay until I fall asleep?' Her eyes drooped, and she snuggled into the pillows some more.

'Very well.'

'You are kind, Kitty-Kat...'

Catrina waited a few minutes until she was sure Aveline was asleep and then slipped from the room. She went along to her father's room to check he was sleeping peacefully but was delighted to see him awake and raised up on his pillows. 'Father, do you need anything?'

He raised his hand. 'Sit, my dear.'

She bent over and kissed his sunken cheek, which had some colour in it for once, and then sat down. 'Do you want a drink?'

He shook his head. 'I'm feeling much better since you came home.'

'I'm so pleased.' She gripped his thin hand. He did look a little better, but he was nowhere near back to good health.

'I can eat a little more now.'

'Then I'll have Cook prepare all your favourites.'

'Once this exhaustion goes, I'll be on my feet again.'

'Absolutely.'

'Tell Whetherby he'll have to press my suits again.'

Her face fell. What could she say? Tell him the truth that their trusted butler was dead or let him believe he was alive until his health had improved enough to deal with it? She fiddled with the sheet and blankets, hedging what to do. When she looked up, he was asleep, and she gratefully left the room.

In her own bedroom, she paused by the wardrobe. Her wedding dress hung on the door after being laundered. Lettie was in the process of altering it. The cream silk gown had been her mother's wedding dress, but the years of storage had taken its toll and now it needed new lace. It pleased her to think that she and her mother were the same size. She wished with all her heart that her mother was here now. Someone who would listen, help her through the changes in her life.

Crossing the room, she stood by the window and stared blindly out. Her neck and shoulders ached from the strain of worry. Aveline, her father, Travis, the wedding, Phillip. It was all too much.

She turned as the door opened and Lettie walked in. 'Where have you been?'

Lettie's face blushed beetroot. 'Downstairs in the kitchens, Miss. I'm sorry.'

'Mrs O'Toole told me this morning that one of the gardeners, Roddy Hannigan has taken a shine to you.'

'I've not encouraged him, Miss, honest.' Lettie's colour deepened.

'I hope not. You're not accustomed to the male sex, Lettie, after years in the cottage.'

'We're just friends, Miss, that's all. I'll not spend my day off with him, Miss, promise.'

Lettie's anxious manner brought Catrina to task. 'Forgive me, Lettie. What you do in your own time is your own business. Of course, you must have friends. How else will you find a husband one day?'

'I don't need a husband, Miss.' Lettie quickly drew the curtains on the night.

Thinking of Travis, of the wasted years, Catrina stopped her with a gentle hand on her arm. 'Everyone needs someone, Lettie. It's a cruel cold world alone. Find a good man to love.'

'Like Mr Millard, Miss?' Lettie's cheeky smile returned, and the tension disappeared.

Catrina grinned. 'Well, at least someone without Mr Millard's temper.'

CHAPTER 10

*N*ervously adjusting a cushion, Catrina paced the drawing room, waiting for Mrs Millard to arrive. The fact Travis wasn't accompanying her and instead had gone to some market to acquire stock, made the interview more terrifying because she had to face her alone. She didn't like his grandmother, never had, and Mrs Millard, she was sure, felt the same in return. How on earth were they going to live under the same roof?

In the past, they had met only as acquaintances in the village. When she was a child, Dr Millard and Ailsa had dined at Davmoor, due to the good doctor's rank as a professional. Though after Catrina's mother died and then the doctor, the invitations fell away, and Catrina grew into adulthood without any associations with Travis's grandmother. However, once Travis defied his grandmother's wishes and began working at the estate as her father's steward, a position Ailsa felt beneath him, Catrina soon became aware of the older woman's stringent opinions on how her grandson could do better than work for the Davies family. Ailsa Millard has used every chanced meeting to utter snide comments in Catrina's hearing. The animosity only intensified once Ailsa knew of Travis's attachment to Catrina.

The crunch of carriage wheels made her spin towards the windows. She watched the older woman being handed down from the carriage by a groom and then shown indoors by Mrs O'Toole.

Smoothing down the blue satin of her day dress, she then fluffed the white lace at her throat and steeled herself to meet the woman who, in five days' time, would be related to her by marriage.

The panelled door opened and Mrs O'Toole entered, smiling reassuringly as Travis's grandmother followed her in. 'Mrs Millard, Miss Davies.'

'Thank you, Mrs O'Toole. We'll take tea, please.' Catrina smiled in welcome at the other woman. 'Welcome, Mrs Millard. I hope you are well.'

'Quite well, thank you.' She bowed her head, making the dark pheasant feathers on her black hat quiver. Although of average height, Mrs Millard had the bearing of royalty, and despite her age, was still striking in looks. With her thin nose raised slightly, she peered around the room, taking in the furnishings, which to the trained eye, were sadly depleted due to Phillip purloining them to pay his debts.

'Please.' Catrina waved her towards the one remaining Louis XV gilt chair, while she sat on the cream and gold striped sofa. Ailsa Millard wore unrelieved black, but beneath her left shoulder she wore a brilliant ruby brooch in the shape of a tiger. 'What a beautiful brooch, Mrs Millard.'

Mrs Millard fingered it, unsmiling. 'A gift from my grandson.'

'He has excellent taste.' Catrina smiled.

'Not always.' Her blue eyes bore hard at Catrina. 'I am grateful you could spare the time to see me.'

Aware of the barb behind the words, Catrina straightened

her back, ready for the fight ahead, and fight it would be, she knew that without a doubt. 'Forgive me for not calling on you sooner. However, my father and sister-in-law are in need of my—'

'I believe they have done without you so far, surely they can survive a half hour without you now?'

'Yes, but—'

'We've much to discuss regarding the wedding preparations. There is hardly any time left to prepare.' She paused. 'Unless, of course, you wish for me not to be involved with the organising?'

'I explained to Travis that the wedding was to be simple.'

'And hardly any guests, from what I gather. Barely a wedding at all.'

Catrina was saved from commenting as Mrs O'Toole and Ida entered carrying tea trays. Catrina caught Mrs O'Toole's questioning gaze and slightly shook her head in answer. They had pre-arranged a signal if Catrina felt the need to escape the older woman. However, Catrina knew she had to go through with the unpleasantness, if only for Travis's sake.

'Shall I pour, Miss Davies?' Mrs O'Toole asked, turning her back on their visitor.

'Thank you.' Catrina allowed the housekeeper to serve them, stretching out the time when she'd have to again converse with the tyrant sitting opposite.

Within a few minutes, Mrs O'Toole ushered Ida out before her and closed the door and Catrina was faced with making polite conversation. As she went to speak about the weather, Mrs Millard placed her teacup and saucer down.

'Miss Davies, I cannot prevent you from marrying my grandson, but be assured that I will do all in my power to prevent you from wounding him as you did several years ago.'

'I have no intention of doing that.'

'Of course, you will, girl,' Mrs Millard snapped. 'It's in your nature. Selfishness and blatant disregard for others is a trait you share with your brother.'

'I beg your pardon!'

Mrs Millard waved her hand lazily. 'Oh, don't look so shocked or outraged. It does you no credit.'

'You know nothing about me.' Catrina seethed.

'I know all there is to know. You spurned my grandson's affections once before, thinking you could do better than him. But let me tell you that there is no man more worthy than Travis. He is a gentleman in every sense of the word, more so than some of the landed men in the country, for all their pedigree and privileges. Men such as your brother, for a start.'

'Spurned Travis?' Catrina jerked forward on her seat. 'Why I left three years ago, and the reasons for it, which include more than simply *spurning* Travis, is my business—'

'And when my grandson is hurting I make it *my* business!' Her dark blue eyes turned nearly black in her anger. 'You aren't good enough for him. I told him so, too. A Davies? He could do so much better. This family is tainted.'

Holding onto her anger, Catrina raised an eyebrow. 'Tainted? How so?'

'Your father's first wife was…what shall we say…unique. Then, she kills herself. Your father marries your mother and devotes himself to her every whim, allowing his son to run wild.'

'That is enough, Mrs Millard.' Catrina's tone was low and menacing, an indication of the boiling rage deep in her chest. She knew nothing about Phillip's mother, but the news that she had killed herself shocked her.

'I'm sorry if the truth hurts.' Mrs Millard straightened her shoulders, her eyes cold. 'Why Travis had to go off and find you is beyond my understanding. He could have had any decent young woman in the district. Why he wanted to join this accursed family is insensible to me.'

'Do not tar us all with the same brush, madam!'

'How can one do otherwise? Your brother is a menace to the area. Tell me, have you been flooded with invitations and callers since your return?'

It hadn't gone unnoticed by Catrina that the silver receiving tray on the hall table by the front doors remained empty of invitations. Not that she cared. Socialising at this difficult time was not something she cared to do.

Ailsa Millard tilted her head sideways, her eyes narrowing. 'Have you any idea of the trouble your brother has been causing? At last count he had fathered five bastards within a fifteen-mile radius. He's raised rents on all his tenants. Yet, sacked half the staff on the estate. He has outstanding accounts with nearly every business in the area. He's rude and arrogant and treats people like scum. The village is tired of it. People have stayed silent against him out of respect for your father, though it won't last much longer.'

Catrina fought the urge to sag against the cushions. She knew none of this. How did this woman know more about her family than she did? 'You seem well informed of my brother's activities, Mrs Millard.'

'I have a respectable position in the village. My late husband was kept in high affection by the people. These same people come to me with their concerns as they used to go to him. Should I turn my shoulder to them? Ignore them? After all, as my own flesh and blood is marrying into this family I should know what he's letting himself in for.'

'Mrs Mill—'

'In one generation, the history and good name of your family has been ruined. And for what? Between you and your brother you've caused enough scandal to blacken the next several generations to come.'

'If, as you say, we have fallen so low, then Travis isn't marrying up as far as you think, is he!'

Ailsa gasped. 'You wicked girl. How dare you compare my family with yours. We may not have had the long-standing wealth and the pedigree as you have but my husband was decent and—'

'Just as my father is, Madam!' Catrina snapped. 'You may disparage Phillip, and he may deserve it, but my father does not. Who are you, Madam to cast these dispersions against us? What gives you the right? By marrying me Travis will gain a lot more than he has now. I should think he'll be congratulated for landing such a union with this family. Why is it only you, someone of no birth or consequence, has the audacity to speak against this family!'

Blinking rapidly, the old woman sat stunned by the outburst. Her mouth opened and shut like a stranded fish.

'As I said earlier, I am nothing like Phillip.' Catrina stood, striving for calm. 'For Travis's sake I have invited you here, so we could become more acquainted, since we are to be related come Sunday, and will be living together. However, you make friendship impossible with your slanderous comments and opinions.'

The other woman nodded and, after a lengthy pause, sighed. Her expression softened slightly. 'I have never begged anyone in my life, Miss Davies, but I beg you now. Don't marry my boy.'

Catrina frowned. 'I love him, and he loves me.'

'You are right. I am of no birth and I married up. Therefore, I know of the difficulties it brings. You and Travis are a worse match than my husband and I, don't you see? A woman can marry up, keep a good house, help her husband progress in the world, but she cannot go down.'

'By marrying Travis, I don't see myself as marrying down.'

'How will Travis cope with you having wealth and property while he is nothing but a simple farmer?'

Catrina saw through her act of painting Travis as a simple soul. 'He is hardly that, is he? He's well educated and used his inheritance wisely to buy property.'

'But he isn't a gentleman born, is he? His grandfather, my husband, was a doctor. True, he was a gentleman's doctor, but what about Travis's father? Lloyd, my own son, wanted to do nothing but paint. Oh, he was good at it, but he died young without reaching his potential.' Ailsa Millard looked down at her gloved hands and then slowly back up to Catrina. 'Travis is the son of an artist, with the same silly dreams and ideals as his father before him. How can he contend with all this?' She waved her hand around the drawing room.

'He is very comfortable within such surroundings. After all, he is a product of your training. As you say, he is more of a gentleman than most who were born to the privilege.'

'He's worked hard to make the farm a success, and for a time it was enough for him. Now he must contend with his wife being more superior than him.'

'What is mine, is his.'

'Don't you know anything of a man's pride, girl?' Mrs Millard scoffed. 'Trying to compete will eat away at him until he is bitter and broken.'

'I don't believe that,' Catrina murmured, but didn't sound convincing even to herself, not after the argument she had with Travis over living on Hugh's estate.

Mrs Millard gracefully rose to her feet. 'All I ask is that you think it over.'

'We are to be married on Sunday.'

'Then there is still time to change your mind.'

'And hurt Travis all over again? Is that what you want?'

'I'd rather him in pain now, than experience a lifetime of unhappiness.'

Catrina stared directly at her. 'You have no faith in either of us, do you?'

'None at all.' With that, Mrs Millard strode from the room.

When the rumble of carriage wheels had died away, the door opened and Mrs O'Toole stepped to Catrina's side. 'Miss?'

Sitting on the sofa, Catrina rubbed her fingers over her eyes. 'Did my father's first wife kill herself?'

'Now, Miss, I—'

'Answer me, please.'

Mrs O'Toole took a deep breath, her large bosom expanding on the rush of air. 'Aye, she did, Miss.'

'Why?'

'It's not my place...'

'I need to know.' Catrina looked sadly at the housekeeper the one woman she could trust with the truth. 'How did you think I felt hearing such news from a stranger?'

Mrs O'Toole pursed her lips and stuck her chin out. 'Aye, well, nosy people like her,' she tilted her head towards the windows where the carriage had just left, 'should mind their own business. Always one to peddle gossip, is that one.'

'Why did Phillip's mother kill herself?' Catrina repeated.

'Nay, that's none of my business, Miss.'

'But you know the story anyway.' She raised an eyebrow at the housekeeper.

'The first Mrs Davies was living in London when she took her own life.'

'Was father with her?'

'No. She'd been banished.'

'Banished?'

'She had been...' Mrs O'Toole glanced around the room, a

blush creeping along her cheekbones. 'She'd been caught in a delicate situation by your good father on more than once occasion and he'd had enough of it.'

'A delicate situation?'

'With men.'

Catrina frowned. 'She had a lover?'

'Lovers.'

'Oh dear. Poor Father.'

'Indeed, Miss.' Mrs O'Toole sniffed, the disgust evident on her face. 'She had her *friends* here all the time. They had wild parties. Oh, the mess they left.' She shook her head, remembering. 'The minute the master left the house on business, she'd invite them all. Often, he came home to find these orgies—' Mrs O'Toole slapped her hand over her mouth, her eyes wide in horror.

'Go on.'

Swallowing, hands fluttering to the keys at her waist, Mrs O'Toole gave a nervous grimace. 'One time your father and the mistress had a huge row. He'd thrown out all these young bucks and well, I'd never seen him so angry. He told her to get out and never come back. She was gone within the hour. Young master Phillip was away at school, his first year, he was about eleven I think, maybe younger. Anyway, she said she'd take Phillip away with her, but she wasn't serious. She had no time for the boy.'

'What happened then?'

'From what I know she lived in a house in London for several years, but your father didn't divorce her and he paid all her household accounts. I know that because Whetherby told me about the bills that came from her.'

'So why did she kill herself?'

'Over a lover apparently. She fell in love with a Spanish man, or so the story goes. He left her pregnant and returned to Spain. She couldn't live without him and topped herself, killing her and the unborn babe.'

'How do you know all this?'

'The staff in the London house. When your father sold the house after the funeral, some of the maids came here to work.'

'Why didn't I know this?'

'Your father made sure such gossip wasn't repeated near you. Not only that, by the time you came along he was madly in love with your mother and those awful times were long forgotten. Everyone in the village admired your mother and they wouldn't speak of the first Mrs Davies out of respect. We did all worry from time to time you would hear of something, especially when Master Phillip came home from school and caused trouble with the village boys, but your father kept you away from it as best he could. Sadly, it's been proven that master Phillip has inherited his mother's traits as far as wild behaviour is concerned.'

Amazed at this family history being kept from her, Catrina stood and patted the housekeeper's hand. 'Thank you for telling me.'

* * *

CATRINA SAT on the chair at her father's bedside and, holding a bowl of soup in one hand, used the other hand to tip the spoon in between his lips. 'A little more, Father, please. You've nearly finished all of it.' His wan smile was her answer and he opened his lips a bit wider. Today, he wasn't so good. After many days of him being in high spirits and he looked to be turning the corner, she'd found him this morning dull of eye and lethargic. She wiped his mouth with a linen napkin. 'Well done. Cook will be happy.'

'I am happy,' he whispered. 'You are home.'

She reached over and kissed his grey-whiskered cheek. 'I'm glad to be home.' In truth she wasn't. At times she was extremely tempted to flee back to the Highland cottage and the simple life Hugh afforded her. In the two and a half weeks she'd been home, she'd run a gauntlet of emotions from rage to tears on a daily basis. Only Mrs O'Toole's never-ending dependability got her through each day.

From the gossip Mrs O'Toole heard in the village, everyone was abuzz with the news that Sir George's daughter had returned and what's more, she was to marry their former estate manager. What Travis's friends and acquaintances thought on the matter she didn't like to ask. It was enough knowing his grandmother, an important person in his life, didn't want the match. She couldn't cope with any more anguish than she had already.

Since her meeting with Mrs Millard, she'd thought hard on what the other woman wanted her to do. And maybe the old crow was right, maybe she was selfish like Phillip, because she couldn't give Travis up. In the quiet hours of the night she would weigh up the pros and cons of marrying him, but come the morning and the prospect of seeing him again, she knew rejecting him wasn't the answer. Somehow, they'd have to work their way through the difficulties of money and properties.

And as if that wasn't enough to contend with, she had the worries of Davmoor Court to deal with. Just this morning, Cook had informed her that only what the Home Farm could produce was what she could use now, as the grocers and market traders refused to put things on account since their last quarter bills hadn't been paid. Unless they started buying supplies from York, they'd have to scale down the menu.

On a daily basis demands for money came in the post from various businesses and people around the country. Of Phillip she saw nothing. He hadn't even sent a letter to

Aveline. Wherever he was, he was in no hurry to return to his pregnant wife. As another day ended without his appearance, Catrina grew more irate at his complete lack of judgement and his selfishness.

As the wedding drew closer, Travis grew more impatient to have her all to himself, but how could she leave Davmoor when her father and Aveline needed her so much? How could she go on a honeymoon, knowing that staff weren't paid and were leaving in droves, that crops weren't being planted, or beasts taken to market?

'Rina?'

Pulled out of her misery, she smiled at her father's use of her pet name as a little girl. 'Yes?'

'Phillip?'

'Away at present.' It was her standard answer, but she was aware he no longer believed her.

'Aveline?'

'In bed. Her baby is due any time soon.' She dreaded to think how soon. Aveline, no matter how much Catrina and Mrs O'Toole tried to ready her for the event, still remained in blissful ignorance of the birthing process.

'Things aren't right. I never see Phillip.' Her father coughed and then let out a long-drawn sigh. 'Why isn't he here?'

Could she worry him with the truth of it? He was so frail, so helpless. She paused in lifting the spoon again, the soup had gone cold. 'I am home, and all will be well again.'

He shifted against the pillows, his gaze watchful. 'Did I imagine I saw Millard?'

'No, you didn't imagine it. He was here yesterday. We tried to talk to you, but you fell asleep.'

'Damn illness.' His eyes held the apology he was too weak to offer.

'Father...' She placed the spoon in the bowl, hesitant to

speak to him about the subject, but knowing she might not get another chance. 'Father, I am to marry Travis Millard on Sunday morning.'

'I know.' His voice was little more than a murmur. 'I knew it was what you wanted that summer years ago.'

'You did?'

'It's not right, Rina. He's not one of us.'

'Tell that to my heart.' She smiled sadly. 'I…I left home because I knew it wasn't right, that you'd never stand for it. I'm sorry if I disappoint you.' Sometimes she wished she could unburden herself to him and tell him the real reason why she left home, but to do that would only hurt him and she gained nothing from that.

He closed his eyes. 'What does any of it matter? All that I hoped for has gone. Phillip isn't the son I imagined him to be. Now, I long to join your mother and be happy again.'

She bowed her head, having no answer to that. After hearing the tale of his first wife, she could understand why he loved her mother so much. They all felt the death of Melody Davies very much, except Phillip, who never allowed her love to penetrate him. He accused her of stealing his father's affection and time and when Catrina was born he turned that same hatred onto her. Catrina was fourteen when her mother died after another miscarriage, her sixth one. At the time Catrina thought she'd die too, of heartache. The house was empty without her bright smile and high laughter. Despite her tragedies, her mother remained cheerful and loving, even to the sullen Phillip, and Catrina missed her dreadfully.

'Rina?' His eyes were still closed.

'Yes, Father?'

'Marry Millard if it makes you happy.'

'It will, but I'd like your blessing, too.'

'You have it. Lord knows, you might make a better deal of

it than Phillip has. Stupid boy.' His breathing grew deep and sleep reclaimed him once more.

Catrina replaced the bowl on the tray and gazed over the bed at the view beyond the window. Dusk was shadowing the countryside in a rosy pink. As spring evolved into summer, the days were getting warmer and longer.

A slight knock made her turn as Mrs O'Toole slipped into the room. 'Miss, your brother has come home.'

Closing her eyes momentarily, Catrina summoned the strength to rise. A trickle of unease ran down her back. 'Where is he?'

'In the drawing room having a brandy.' The tart look on the housekeeper's face said more than her words.

Taking a long breath, Catrina left the bedroom and went downstairs. The time had finally come for her to face him, the one who should have been her champion, her protector. Instead, she faced her tormentor. Clasping her trembling hands in front of her, she lifted her chin and walked into the room.

CHAPTER 11

*P*hillip was reclining in the wing-backed leather chair by the unlit fireplace, nursing a balloon glass in his hands, but he wasn't alone. Opposite him sat a tall thin man, swarthy in looks, dressed in black and with a direct stare as Catrina stepped nearer. He ran one finger over his black moustache.

Catrina switched her focus back to Phillip, her heart pounding. Her stomach tightened at the sight of him in dirty, stained clothes with two days' worth of stubble on his chin. She was shocked at how fat he'd become. A large stomach filled out his shirt and strained his waistcoat. He had more than one chin and his arms were as thick as her two legs together. He looked grotesque. And she knew with an inborn sense of instinct that sober or drunk he was still a monster. That part of him at least hadn't changed. 'Ph-Phillip.' She cleared her throat. 'Phillip, I-I need to speak with you.'

He raised his head and blinked. 'Catrina?'

'Yes.'

'What the hell are you doing here?' he slurred, his eyelids heavy.

'I've come home.'

'What the hell for?'

'To see Father.' Her nervous tension made her legs feel like they were made from custard.

He grunted. 'Is he still alive?'

'Yes.' What a thing for him to say, but did she expect anything different from such a man?

'How long have you been here?' He leaned forward, swaying in the chair.

'Twenty days.' She flicked a look at their guest. 'Excuse my brother's rudeness, I'm Catrina Davies.' She held out a shaking hand and he rose to bend over it.

'Darius Smith.'

'How do you do, Mr Smith?'

'Very well, thank you. And please call me, Darius.' His smile was silky smooth in a deeply tanned face.

Phillip stuck out his empty glass towards his friend. 'Darius is a bloody foreigner.'

Mr Smith stiffened at the insult before controlling his emotions and relaxing his shoulders. Embarrassed, Catrina gave him a polite smile as he addressed her. 'My father is English, my mother is not. Her family came from Persia.'

She nodded and wanted to escape, despite her good intentions of helping Aveline. She must have been mad to think that the years would alter Phillip, that he'd be the loving brother she always wanted. 'Are you staying the night, Mr Smith?'

'Yes, thank you.' He stared at Phillip, who belched loudly. 'Your brother and I have business to discuss in the morning.'

'Very well. I'll go and see that you have a room prepared.'

'Thank you, Miss Davies.'

'Catrina!' Phillip tried to lurch to his feet, but with his rump halfway out of the chair he sighed and gave up. 'I need a bath, food and clean clothes. Can you see to it?'

She glared, repulsed by him. 'No, I will not!'

'Bitch.' He shrugged. 'Ring the bell then, I'll order the maid.' He held out his glass. 'Fill us up again, Smith, there's good man.'

Good God, how was she to stand this? Fear gave way to anger. Mortified by Phillip's rudeness towards his guest, Catrina snatched the glass and placed it on the drink's trolley in the corner. She kept her temper in check, but it was hard. 'You've had enough, Phillip. Go upstairs and get into bed.'

'Not with Aveline.' He screwed his face up, lifted his leg and let out a rumble of gas.

She closed her eyes, utterly revolted. 'There are other rooms.'

Phillip yawned. 'Hey Smith, if you're looking for company my sister will be willing I'm sure. How have you been supporting yourself, sister dear?'

Her blood ran cold and a wave of dizziness came over her. No, not again. Feeling like a trapped animal, she began to panic. He wouldn't. He couldn't. She couldn't breathe. Terrified, she stared from Phillip to Smith.

Darius Smith was beside her in seconds. 'Miss Davies! Are you all right?'

Recoiling from his touch, she gaped wordlessly at him, then fled the room with Phillip's laughter chasing her.

After a restless night, in which she asked Lettie to sleep on a trundle pallet by the bed, Catrina rose early. The May day was already warm, despite the early hour and she dressed in a light linen skirt the colour of wet sand and a white blouse with a lace collar.

Checking on her father and finding him still asleep, she slipped from the back entrance of the house and out into the gardens. She wandered down to the orchard, the scent of blossom enticing her. The crab apple trees were a special delight showing off their pink flowers and crimson buds.

The sheer beauty of the orchard in full blossom did much to restore her shattered nerves as she made plans for the day. She'd promised Aveline another walk in the knot garden after their successful attempt a couple of days ago. The sheer joy on Aveline's face was wonderful to see as she sniffed the flowers and picked bunches of bluebells that formed square patches of blue inside the hedge patterns. Then, emboldened by the sense of freedom, Aveline had urged Catrina that they should go further away from the house, down to the spinney and duck pond. After an hour of gentle strolling and feeding the water hens, they returned to Aveline's rooms and shared a tray of tea before Aveline rested.

Only, now, would Aveline want to spend the day with Phillip? If so, she was welcome to him.

Leaving the orchard, she strolled along the lane that led to the estate's home farm. Here the hawthorn hedges were in plentiful flower, and below, sheltering in the ditch at its base, grew wild purple hyacinths. She thought to pick some for Aveline later. Her thoughts turned to Travis. What was he doing at that moment? Would he call on her later? Was he thinking of her, of their wedding day?

'Good morning, Miss Davies.'

She nearly jumped out of her skin as Darius Smith strolled out of a field gate on her left. 'Good morning.' Ducking her head, she turned and hurried back towards the house, her peace shattered.

'Please, Miss Davies, do not fear me.'

Hesitant, she chanced a look over her shoulder at him and found he'd remained where he was. She stilled her trembling and fought for composure. 'I...I...'

Mr Smith tilted his face up to the sky. 'Isn't it a beautiful morning?'

'Yes.' She watched him for a moment and believed he caused no threat to her in the open. Several farm workers were in shouting distance. The grooms were in the next field turning out the horses.

'I hope you don't mind me walking the grounds without invitation?'

'Not at all. Guests are welcome to use the house as they see fit.'

'Thank you.' He paused by the hedge and plucked off a hawthorn blossom. 'I apologise for arriving unannounced. I assumed Phillip had sent word ahead.'

'My brother wouldn't think to be so courteous.'

He dipped his chin in acknowledgment, but remained silent, his dark eyes assessing.

'Please excuse my brother's appalling manners last night.'

'I know how Phillip is. Do not worry. I'm accustomed to it.'

'Then why do you remain friends with him?'

'May I be blunt?'

'Yes.'

'He owes me a great deal of money. I'm staying *friends* with him until he repays his debt.'

Catrina couldn't stifle the groan that escaped. Just once she wanted to hear something good about Phillip. All her life he had been a troubling menace, and she was so tired of it. 'I am sorry for your plight, really I am, but there is no money.'

'I thought as much.' Hands thrust in his black trouser pockets, he sauntered towards her. 'After my walk this morning I can see the estate isn't up to the standard I expected, or that Phillip boasted about. He has duped me.'

'I'm sorry.' Shame filled her. Was there no end to the misery Phillip created? Her father would be humiliated if he knew.

'Don't be. It wasn't of your doing.' Darius Smith stared out across the gardens and to the distant fields beyond, which were yellow with buttercups. 'However, I will get what is owed.'

The tone of his quiet voice sent shivers down her back. 'I don't know how that will be possible.'

'This estate will do to start with.'

She jerked as though he'd slapped her. 'The estate?'

'Yes. Phillip can sign it over to me.'

'But you cannot have the estate, that's absurd. It is for the next generation of Davies. It is our family home, has been for centuries. My father won't allow it.'

'That is not my problem. Phillip owes me.' The look he gave her showed ruthless determination and she adjusted her assessment of him. He was a threat, a very real threat.

He didn't stop her this time when she rushed back to the house. Her thoughts whirled. She flung open the scullery door and flew into the kitchen. Her shoes skidded on the wet floor tiles.

'Hey, look out!' Nell, the scullery maid shrieked, then realised who she spoke to and scrambled to her feet, nearly knocking over the bucket in the process. 'Eh, I'm sorry, Miss.'

Catrina waved her away and sidestepped the bucket and made for the big green baize door leading into the service corridor.

'Is everything all right, Miss?' Cook asked, coming up into the kitchen from the cellar. She carried rinds of bacon on a marble slab.

Her hand on the doorknob, Catrina paused, frightened, and the look on the kindly Cook's face didn't help her resolve to stay strong. 'I doubt it ever will be again, Cook.'

She left the kitchen, intent on seeing her father, but noise from the morning room halted her. Warily, she peered into the bright room, decorated in shades of apple green and cream, expecting to see Phillip down. But the maid, Ida, was alone in the room, filling the coffee pot. 'Good morning, Ida. Has Master Phillip been to breakfast yet?'

'Good morning, Miss. No, he hasn't. I took up a tray to his room, Miss.'

Sitting down at the table, Catrina frowned. 'Which room?'

'Master Phillip slept in the blue guest room, Miss.'

Catrina prayed for patience. How could Phillip not stay with Aveline? He'd know she'd be eager to see him after weeks apart. Would he ever change? Just once she hoped to see something in him she liked. Something that would redeem him.

She managed a smile for Ida, who piled her plate for her and she ate because she knew her body needed food. Within ten minutes, she'd done enough justice to the breakfast Cook provided, but wasn't really aware of actually eating it. Her thoughts swirled in her mind and she once more wished she'd never returned home. Wiping her mouth on the napkin, she glanced up as Darius walked in. Unable to hide her distrust and anger, she swept from the room before he could speak to her.

In the hall, she was about to go upstairs when she heard talking and giggles coming from the billiards room. Frowning, believing a maid was wasting time, Catrina entered the room. 'Aveline?' She stared at her sister-in-law, still dressed in her nightgown, kneeling by the billiard table. 'What are you doing?'

'Searching.' Aveline tried to rise from her knees and Catrina hurriedly went to assist her. 'Thank you, Kitty-Kat.' Aveline panted, clasping her hands over her large stomach.

'Why are you downstairs?' Catrina helped her to the door.

'Phillip's home isn't he?' Her wide-eyed look of innocence was difficult to lie to.

'Yes, he is.'

'I was looking for him.' Aveline giggled. 'He's hiding from me!'

'No, no, he's not at all. He arrived late and didn't want to disturb you so he slept in one of the guest rooms.'

'Really?'

'It's true.'

'Aren't I silly.'

'Let's get you back upstairs and into bed.' Together, they slowly climbed the staircase and Catrina was thankful when they made it to the top without seeing anyone. Shuffling along towards the east wing, Catrina heard a stifled cry and an answering harsh murmur coming from the guest room on her right. She walked a bit further and then released Aveline's arm. 'Go back to bed and I'll be along in a minute.'

'Can you bring me some hot chocolate?' Aveline hobbled on, holding one hand on her stomach, and the other against the wall for support.

'Of course. Hop into bed now.' Turning back, Catrina stepped quietly to the guest room and listened. Again, came the sound of a muffled sob. Thinking perhaps a maid was ill, she opened the door and stopped. Before her stood Phillip, with his back to her and his underwear down around his ankles. He had a firm grip on someone in front of him and when Catrina moved to the side, she saw that a maid was bent forward over the end of the bed railing, her black skirts up, revealing her naked buttocks.

'Phillip!' Catrina screamed, close to fainting at the sight.

He whirled around, his pudgy face red with effort at trying to get his way with the girl. 'Get out, you stupid bitch!'

Without thought, Catrina grabbed the vase from the console table near the door and flung it her brother's head. He ducked, and it smashed onto the floor on the other side of the bed. The maid screamed, and finding herself free, ran from the room.

With his penis now shrivelled and hanging limp, Phillip turned away muttering the foulest language she'd ever heard. Heart thumping as though she'd run a mile, Catrina staggered from the room. She managed to make it to her own room before she vomited. While Lettie fussed and petted her, Catrina flopped onto her bed and tried to ignore the images of that black night when, in a dusty corner of the attics, a faceless man had done the same to her.

* * *

TRAVIS DUCKED his head to enter the warm farmhouse kitchen. Molly, the maid of all work, and his grandmother were sitting at the well-scrubbed pine table, studying recipes. 'This looks promising. Are we to have a feast tonight?' He grinned, shaking off his wet outerwear and hanging it up in the scullery. 'My word, this rain doesn't want to stop.'

'And if you keep going out in it, you'll catch your death, my boy,' his grandmother harked at him as he re-entered the well-lit kitchen.

'I hope it stops for tomorrow.' He smiled at the two women. 'I can't get married in the rain.'

'What is a bit of water, for heaven's sake!' his grandmother snapped.

Ignoring her, he smiled at the maid. 'Any tea in the pot, Molly?'

'Aye, sir, in a minute there will be.' Molly slid off the stool and set about brewing some tea. Although not old, Molly remained unmarried at twenty-eight due to a club foot. His grandmother had taken her under her wing when the girl found it tricky to obtain work after her parents died three years ago.

Pulling out a chair, Travis sat and glanced at the old recipe books. 'What's all this about then?'

'Food for the wedding.' His grandmother packed them away into the pine dresser against the far kitchen wall.

'There is no need.' He frowned. 'I told you that we're having a light luncheon at Davmoor. I thought you discussed this with Catrina?'

'Yes, well…' His grandmother fiddled with the lace cuff of her sleeves, not meeting his eyes. 'I was thinking that perhaps we could also have a small gathering here, the following day, for our friends.'

'A party here?'

'Why not? She's not invited many people to the wedding breakfast, if you can call it that. A light luncheon indeed. It's a mockery that's what it is.'

'Grandmother,' he warned.

'Have you given thought to our friends and acquaintances? They'll be insulted not to be invited to your important day. She may not want to celebrate, as is normal, but we must make something of it or be the butt of jokes for years. It's a disgrace to the Millard name.'

'But is that such a good idea?' He accepted the cup of tea from Molly with a smile of thanks. 'I mean, Catrina will need time to adjust to living here. Does she need to entertain the first day of being married?'

'I shall be organising it. Catrina only needs to converse with our guests.' Her tone was cutting, as if to say the girl should be able to manage that at least.

He waited for Molly to go into the scullery to do some work before leaving the table and walking closer to his grandmother. For too long she had got her own way with him, and it had to stop. Tomorrow he was to be a married man, he didn't need his grandmother mollycoddling him, organising his life as she saw fit. Before, he fell in with all her plans because it suited him and stopped her from nagging, but not anymore. 'You should have asked me about all this.'

'Why?' Her eyes widened innocently, a look she had perfected over the years when she wanted her own way. 'Am I no longer allowed to host a party anymore?'

'Please don't be difficult. I know there will be adjustments for us all.' He placed his hand on her arm, praying this new arrangement would play out. 'We can make this work if we try hard enough.'

'No, you mean you want *me* to try, not her. It'll be me doing all the adjusting. I've run this home for years, but now I must move aside like an unwanted old dog.'

'Nonsense.'

'I should have stayed in my own home and not come here when you bought the farm, but I thought I'd be needed.'

'And you were.'

'I see it clearly now.' She nodded her head, her eyes cold. 'Out with the old and in with the new.'

'I'm getting married, Grandmother. It was bound to happen sooner or later.'

'Yes, and I was looking forward to the day you brought your new bride here, but never did I think it would be *her* from Davmoor!'

He ran his fingers through his damp hair. Never in his life did he think it would be so difficult to marry a woman that he loved. But then, he wasn't marrying just a girl from the village. No, he was marrying a Davies.

'Have you noticed that her belongings aren't here yet?' His grandmother walked to the doorway that led into the hall and the front of the house. 'It doesn't look like she is too keen to leave home, does it?'

'Her luggage will arrive tomorrow afternoon.'

'So that will be another thing I'll have to organise, will it?' Her face tightened with annoyance. 'And how many servants is she bringing? One, two, five?'

'Only Lettie.' He sighed, tired of defending every word he

uttered. Just once he'd like his life to run smoothly, was it too much to ask?

'You'd have been better off moving into Davmoor and living there.'

His head jerked up at that. 'What do you mean?'

'She'll never settle in here, lad.'

'She will, if you let her.' God, why was she being so obstinate? It exhausted him fighting her every step of the way.

His grandmother shook her head sadly. 'You're deluding yourself. Every day she'll be racing off to check on her father and that sister-in-law of hers. You'll find she will have a thousand excuses to be at Davmoor. We'll never see her.'

'Then you'll be happy then, won't you?'

'And you know that good-for-nothing brother has turned up, don't you?'

Travis stiffened, hating the man with all his being. 'When?'

'Last night, apparently. Mr Clarkson told me this morning when he brought our post. As if we need more trouble. God knows what the wretch will do this time.'

'He'll be on his best behaviour if I have anything to do with it.'

'Hah! You? What makes you think he'll listen to anything you have to say?' she snapped at him.

At that moment his high esteem for his grandmother faltered. 'You don't know everything, Grandmother.' He flung back his chair, anger pulsing through him like hot iron.

'Travis, love...' His grandmother backed down, knowing she had gone too far.

'I'd like nothing more than to wring Phillip Davies's neck, but I won't because it'll do nothing but cause more trouble than he's worth. But don't think for one moment that I wouldn't do it, Grandmother, and do it gladly.'

127

She reached out a hand to him, her face soft with affection. 'I know, lad, I know.'

He ignored the hand and stalked to the scullery door. 'And cancel that bloody party!' He stormed from the kitchen and out into the rain again, allowing the door to slam behind him.

Out in the cold afternoon weather, he headed for the warm comfort of the stables. Old Jim, his only stablehand had gone into the village with the horses to the blacksmith, so the tackroom was quiet.

Sitting down on a wooden stool, he rested his feet up on the wall that held all the harnesses and equipment. The smell of hay and leather mixed with the aromas of molasses and manure. As normal, his thoughts drifted to Catrina. Tomorrow they would be married, but he had the feeling that their problems would only be beginning not ending by the marriage.

He hadn't expected Phillip to show up and cursed his timing. Catrina would be unsettled by his appearance. Travis wished he was there to support her. Although, if he was faced with Phillip he'd likely knock the man to the ground and more. Damn Phillip!

The whole situation was spiralling out of control. In an ideal world, he'd find his grandmother somewhere else to live, but he couldn't and wouldn't do that. She'd taken care of him since his parents' death when he was a brooding youth with an uncertain future. It wasn't until he came to live with her and Grandfather that he gained some direction in his life, some purpose to do well and make them proud of him. How could he repay her for giving him the chance to escape the bohemian life his father adored by sending her away?

Yet, was it fair to Catrina to bring her into another woman's house and expect her to feel comfortable and at home? He knew she had responsibilities at Davmoor and he would accommodate her needs to go between the two houses. Only, it grated in his gut to think that one day she would also have Hugh's vast estates and wealth. How was he to deal with her going to Gloucestershire as well as the time she spent at Davmoor?

And what of his dreams and ideas for the future? How was he to improve his farm and not be tempted to the money Catrina will get from Henley?

He looked out through the wide stable doors back to the farmhouse. Although not small, the house was nothing in comparison to Davmoor, or Henley's estate. Would it be enough for Catrina? Was his love for her enough to keep her this time? She didn't really need him, she never had. She hadn't come to him when she was attacked, had she? No, she'd run away instead of trusting him to take care of her.

He ran his hand over his face, his heart aching for answers his mind couldn't give him.

Unable to cope with the silence of the stable he jerked to his feet and headed out over the fields.

CHAPTER 12

*R*ain from heavy, low clouds tapped against the windows, bringing dusk forward an hour or two. The sunshine of the last week was replaced by dull, grey skies and a damp cold wind. Catrina had a fire lit to give some warmth to the library. The gloomy weather reflected the sombre mood of the house.

Catrina checked the shelves for her favourite books to pack. It seemed a little surreal to her that she was spending her last night as a single woman packing. Upstairs, Lettie was sorting through which of her clothes to put in the trunks.

Selecting *David Copperfield* from a high shelf, she studied the red leather spine, but her mind wasn't on books. Since Darius Smith's declaration to have the estate, she'd spent hours trying to work out a solution. She must talk to Phillip about it, but the thought of facing him made her sick to the stomach.

With Mrs O'Toole's help they had identified the maid Phillip abused. The girl was from the laundry, recently and cheaply employed when the older staff had left over non-payment of wages. Thankfully, Phillip hadn't managed to go the whole way with her and Catrina's arrival in the bedroom saved her from complete ruin. Mrs O'Toole believed the girl to be a little slow, one of the orphaned girls she'd hired when the original staff left. The girl had willingly gone with Phillip not understanding his intentions.

A slight knock preceded Mrs O'Toole. 'Miss, Mr Millard is here.' She stepped aside for Travis to enter the library.

'Travis, you're soaked through!' Catrina rushed to him, worried by the anxious look on his face. 'What's happened?'

'Nothing, nothing.' The tight line of his mouth eased into a warm smile. 'I had to see you.'

'Without a coat?' she tutted. 'Look at you. You'll catch your death.'

'That's what Grandmother said.'

'Then we at least agree on something.' She turned him towards the fire. 'A towel, if you please, Mrs O'Toole and some brandy.'

Once the housekeeper left, Catrina poked some heat into the fire and added more coal. She glanced at Travis as he crouched beside her, holding his hands out to the flames. 'Are you sure everything is all right?'

'I've come to ask you the same question.' He straightened, his gaze earnest. 'Are you certain in your mind that you wish to marry me?'

She gently stroked his cheek, feeling the roughness of his stubble growth. 'Yes.'

'Can you live at the farmhouse?'

'I'll do my best to fit in. Living in a farmhouse doesn't worry me at all. If I can live in the cottage in Scotland I can be equally as comfortable in the home you provide.' She looked away, knowing her words weren't coming out as she wished. 'It's not going to be easy because of your…'

Mrs O'Toole bustled in and gave Travis a white hand towel, which he wiped over his face and head, while Ida placed a tray holding the glass of brandy onto a low table in the middle of the room.

When they were alone once again, Catrina sighed, her mind whirling. Travis took her hand in his cold ones and kissed it. Her heart constricted with love for him and not for the first time did she wonder why nothing was simple in her life.

'Talk to me,' he whispered. 'Tell me all your thoughts.'

'I want nothing more than to be your wife...'

'But?'

'But I feel pulled in other directions. So many things aren't right here, and I'm needed to oversee the estate, which Phillip continually abuses and abandons, not to mention his wife. Then there is Father.'

'Grandmother said that you'd hardly be at the farm, once we are married, and that issues here will take all your time and energy.'

Tears welled in her eyes and blindly she gazed down at their joined hands. 'I'm sorry. It's just that after being away, wallowing in my own self-pity I feel like I've deserted Father when he needed me most. He cannot rely on Phillip. I'm all he has.'

'I understand.'

'Oh, I know I cannot do much and that it might be all too late anyway, but I must try, Travis. Somehow I have to regain what Phillip has gambled away.'

'Darling.' He squeezed her hands and as she looked up at him a single tear slipped over her lashes. 'Don't cry, my love.' He traced her jaw line with a fingertip, stopping at her chin, which he gently tilted up so he could kiss her lips. Staying only an inch from her face, he locked eyes with her. 'I love you.'

'And I you,' she whispered.

'I'm glad to hear it.' He winked and grinned before giving

her another kiss. Taking a deep breath, he stepped back and straightened. 'So, I've decided that instead of you moving to the farm, I'll come and live here with you until things are sorted out.'

Catrina blinked, wondering if she had heard correctly. 'You'll move here?'

'Does that meet with your approval?' He gave a half smile.

'But what of Bottom End?'

'It's only five miles away, sweetheart. I can go there each day if need be, but I sense you're in need of my help more than the farm. At the moment, I have good men assisting me and I can leave them to do what needs to be done. Whereas here, there is chaos.'

'You don't know the half of it,' she murmured.

'Well, you can soon set me straight about it. Yes?'

She didn't know what to say. An overwhelming sense of love and guilt filled her. 'You'll live here at Davmoor, leave your home, for me?'

He clicked his fingers dismissively. 'Is that all I'm doing?' Laughing, he pulled her roughly into his arms. 'I can live anywhere, as long as I'm with you.'

Catrina hugged him close to her and kissed him all over his face. The fierce affection she felt for this man robbed her of breath. 'Thank you!'

THE RAIN of the previous night had washed away the dust and given the flowers a refreshing drink. The countryside sparkled as the sun poked through the last of the sketchy clouds and gave people something to smile about.

Catrina, dressed in her wedding finery, left her bedroom and went to see her father. Opening the door, she entered his room and then stopped.

'Surprise.' Her father stood by the bed, wearing a dark suit, complete with a ruby red cravat and silk waistcoat. His face held the grey tinge of illness, but his eyes shone with determination. 'I had some help. Mrs O'Toole was in on it.'

'You aren't well enough to leave your bed.' Catrina, full of concern, hurried to take his arm as he swayed a little.

'Nonsense.' George Davies lifted his head proudly. 'How could I let my only daughter get married without being there to give her away?'

'Father, I—' She turned as Mrs O'Toole entered the room.

'There you both are. Good.' Mrs O'Toole, wearing her best dress of deep steel grey and a black bonnet with a white spray of flowers on it, gestured behind her. Roddy and Flynn, the two remaining gardeners nervously stepped into the bedroom. 'Come along, hurry up.' Mrs O'Toole ushered them in. 'Now then, Master, if you'll just sit on the chair there, the lads will take you down and out to the carriage.'

'Mrs O'Toole.' Catrina's eyes widened. 'I hardly think—'

'Now, Rina, stand aside so I can be taken downstairs,' her father insisted.

Stupefied, Catrina watched the two brawny men carry her father downstairs for the first time in two years. Shock gave way to apprehension as she hurried after them. She fussed all the way down the stairs and outside to the carriage, but Roddy and Flynn were careful and cheery, cracking jokes to amuse their master, while Mrs O'Toole harangued all the other servants into the rest of the estate's transports going to the church.

'Kitty-Kat!'

Catrina looked back up at the east wing to see Aveline waving from her opened bedroom window. She waved and smiled, then once her father was settled into the seat, she entered the carriage.

The short journey to the village church allowed her to

fuss some more over her father but, after a few moments, he took her hand and held it firm. His quiet presence calmed her, and she trusted him to know what was best for himself, if only for this day.

Roddy and Flynn carried him down the narrow aisle inside the cool stone church and placed him at the end of their family pew. Catrina walked slightly behind, nodding to the odd guest and trying to relax. It was only when her father was comfortable did she look up and focus on the man she was to marry.

Travis wore a dark suit of finest wool, his waistcoat and cravat were of embroidered gold silk. Best of all, was the loving gaze he bestowed on her. Taking his hand, she respectfully stood at his side and listened to Mr French, the vicar, say the words she longed to hear.

When, at last, she was joined by law to Travis, Catrina turned to smile at him, knowing that whatever lay ahead she had him by her side.

'We did it, at last.' Travis kissed her as they signed the register. Her father and Mrs Millard acted as witnesses. Ailsa's smile was more of a grimace as she wished Catrina a happy life, but her father shook Travis's hand with joy on his face.

Outside in the sunshine, she gripped Travis's arm as well wishers came to congratulate them. A select few were going back to Davmoor for refreshments, so the rest of the village used this time to speak to the happy couple. Catrina noticed that Ailsa Millard stayed at the back of the group, her face as sour as unsweetened rhubarb. Beside her stood Travis's cousin Estella and her husband, Mr Baldwin. The three of them watched on, showing no warmth between them.

'Shall we go?' Travis whispered into her ear, leading her along the church path towards the waiting carriages.

'Yes. I see Mrs O'Toole is having a difficult job of prising

Father away from people. They've not seen him in such a long time, but he's tired.' She shook hands with Mr Brown the butcher and his round little wife and moved a couple of steps to shake the hand of Miss Beasley, the village school teacher.

'We shouldn't have married after Sunday service,' Travis groaned. 'We'd been better off to do it early one morning mid-week.'

'I hope they are happy for us.' She smiled and nodded greetings to more acquaintances, people she hadn't had the time to speak to since her return.

Finally, they made it to their carriage and were soon trundling away back to the estate. Travis kissed her all the way home, making her giggle and blush like a girl. Only her laughter disappeared as the horses slowed in front of the house and Phillip stood on the steps, his face furious.

'Don't let him spoil our day,' Travis muttered, climbing out and then handing her down. 'If he starts, I'll knock him down and more.'

'Where is Father?' Phillip snapped. 'Why isn't he in bed?'

'He wanted to attend our wedding.' Travis's cold tone stopped Phillip from advancing closer to Catrina.

Phillip glared from one to the other. 'Was he well enough? I thought he was at death's door?'

Gathering her skirt, Catrina feigned a cheerful expression. 'Not at all, Phillip,' she lied. 'He's feeling very well indeed and wanted to join the celebration.'

The puce colour drained from Phillip's cheeks to a ghastly shade of white. 'He's better? So suddenly?' He followed after them as Travis and Catrina went through to the drawing room. Guests were coming up the drive and the last thing she wanted was an argument with her brother. She turned a stunning smile on him. 'Would you care to stay for some refreshments, Phillip? And perhaps converse with everyone?'

He blanched and backed towards the door. 'God, no. Not with them lot. Mix with villagers and the like? I think not. I'm off for a ride.'

'And Mr Smith? Where is he?'

'Around somewhere, I don't know nor care. Just as long as he's not with me!' Phillip strode from the room as the first of their guests arrived.

'Mr Smith?' Travis asked quietly, waiting for Doctor Robinson and his pretty wife to join them.

'I'll explain later.' Catrina kissed Travis's cheek. 'Play host, darling, while I see that Father is settled upstairs.' She left the drawing room as guests mingled outside. Mrs O'Toole shepherded in Roddy and Flynn, who carried in their master on his chair. Catrina took her father's hands. 'How do you feel?'

'Tired, dear, but happy,' he replied. 'I'll go up and have a nap.' As Catrina went to go with them upstairs, her father waved her away. 'No, don't come up. Stay with your guests. These lads will see to me.'

Mrs O'Toole nodded. 'I'll just get Ida started on the serving and then I'll go up and check on him. Doctor Robertson is here if needed.'

'I can't believe Father did it.' Catrina watched the men struggle up the stairs, carrying the chair between them.

'He's been planning it for days.' Mrs O'Toole patted Catrina's arm and then whirled off down the hall to the kitchens beyond.

About to walk back into the drawing room, Catrina hesitated as Ailsa Millard, dressed all in black, stood by the front doors. They gave each other a long look before Catrina stepped forward. 'Mrs Millard.'

'So, you won,' the older woman muttered.

'It's not about winning or losing.'

'Isn't it?' Ailsa raised a lofty eyebrow. 'You were successful in getting your own way. You made my grandson leave his property to come here.'

'It was Travis's suggestion and his final decision.'

'You could have swayed him otherwise, but instead you selfishly agreed to it. A true Davies, after all.'

'He understands how it is here. That I cannot leave right now.'

Ailsa stalked past her only to pause by the doorway. 'You'll regret all of this, you mark my words.' Then, pasting a false smile on her face, Ailsa sailed into the drawing room to kiss Travis's cheek and to talk to people she knew.

Catrina turned away, only to find Darius Smith watching her from the end of the hall. He bowed his head to her, his dark eyes assessing, before he walked into the library.

CHAPTER 13

*S*nuggled against Travis's back, Catrina listened to his breathing as he slept. A smile played on her lips as she thought of their lovemaking only hours before. Travis was insatiable, wanting her at all times of the day and night. It was as though he was making up for lost time. Not that she was complaining, she found his constant attentions delightful. There wasn't a safe time or place as to when he didn't come to her and kiss her soundly and make love to her. The house was filled with their laughter as he chased her, begging for kisses and more. They'd made love in strange places, with Travis locking the door to whatever room they were in and ravishing her on tables and chairs. A simple horse ride turned into a romp in the wood or cavorting in an abandoned barn.

Many times, they'd been caught kissing by the staff and blushing Catrina would push Travis away, only for him to laugh and kiss her all the more. The relaxed five days since their wedding on Sunday had been helped by Phillip and Darius Smith leaving for York early Monday morning. She didn't know how long they would be gone for, but with their presence removed from the house she felt a sense of relief. That, and her father's improved health had allowed Catrina to enjoy some special time with Travis and for a while at least, forget the troubles awaiting her attention.

Sighing, Catrina watched the moonlight shadowing the walls through the opened curtains. The warm night air stole through the sash window, gently lifting the lace curtains. Dawn was close, and another sunny day expected. Her eyes were heavy, but sleep wouldn't come. Unlike Travis, she couldn't always fall asleep so quickly.

She rolled over to her other side and then back again, not finding a comfortable spot in the hot bed. After so many years sleeping alone, it was hard to share her bed with another. When she tossed again, she disturbed Travis and forced herself to lie still. In the quiet, an owl hooted outside. She closed her eyes.

A bang woke her. For a moment she lay without moving, confused if she'd actually heard something or not. Then came another sound.

Leaving the bed, Catrina shrugged on her linen dressing gown and glanced at the clock on the mantlepiece. Ten minutes past five. Dawn was breaking, filling the room with a golden pink glow. The balmy heat of the night lingered and gave a hint of a hot day to come.

The sound came again. Who'd be up at this time? The servants? Had Ida dropped something? Perhaps her father had woken and needed help, or Aveline?

With her slippers on, Catrina slipped from the bedroom and peeked in her father's room, but he was sleeping soundly. Heading along the east wing, past one of the guest rooms, she heard shuffling. A trickle of unease slid down her back. Who would be in there and why? She opened the bedroom door.

Phillip turned from the suitcase he was throwing items

into. His hands were shaking and there was a stain on his shirt, stubble coated his podgy jaw. 'What do you want?'

She ventured a little further into the room, but stayed near the door. 'When did you arrive home?'

'A few minutes ago.' He continued packing, his movements jerky and unsteady. Several more trunks were opened at the end of the wide bed.

'What are you doing?'

'Must you be so dense?' he snapped. 'What does it look like?'

She took in the large amount of luggage he was packing. The drawers were open and empty, along with the wardrobe. 'You are going away again?'

'Very clever.'

Ignoring his sarcasm, she weighed up what to say next. That he'd returned home at dawn, drunk, didn't surprise her, but to be packing to leave again so soon filled her with alarm. He was taking everything with him. This wasn't a simple visit somewhere for a few days. Her annoyance grew. 'Did you come alone?'

'Yes.'

'Will we be seeing anymore of Mr Smith?'

'I won't be, no.' He crammed more shirts into the trunk.

'Phillip, you have to stay. There are things to discuss. We haven't had the chance to sort issues out yet. I know about your gambling, the debts and—'

His grey eyes, so unlike her tawny brown ones, narrowed with hatred. 'You know nothing, little sister. You've been away for years and come back to gossip. Don't listen to every tale your husband tells you.'

Her anger rose hot like a boil. 'Gossip? Is it gossip that sold acres of the estate? Is it gossip that has accounts unpaid.'

'Be quiet. You know little about it.' He strode to a tall cabinet in the corner and opened it to reveal a decanter and glasses. After pouring out a large measure of brandy, he threw back the contents.

She glared at him. 'How long did Aveline's money last?'

'Not long enough to be saddled with her for life.' He sneered and drank another glass dry.

'I am ashamed of you. I always have been.'

'Do I look like I care what you think of me?' He snorted and swayed slightly. 'Besides, you can't berate me about causing gossip. You've been doing it for years.' His top lip curled in disgust. 'Millard. Good God, after all that nonsense a while back you've gone and married him.' He swung away to refill his glass. 'You are his wife instead of his whore.'

'Shut your filthy mouth!' her fist clenched into her nightgown.

'Shaved too close to the bone, did I?' Phillip laughed and reached out to tug at the bell pull. 'Us Davies are a sorry lot. I marry the lunatic and you marry the hired help. No wonder Father wants to die or did.' He gave her a look of hatred. 'How long do you think this period of *good health* will last this time? A week, perhaps two? God, who'd have thought he'd last so long?'

She trembled so much she thought she'd fall. How she hated him. With effort, she tried to control herself. Since the wedding, her father had rallied, buoyed by the good spirits of seeing everyone again and having Travis to talk to each evening. But she knew it wouldn't last. Doctor Robinson warned it could be the high before the low, and, he'd been right. Only last night her father's appetite had dwindled again and he had no wish to leave his bed. 'And when Father does die the creditors will come calling, won't they? Will we lose everything, Phillip?'

His blood-shot eyes peered at her. 'No, not everything.'

'Yet my dowry has gone.' She'd found out that piece of

information from their solicitor at the wedding breakfast. 'How did you manage to get hold of it?'

'Father signed papers.'

'Did he know what he was signing at the time?'

'I bought us some time, so be thankful.' Phillip tucked a handful of gold trinkets into his pockets. 'Besides, you've got a husband now to provide for you. Go live on his little farm and raise a dozen brats and stay out of my business.'

'How else did you buy some time and keep the creditors away?'

'I've sold the terraced row in Leeds and the glass factory in Bolton.'

Her blood ran cold. 'What do we have left?'

He picked up his glass again and drained it before waving it in the air. 'This, though it's mortgaged to the hilt.'

'The house and estate? Nothing else?'

'Not much.'

'And what of Darius Smith? He says you owe him an enormous amount, that the estate's worth doesn't even cover it. Is that true?'

Phillip shrugged and banged the lid of one trunk closed. 'Smith is a greedy bastard. I've already given him a capital little boat yard in Newcastle, but it's not enough. He's no sense of friendship.'

'Do you? Do you have any sense of decency left?'

'According to some, I never had any decency.' A look of hate came to his face. 'They said I was the image of our grandfather, the one who used to terrorise the village with his debauchery, his wildness and fondness for drinking and gambling. They said I would grow up to be just like him...just because I resembled him.' He gave her a piercing stare. 'Village women would turn from me and I was only a child. I wasn't allowed to talk to their children.' He stepped to the bed, his shoulders bowed. 'Ailsa Millard was one of the women, who when I returned from school as a young man made my life hell. I heard her in the village one day say I was no good, bad. The other women listening nodded and agreed. They didn't know anything about me.'

'They knew you rejected my mother.'

'I was a child...' He shrugged and shook himself like a dog. When he turned around to face her, the evil smirk was back. 'They all thought me to be bad, so I gave them what they wanted. I went out of my way to cause them insult. Everything they had accused our grandfather of doing, and therefore me included, I made sure I did it.'

'So, the village women are the reason you became wicked?' she scorned.

'It was easier than trying to show them I could be good.' A sinful sparkle shone in his eyes. 'I found a had the knack to be the scoundrel. I was, after all, just like grandfather!'

'But why do you hate me so much? I've done nothing to you. Yet, you've treated me with contempt all my life. You even allowed me to be...raped by your friend.'

His expression tightened, the light in his eyes become bleak. 'I didn't mean for that to happen. How was I to know he'd go so far?'

'You encouraged him to chase me, knowing full well he was drunk and lust-filled...'

'Yes, well...' Phillip glanced away and fiddled with a shirt spilling out from his luggage. 'Pollack also paid the price.'

'And I didn't?'

'When he realised what he had done he offered to marry you, but you'd gone.'

'As if I would have married the man!'

'Pollack left for the West Indies a few weeks later. I've not seen him again.'

'Are you sorry it happened, Phillip?' Would he at last be a man, a brother and say what she wanted to hear?

'I've got to go.' He turned away from her.

'Even now you cannot be the person I hoped you could be.'

'Go away, Catrina. For God's sake just leave me alone.' He fastened a portmanteau. 'Where is that blasted maid?' He closed and locked another lid. 'I must leave straight away.'

'Why? Do you realise what time it is?' From the corner of her eye she saw Ida standing in the hallway, her eyes wide and terrified.

He strode to the door and yanked it open. 'There you are, you idiot.' He glared at Ida. 'Get in here and have those trunks taken downstairs. Have the carriage brought around and be quick about it.'

'She can't lift them, Phillip. Have some sense,' Catrina scoffed. 'Ida, go down and ask Roddy and Flynn to come and help, please.' The maid scurried away, and Catrina turned back to Phillip. 'How are we to manage with all these debts?'

'Ask Father.' He chuckled without humour. 'Or ask your husband.'

'We could lose the estate!'

'Good!' Phillip pulled on his suit jacket. 'I'm tired of the bloody lot!'

'And how will we all live then?' She wanted to scratch his eyes out.

'You can go to your husband's property and take the rest of them with you.'

'And you? How will you live?'

He gave her a calculating look. 'There are many opportunities in America, sister dear.'

'America?' The warmth drained from her face. 'You're leaving us altogether?'

'I'm done with England.' He smiled a sickly sly grin. 'For good.'

A scream rent the air and Catrina jumped. They both turned to the door as the scream came again, louder.

'Aveline.' Catrina ran to the door. 'Quickly, Phillip, it's the baby.'

'No.'

She stopped and stared. 'No?'

'I don't care about her or the scrap she'll bring into the world.'

'But—'

'Do you think I want an imbecile child as well as a wife?'

'You don't know the child will be affected.'

'What, with her as its mother? What do you think? I'm not staying to find out either.' He grabbed a leather carryall.

'Then you shouldn't have married her, should you!'

'I didn't realise she was so bad back then. After we married and we…we…Jesus Christ!' He ran his hands through his hair, making it stand on end. 'I can't do it, Rina. I can't face it. She not right in the head and the child will be the same. It's all too much.'

'You filthy coward.' Other screams came, higher and more urgent than the ones before. Catrina glared at him. 'Help me settle her down, at least. She'll be calm with you. For some reason she thinks you are wonderful.'

'No.'

'Yes! For once in your greedy life, Phillip, think of someone else.'

He hesitated, then reluctantly went with her to the east wing. They saw Ida on the landing and Catrina told her to fetch Mrs O'Toole and to get one of the staff to ride for the doctor. The screams now alternated between deep guttural moaning and wild hysterics.

Phillip hesitated in the sitting room of the suite. 'I can't go in.'

'Shut up, for heaven's sake.' The door to the bedroom was

146

closed and when Catrina turned the handle she found it locked. She pounded on the wood. 'Aveline, open the door.' A pitiful whining came from the other side. 'Phillip, talk to her.'

He pounded his fist on the door impatiently. 'Aveline. It's Phillip.'

'Phillip?' The word was barely heard.

'Yes, open the door.'

'Been sick, Phillip. It hurt.'

Catrina stared at him. 'She's in labour I think. Get the door open.'

He rattled the handle and then thrust his solid weight against it, but it didn't budge. 'Aveline, come and unlock the door. Be sensible.' Whimpering was all they heard.

'She might not be able to move, Phillip. You'll have to break the door down.'

Scowling, he shook his head. 'That's an oak door and not cheap.'

'And Aveline needs help.' Catrina twisted the knob again, cursing her brother's attitude. 'Aveline, can you get to the door, dearest?'

'Catrina?' Travis hastily came to her side, tucking his shirt into his trousers as he did so. 'What's happening?'

'Aveline has locked the door. We think she is in labour.'

'Here, Miss.' Mrs O'Toole panted up behind Travis, separating a key from the bunch that hung at her waist. She handed it to Catrina. 'Roddy's gone for the doctor.'

'Why do you have a key?' Phillip demanded at the housekeeper. 'No one should have a key to my wife's personal rooms.'

'The doctor advised it months ago, Master Phillip.' She gave him a hard look that spoke volumes.

In her haste, it took Catrina many frustrating moments to get the door unlocked, but finally she pushed it open and they rushed in only to stop in horror at the scene before them.

Blood seemed to be everywhere, on everything. The sour smell of it filled the room and their noses. Catrina's stomach churned, and she heard Phillip swear a vile oath and gag. Aveline was sitting on the floor by the bed, which was stripped off all its coverings. Her white nightgown was ripped and soaked in red. Blood oozed out from between her legs, staining the carpet in a dark pool. What appeared like a blue cord lay between her thighs. Her wide, child-like eyes were glazed and unfocused while her fingernails tore at her scalp.

Mrs O'Toole was the first to recover. 'Now, my pet, let's have a look at you.' As she reached to help Aveline up, there was a flash of silver. Mrs O'Toole cried out and stumbled back. Aveline's face twitched, a pair of scissors in her hand.

Catrina and Travis rushed to help Mrs O'Toole, dragging her back out of harm's way. They sat her on a chair by the door leading to the sitting room. Travis kept his arms around her for support as blood trickled out of the wound in her arm.

'Find something to bind up the wound,' Catrina demanded of Phillip as she put pressure over the hole, but he kept staring at his wife. 'Hurry, for God's sake.'

'I'm all right, Miss.' Mrs O'Toole grimaced in pain, giving lie to her words. 'It's nowt but a scratch.'

'It's deeper than that I'm afraid. It'll need stitches.' Catrina glanced back at Aveline, but her sister-in-law hadn't moved from the floor.

Phillip returned from the sitting room, holding a silk scarf. 'Will this do?'

'Yes. Tie it quickly.' Catrina moved her bloodied hands away from the stab wound and the blood ran freely again down Mrs O'Toole's sleeve.

'I can't do it.' Phillip thrust the scarf at her, a horrified look on his face.

Grabbing the scarf, and cursing her unreliable brother to hell and back, Catrina quickly secured the material around the housekeeper's arm. 'Hopefully that will help until the doctor arrives.'

'What do we do about her?' Phillip glared with revulsion at his wife.

'She's scared.' Catrina wanted to go and comfort the poor bewildered girl, but with the scissors in her hands she dare not step closer.

'Miss, the doctor's here.' Ida rushed into the room, breathing hard. 'Roddy found him down the road. He'd been at Mrs Percival's house and was on his way home. Poor old Mr Percival died during the night.'

'Be quiet, girl,' Mrs O'Toole barked. 'Get downstairs and tell cook to heat plenty of water, then bring some towels. You know what to do, so look sharp.'

'Good God!' Doctor Robertson strode through the sitting room doorway towards them. 'What has happened here?'

'Aveline, in her fright, stabbed Mrs O'Toole,' Travis told him.

Robertson knelt beside Mrs O'Toole and peered under the scarf. 'Binding the wound is the right thing to do. Are you feeling faint, Mrs O'Toole?'

'Strong as an ox, Doctor.' The housekeeper jerked her head towards the bed. 'Mrs Davies needs you more.'

Catrina nodded towards Aveline. 'She's in labour and terribly frightened.'

The doctor took in the bloody state of Aveline. 'She's not in labour any longer. I can see the cord.' He froze. 'The baby has been born.'

'Born?' Stunned, Catrina stared, while Phillip moaned and backed towards the door.

'I thought that too,' Mrs O'Toole murmured, her face the colour of putty.

'Then where is it?' Catrina couldn't believe she was in this nightmare and was thankful Travis was close for her legs threatened to buckle beneath her.

Doctor Robertson took a step towards Aveline. 'Mrs Davies, it's me, Robertson, your doctor. Remember?'

Aveline ignored him for a moment and then slowly gazed up at him. 'It hurt. Dreadful thing. I was scared.' She trembled violently. 'I can't move.'

He took another step closer, wary of the scissors she clutched. 'Where's your baby?'

'Baby?' She stared open-mouthed. 'What baby?'

'Your baby? The one you just gave birth to, with all the pain.' He crouched low, close but not within striking distance. 'Can you tell me?'

'I want my baby.' Large fat tears tripped over her lashes. 'A sweet baby with a bonnet on.'

'Yes, that's right.' Abruptly, Robertson pivoted on his heels and went around the bed and they all saw what he saw, a trail of blood dotting the carpet. The trail led to the window. Carefully, Robertson pulled the curtains aside and a soft warm morning breeze and sunshine flowed into the room from the open window. Leaning forward, the doctor looked over the edge and down.

Phillip gasped, his face tinged green. 'Christ in Hell! She threw it out of the window, didn't she?'

'No!' Catrina's hand went to her throat as Robertson rushed from the room, calling for Travis to go with him. She desperately wanted to follow them and see for herself if the baby lived, but Phillip left the room after the doctor and Travis instead and so she stayed with Mrs O'Toole and Aveline.

The minutes felt like hours until the doctor came back

into the sitting room. He carried the baby wrapped in a thick blanket and gently laid it down on the blue and white striped sofa. Ida followed him carrying more blankets. While Travis opened the medical bag and placed it by Doctor's side.

'Does it live?' Catrina whispered through the bedroom doorway.

'She does, but barely.' Robertson rubbed warmth into the tiny body. 'Can you assist me please, Mrs Millard. We must warm the child.'

Catrina left the bedroom. 'Ida, have the fire lit immediately.'

Mrs O'Toole, her hand holding the scarf in place, joined them in the sitting room. 'There's baby garments in the basket over there.' She nodded to a long narrow wicker basket by the side table. 'They've just been washed and Mrs Davies was looking at them only yesterday.'

Robertson continued to rub and check the baby. He looked around 'Where is Mr Davies? I'll need some help with his wife.'

'Didn't he go down with you?' Catrina asked, glancing up from the baby.

'No.' He checked along the baby's limbs, which were now turning a slight pink colour.

'I'm sorry. I don't know where he has gone.' She stared out through the sitting room door, willing her brother to come back into the room and help take some of the responsibility.

'When I went through the kitchens I asked your Cook to heat up some milk for the infant. We must pray it's not too late.' He turned the baby over and she gave a small faint wail as he ran his fingers down her spine. 'Thankfully, Mrs Davies had wrapped her in the thick blankets from the bed. She landed in the bushes below the window. The blankets cushioned the fall. It doesn't seem she's broken any bones. Babies are soft that way.'

Gazing at her niece, Catrina's heart constricted at the puny little body and the angelic tiny face. 'Do you think she was out there long?'

'No, I don't. She wasn't that cold, maybe only minutes. But if it had been any longer, well…'

Ida sat back on her heels and added more kindling to the small blaze she'd started. 'Shall I get the baby's milk, sir?'

'Yes, do that.' Mrs O'Toole answered for the doctor. 'And tell Cook to use those feeding bottles I ordered, the ones with the smaller teats. And get the men from outside. We'll need help in here.'

Ida rose from her knees, her thin face serious. 'Roddy was packing the carriage with Master Phillip's trunks when I looked through the window as I came up.'

'Then find someone else. Now get down stairs for that bottle and be quick about it.' Mrs O'Toole used her good arm to wave the girl away.

That her brother was running away didn't concern Catrina at that moment. He was beyond her forgiveness. She'd washed her hands of him once and for all. She hoped she never saw the cowardly slug again. What concerned her now was seeing that the baby lived. She peered at the little face and when it screwed up its features and let out a long wail they all breathed in relief.

Robertson bundled the baby tightly in a warmed blanket and then handed her to Catrina. 'She'll need careful watching. Can you try to feed her when the bottle comes? Aveline won't be in any condition…'

In their desperate bid to see to the baby they'd forgotten about Aveline. They all glanced through the bedroom doorway and were thankful to see her still sitting on the floor by the bed.

Cradling the precious bundle close, Catrina sat on a chair near to the fire. She was surprised by the lightness of the baby. Taking a closer look, she became awed by her perfect features, but as the baby hadn't opened her eyes or done more than utter the odd feeble cry, she was worried it was dying. She glanced up to the doctor to say so, but he was in deep conversation with Mrs O'Toole and only broke apart when Ida rushed in with the feeding bottle. Behind her came Mr Thatcher, the old head gardener, Hannigan and Carter, the grooms.

Robertson turned Travis. 'We must move carefully near Aveline, slowly and quietly.' He nodded to the men, who were all looking unsure and ill at ease. 'This won't be pleasant, but your help is very much needed. Mrs Davies isn't herself at the moment and is fragile.'

In the doorway Phillip appeared, dressed for travelling. 'Catrina. I must speak with you.' He pulled on his gloves, not raising his head. They all turned to stare at him in amazement.

He couldn't even look them in the eyes. Shame washed over her at his weakness.

'Mr Davies,' Robertson stepped forward. 'I'll need your assistance, too, in getting your wife into bed so I can check her condition.'

'Like hell I will.' Phillip's head jerked up and he backed from the room, his expression one of loathing. 'She can rot as far as I'm concerned. I want her committed. She mad. Insane. A murderer! She killed the child.' He held onto the door jam, all pretence of sophistication gone. Fear blazed in his eyes. 'God Almighty this will ruin us all, don't you see? It'll be the end I tell you!' He ran from the room and they let him go.

The outdoor staff moved restlessly and Robertson gave them the nod to proceed into the bedroom. Catrina, holding the baby close, took the strange curved bottle from Ida and tried to insert the nipple into the small mouth, hoping she was doing it correctly. 'Come on, little one. You must drink now.' Gradually, the mouth puckered and sucked. Catrina smiled as the baby drank. 'Good girl.'

A moment later Robertson returned to her side. 'Mrs Millard.'

She looked up from gazing at the baby in her arms. 'Look she's drinking. That's good, yes?'

'Yes, most gratifying indeed.' Robertson's handsome face was grey with fatigue. 'Mrs Millard, Catrina, Aveline is dead.'

Catrina stared at him. 'Dead?'

'She stabbed herself.'

Catrina looked past him into the bedroom. There on the floor, slumped against the side of the bed was Aveline. The scissors sticking out of her chest created a river of blood down her body.

CHAPTER 14

*H*er father might be dying, but he wasn't stupid and knew that something had happened. Catrina, with Doctor Robertson present, told him the news about Aveline, softening the blow with details of his grand-daughter who had survived the last twenty-four hours and taken small amounts of milk every three hours.

'We have called the baby, Ava, Father. It's close to her mother's name and we, Travis, Mrs O'Toole and I, thought it fitting.' Catrina squeezed his hand.

After a long moment, he spoke. 'And Phillip?'

'Away, Father.' Catrina rose from the chair. She would never forgive Phillip for his behaviour. It disgusted her beyond words. She knew she'd been a coward, hiding up in the Highlands, not wanting to face a life of misery as a spin-ster in her father's home, with Travis in eyesight but never to be hers. However, Phillip even outshone her in the stakes of spinelessness.

'He'll be back for the funeral?'

'I'm not sure.' She tidied up his blankets. 'I'll leave you

with Doctor Robertson and I'll come up again later to sit with you.'

'Rina.'

She paused. 'Yes?'

'The funeral…when is it to be?'

'Friday.'

'It is for the wrong person. It should be mine.' Her father's voice held a steely determination and she had no answer for him. Quietly, she left the room and headed downstairs.

'Ma'am,' Ida met her at the bottom of the staircase.

'Yes?'

'The nursemaid has been interviewed by Mrs O'Toole and she is waiting in the kitchen.'

'Mrs O'Toole should be resting. I could have interviewed the girl.' Catrina tutted. 'Is this girl suitable?'

'Aye, Ma'am. Mrs O'Toole approves of her. Would you like me to send her into the study?'

'This girl, what's her name again?'

'Penny Mately. She's Cook's cousin's niece. Recently widowed and just had her twenty third birthday. Sensible and clean, too.' Ida blushed, realising she knew and said too much.

'Then if Mrs O'Toole and obviously Cook approves of her I'm sure she'll be fine. Show her up to the east wing and help settle her in. I'll see her this afternoon.'

Ida bobbed a quick curtsey and fled back down the hallway to the service end of the house.

With Mrs O'Toole in bed resting her injured arm, or meant to be, her work and supervision was now Catrina's, but instead of heading to the study and dealing with menus, accounts and staff issues, she opened the front door and went outside to feel the sun on her face. Though, on second thoughts that was a mistake. Seeing the neglected and unkempt gardens depressed her further. She was about to return inside when a horse and rider trotted down the drive. Gladness lifted her heart at the sight of Travis.

'You came out to meet me? Were you spying from the window?' he said as he drew closer and dismounted.

'I came out for air and a turn around the garden while the sun is out. Though the sight of it only deepens my gloom. Old Mr Thatcher can't see to the gardens properly. They're too much for him now.' She raised her face for his kiss. 'Is everything well at the farm?'

'Yes, all is in order. It dare not be with Grandmother watching over them. Where's the groom?' He looked towards the wall arch leading to the service quarters.

'Does it surprise you that one hasn't come running? Staff have been leaving daily due to lack of wages and I can't blame them.' Arm in arm they walked around the side of the house, leading the horse. They had to bend their heads through the arch as a creeper had grown beyond management and hung low in great swathes ready to strangle an unsuspecting visitor. 'Carter and Hannigan left this morning. I gave each what money I could, only they were still short. They are good men and didn't press for the rest of what is owed them, though I did give them glowing recommendations. They were sorry to go, but how could I persuade such hard-working men to stay after they saw Phillip leave himself the very day his child was born? Everyone knows he is not likely to return for a long time. I couldn't look them in the eye and say yes wages are secure because I don't know if they are.' She sighed, shoulders aching with the strain of it all.

Travis glanced around the stable yard. 'Is there anyone left to tend to the horses?'

'Just a boy, Freddie.' She pointed to the empty stalls. 'Phillip sold all but the carriage horses, and he has those with him at the moment. If he does go to America I expect he'll either send them back or sell them.'

'Knowing Phillip, he'll have sold them and turned off his driver.' Travis began unsaddling his horse. 'Old Jones has been working here his whole life. He'll likely return and tell you what happened either way.'

'Yes. And despite there being only your horse here, Jones can stay for his bread and board as long as I can afford food.' Tears welled. The damage done seemed insurmountable. How would it ever be put right? Years of loyal servants were being treated so callously. Her father would never approve. She wondered if there was anything left to sell in the house which could safeguard next year's wages.

Travis dumped the saddle and cloth over a wooden rail. 'I'll pay the staff wages I told you that.' He took her chin and raised her face for his inspection. 'You look tired, my love.'

'I am tired.' She savoured his kiss and for a moment they simply stood and embraced. 'You can't pay the bills forever, Travis. I'll have to reduce more staff.'

'Let me tie up young Monty here.' He patted the gelding's head and led him into the stables where Freddie came running from cleaning out a stall and took him away. 'Now I am yours for the day,' Travis said returning to her side. 'Let's walk down by the lake.' He nodded towards the sloping lawns and they strolled that way.

Catrina lifted her face to the sun, enjoying the warmth on her skin. The air smelled of summer. Blossoms of the maple trees peeked out between new leaves and if the estate's debts didn't pressed down on her Catrina would have sat on the clover lawn and idled the day away.

'Did Mr French arrive?'

'Yes. The funeral is set for Friday. Mr French confirmed this morning when he came to sit with Father. Father is taking it badly.'

'And what of Phillip?' Travis took her hand and placed it through his arm. 'Do you really believe he has gone to America?'

'Yes, I do. He wants to get as far away from his responsibilities and creditors as he can. From what I can gather from the conversations I've had with Father is that Father signed over a great deal of his business concerns to Phillip as well as full control of the estate.'

'So he has nothing to gain by staying then, if there is no more money to come his way?'

'Exactly.' They paused at the water's edge and watched the ducks glide serenely across the dark lake, their ducklings fanning out behind them. A green dragonfly hovered over the water lilies. The marsh irises were in bud the white flowers of the bitter cress dotted the lake's banks. Despite the prettiness of the area her thoughts remained on her brother. 'Phillip has managed to get his hands on all the money and waste every penny of it.' She turned her back on the lake and gazed up the slope to view the house and gardens. All she saw was the need to spend money. The dreaded attics, which she never visited, but had been reported to her, had damp patches were rain was starting to leak in, some parts of the brickwork needed new mortar. The chimney sweeps would have to come before winter, and likely the window frames could do with fresh putty. How on earth could she pay for it? She only had one answer. The same answer that kept coming to her every day. 'I'll have to swallow my pride and go to Hugh.'

Travis stared at her. 'Hugh Henley? Why?'

'To beg for a loan.'

'There's no need for that, not yet. What I have is yours. I know it's not a lot, but we can survive on it.'

'Thank you, but the farm cannot pay for the upkeep of the estate.' Silence stretch between them as they battled their thoughts. Catrina knew what Travis was trying to help her, but he didn't have the capital to do so.

'There are other alternatives, Catrina, as I've mentioned before.'

She stiffened. 'You propose that I close the house down, let go of the staff who have lived here for years and move at the farm?'

'I know it would pain you, but—'

'And my father?' her voice rose. 'Could you witness him being evicted from his own home? Can you imagine what that would do to him?'

Travis took his hat off and banged it against his leg. 'Certainly, it would cause anguish.'

'Anguish? It would kill him.' She glared at him, wishing that he had a better way to help her. The damn farm was all he thought about. Why couldn't he see that such a move wouldn't do anyone good? For sure she and Ailsa would likely come to blows before the first day was out.

'As I see it there is no other choice.' His tone was tight and his lips compressed into a thin line to hide his frustration but she knew of it.

'But there is. I can borrow against what Hugh has promised to bequeath me.' She started walking towards the house. Now the decision was made and aired, she intended to act on it. 'Hugh will grant me a loan I'm sure of it.'

'Why saddle yourself with more though?' He strode alongside of her.

'It won't be debt. Hugh's estate will be mine anyway or will be one day.'

'That's morbid and selfish.'

'It's a fight for survival, Travis.' She wouldn't give way on this. Someone had to make a stand before everything was lost.

'I think it is rather rude to be honest.'

She rounded on him. 'I'm not wishing for Hugh to die.'

'It sounds like it.' His face was as angry as hers. 'It's as though you can't wait for the event so you can use his money to save this place.'

'Well, someone has to.' She glared at him. 'Am I supposed to let the estate fall to ruin? The bank is breathing down our necks with every letter they write.'

Travis ran his fingers through his dark hair. 'It's not your responsibility, Catrina.'

'It's my home.'

'And so is my farm. Close the house up and come live at the farm. Forget all the worries, all the duties that aren't yours but those of your bastard brother.'

She stormed away from him. 'Don't be simple! With Phillip gone it all becomes mine to deal with.'

'Not legally.'

'No, but morally. Father would want me to do something.'

'And what of your duties to me, your husband.'

She whirled around so fast he nearly bumped into her. 'How dare you make me choose when you said, you *promised*, you'd help me set things right.'

Travis gripped her arms, a desperate plea in his eyes. 'You don't understand. You don't see what everyone else does. The estate is past saving, as are Phillip's debts. There is nothing here. You cannot fight against the tide of destruction Phillip has created.'

'I have to try.'

'Why, for God's sake? You ran away from here once before easily enough. You can do it again.'

'Yes and look what I came back to. If I'd stayed...if I'd been here I could have...perhaps Father wouldn't have...I'd...'

'Yes?' he jeered. 'What could you have done? As a daughter, as a sister?'

'Things might have been different.'

'Well, you could have married Arthur Seaton. He has the wealth needed to fix this place.'

'I wouldn't have married him.'

'Nor me either I'm guessing.' His eyes were hard as granite.

'You are probably right. That's why I didn't stay!'

He let go of her arms and stalked away a few steps before turning back to her. 'You have to let it go.'

'No, I don't, and I won't. Hugh will help me.'

'Don't be so foolish, Catrina! You'll be pouring more money into this place than is sensible and for what reason? This place isn't yours and it never will be, don't you understand? At any time, Phillip can come back and banish you from ever setting foot here again.'

His words cut her like broken glass. Catrina straightened her shoulders and raised her chin. 'It might not be mine, but it will be Ava's eventually. She has no parents. I will do it for her.'

'You'll do more for her by taking her away from here.' A muscle clenched in his jaw.

'Oh, take her where exactly? Five miles down the lane to your farm? Is that it? Let her grow up in the shadow of the estate and all the while never allowing her to live here, her rightful home?'

His shoulders drooped, the fight leaving him. 'At least at the farm she will be happy, but then we both know that you will not be.' He gave her a sad smile. 'Am I right?'

She steeled herself not to waver. 'I have to do what I think is right.'

'Right for whom, Catrina? What are you trying to prove?' He walked past her without looking her way and she half reached out to him, but let her hand drop before she made contact.

* * *

IN THE DYING SUNLIGHT, grey gulls wheeled and cried over the wharves, beady eyes trained to find any scrap of food spilt from unloaded crates or unwary people. Fishing boats at anchor bobbed slightly, their decks quiet now as workers left to go home or visit the nearest tavern to wash away the grime of a hard day's work.

Further along the docks, larger ships waited for cargo, either human or produce. Dusk didn't hide the fear on the foreign faces as they made the next step on their journey to pastures new. Accents from all over Europe vied to be heard along the busiest port in the world – Liverpool.

In the weak light of a street lamp just lit, Darius Smith climbed down from his carriage and nodded to his head man, Seavers, before glancing around him. Seavers slipped away to whisper a word to the two men sitting up top beside the driver. Three weeks. It'd taken three weeks to track down the whereabouts of his quarry. It'd been an interesting hunt. Davies had gone to ground in London until word came of his desperation to sell off items to fund his new life in America. From a distance, Darius had watched and waited.

Twitching his long coat from around his knees, he strode into the ancient tavern opposite. Dark, noisy, stinking of stale ale and sweat and bursting with people, Darius ignored it all and headed straight for the back room tucked down a narrow hallway beside the staircase.

'Well do, Mr Smith.' The tavern owner, Isaacs, followed him into the small room and, pulling a damp cloth from his waistband, gave the wooden table a wipe even though it was spotless. 'A hearty meal you must be wanting, sir?'

'Is he here?' Darius pulled off his leather gloves and slapped them onto the table.

'Aye, upstairs. Third door on the right.' Isaacs tucked his

cloth back into his waistband. 'He's been drinking all day though. I had to help him up to bed not an hour since. I doubt you'll get any sense from him tonight.'

'Blast it.' Darius shrugged off his heavy coat and Isaac jumped to collect it. 'Have food sent out to my men and I'll take a meal in here.' He sat on a green padded chair as Isaacs left the room. His fingers tapped the wood of the table as he thought. He'd wasted enough time in playing the gentleman with Davies. The fool owed him too much for pleasantries to be of any use now. He didn't know why he'd waited so long to extract what was his. But then, if he was honest he did know.

Catrina.

Throwing his head back, Darius closed his eyes and pictured her. Her smile, the intelligent look in her eyes, the way light caught the gold in her chestnut hair. How in God's name did a maggot like Davies end up with a sister as magnificent as her? His blood ran hot at the mere thought of her. He had to possess her.

A bang in the taproom and raucous laughter brought his attention back to the situation at hand. Phillip Davies. Darius rose, knowing he wouldn't enjoy a mouthful of food while ever that gluttonous pig lay above his head sleeping.

It took but a moment to locate Davies' rented room upstairs. The door wasn't even locked. Darius stood beside the bed while Phillip snored heavily, spread out on his back. The man's shirt and waistcoat stretched tight across his large stomach and he didn't look as if he'd shaved for days. Perhaps he thought growing a beard would aide his flight to freedom.

Fighting the urge to slit the man's throat while he slept, Darius kicked him awake instead. Groaning, Phillip rolled over and mumbled. Incensed, Darius kicked him again. 'Get up you fat bastard!' He grabbed him by the lapels and then saw the water jug. A quick toss of cold water over Phillip's head made him smile as his former so-called friend gasped and blundered around the bed like a beached whale on a sandbank.

Stepping forward, Darius gave him a stinging back-handed slap to the face. 'Come on, you cheating dog!'

'What? What...' Phillip struggled to a sitting position, popping a waistcoat button as he did so. 'Who dare—'

'I dare,' he said very quietly. He stepped back as Phillip's face changed colour and then swore as the bloated fool vomited over the floor. The acrid smell filled the room and Darius whipped out a handkerchief to cover his nose. 'You sicken me.'

Bleary eyed, Phillip looked up and moaned. 'You.'

'Yes. Me.' He walked across and opened the small window out an inch or two to breathe in the salty air. Muted voices from below drifted up.

'Trust you to find me. You're like a rat terrier, won't let go.'

Darius turned smiled. 'Enough of the praise, friend. To business.'

Flopping back against the pillows, Phillip threw one arm over his eyes. 'Come back when I'm feeling better.'

'You never will feel better, Davies.' Crossing the room, he opened the door, startling a passing serving maid. 'You there. Have hot water and food brought up. Strong tea.' The maid scuttled down the stairs and Darius shut the door. 'Wash and shave, then eat.'

'Why?' Phillip murmured.

'Well, unless you have the estates' deeds in your luggage, we'll have to journey to your solicitor. Where is he, York or London?'

Phillip slowly sat up. 'Deeds?'

'What else would I want from you?' He lounged against the door and inspected his fingernails.

'I thought you said the estate wasn't worth the money owed?'

'I changed my mind.'

'If you'd just wait—'

Springing from the door, Darius resisted the urge to throttle the man. Taking a deep breath, he fought for calm. 'I have been patient enough. Wouldn't you agree? So tonight we travel to get the deeds.'

Phillip's gaze darted to the pile of luggage filling one corner of the room before he quickly looked away and ran his hand through his thinning hair.

Darius smiled. 'So, you carry them with you?'

'No. Why would I?'

'Why indeed. Perhaps to sell once you'd crossed the Atlantic?'

'Absurd. The deeds are with all my important papers with my solicitor in York.' Phillip's hands shook, and he straightened his rumpled waistcoat and shirt.

'Really? Do I need to ask my men to come up here and search your belongings?'

Vile swear words issued from Phillip's mouth. He grew red in the face from rage as he ran out of curses and insults.

Far from offended, Darius laughed. He'd won. 'Enough now, man. Let us get this done and then we can have a drink to celebrate.'

'What do I have to celebrate you son of a whore.' Phillip stumbled over to his luggage and unclipped a small trunk.

'A new life in America.' Darius ran a finger over his moustache.

'New life. Huh.' Phillip searched through numerous documents. 'Without money I have nothing.'

'Because I'm feeling generous, how about I give you, as a parting gift, a small amount to help you on your way.'

Phillip looked sceptical as he handed over a thick roll of paper tied with black ribbon. 'Oh? In return for what?'

'Nothing. I have everything I need.' He untied the ribbon and began reading.

'Lucky bastard. You have everything and I nothing.' Phillip shrugged and sighed. 'It's a relief actually. I don't have to worry about any of it anymore. Good riddance, I say. I've hated my life as long as I can remember. That estate was a noose around my neck. I never wanted it. If it had been closer to London, somewhere fashionable it might have been different. But stuck in Yorkshire?' He snorted in disgust. 'What good can that do for a man? The world is in London, or New York.'

'Then why did you sell your London townhouse?' Darius murmured as he read, not really caring for the answer.

'Had to. The bank pressured me...' Phillip sighed heavily. 'I need a drink.'

'No.' Darius turned another page. 'You need a clear head to sign. In the morning we will finalise the arrangements. Then you won't see or contact me again.'

Swearing softly, Phillip turned to the window and looked out. 'Actually, there's one last thing you can do for me, if it pleases you.' He turned. 'One last thing.'

'And it is?' Darius looked up from studying the sheaf of papers and jerked at the cold stare of Phillip's eyes.

'Kill them. All of them.'

CHAPTER 15

The hot June sun baked the village church as the mourners made their way out of the cool stone building and into the bright sunshine. Many people, those who couldn't fit into the full pews, stood by the open grave waiting for the polished mahogany coffin to be carried out.

Catrina nodded and murmured thankyou to the old friends and acquaintances who'd travelled to honour her father. The large number of people who'd gathered gave her hope that the Davies name wasn't totally destroyed by Phillip's behaviour and that, despite all, George Davies had been loved and admired.

As Mr French intoned her father's favourite verse while his coffin was lowered into the ground, Catrina gazed, dry eyed, at the spray of white roses covering the lid. Then, raising her head, she stared at the beech trees lining the perimeter of the graveyard. A great many birds were enjoying the sunshine, warblers, house sparrows and she even spied a greenfinch on the stone wall beneath. For a moment she blanked out everything but the twittering birds.

'Are you all right?' Travis whispered close to her ear.

'Yes.' She gave him a brief smile, but there was no return gesture from him. In the weeks since Ava's birth they'd grown apart and her father's death a few nights ago hadn't brought them closer. It pained her that they couldn't see eye to eye on the important issue of money and the future of the estate. If she had the strength to grieve over her father and the sorry condition of her marriage she would have, but the stress and worry of keeping the estate alive had driven every emotion out of her. She'd lost count of the long nights she stayed in her father's study working on the account books, looking for ways to curb expenditure and find income. Yesterday the annual Inland Revenue bill for the servants and animals had arrived in the post and the thought of not being able to pay it nearly made her collapse. Still, next year the bill would be a lot less with no carriage and fewer male servants to account for.

'Mrs Millard.' Mr French patted her arm, bringing her back to the moment.

'Thank you, Mr French. It was a very fine service.' She smiled and shook his hand. 'We're having refreshments back at the house. Will you come?'

'I will indeed.'

She smiled and over the heads of others saw Mrs O'Toole ushering the staff onto the cart. She'd be there to greet the mourners.

'Catrina?' Travis waited a step away. 'Ready?'

Taking a deep breath, she left the gravediggers to complete the task of burying her father, and after a moment beside her mother's grave, she headed for Travis's carriage. The one Phillip took never returned, only Jones did, by train, and it was he who now drove Travis's vehicle.

Somehow, she managed to make it through the afternoon. Her head felt as though it was full of cotton fibres. She assumed she spoke the right words and conducted herself properly towards her guests but as the last one left she found she couldn't remember a thing she'd said.

'So, Mr Kelthorn didn't make it.' Travis, pulling loose his black cravat, stood by the fireplace which was filled with a large bouquet of bluebells.

'No. There has been no word from him. I don't understand what prevented him from coming today. He's been Father's solicitor for a good many years.'

'Maybe he is unwell.' His tone indifferent, he folded the cravat and tucked it into his trouser pocket. 'Besides, we know what he has to report. Everything is, or already has been, left to Phillip and he's squandered it.'

She had nothing to say to that and so an awkward silence stretched between them. Since their argument by the lake, nothing she said or did seemed to penetrate his coldness towards her. He wanted her to bend to his will, but it was impossible. With her father dead and Phillip no doubt across the ocean, Davmoor was her responsibility. Naturally, she acknowledged it didn't have to be. She had every right to close the house up and live with Travis at Bottom End, but she couldn't do it. Something stopped her whenever she thought to heal the rift between her and Travis. He would be happy and loving again if she went to the farm. So why didn't she do it? Why did she fight to stay here in a crumbling estate? She didn't know. It wasn't as if she had a deep abiding love for the house. True, it was her home, she'd been born here, but she hadn't always been happy. The attics and what happened that dreadful night haunted her every time she stood on the landing and glanced at the narrow staircase leading up to them. It wasn't as though she had many good memories here either. Her mother died young, and afterwards her father existed in a half world full of pain and longing for his dead wife, and Phillip was continually spiteful. If she was honest she couldn't say she loved her home with passion, not like her father and grandfather had done. Yet, the thought of walking away, of living only five miles from it seemed ridiculous, cruel even. And she couldn't do it. She was hurting Travis, damaging their marriage, but she couldn't alter her feelings.

'Now then, Ma'am.' Mrs O'Toole came back into the drawing room and looked from her to Travis. 'A light meal? Cook will make something tasty for you both.'

'No,' Catrina raised her hand, 'no, thank you. I'm not hungry. I would rather a long hot bath if I may?'

'Certainly.' Mrs O'Toole's face was all concern. 'It's been a trying day, so it has. I'll have Ida see to it immediately. Mr Millard?'

'Nothing for me either. I'm off to see my grandmother.'

Catrina glanced at him as she rose. 'Now?'

'There's still an hour or two of daylight.' He left the room without another word.

Catrina felt the prick of tears and closed her eyes. She wanted to reach out to him, needed his arms about her. How could she close the breach between them? Would the news she believed to be with child heal the gap?

* * *

A FOX CRIED into the silence of the night as Travis turned on the doorstep and kissed his Grandmother's soft cheek. Golden light spilled out from inside the warm kitchen and he found it difficult to leave. It annoyed him that he had to. This was his house, damn it. Pushing the thoughts away, he summoned a smile. 'I'll come back tomorrow. The roof on the hay barn needs repairs. I want it repaired before harvest.'

'Why don't you just stay the night?' She pulled the lapels of his lightweight coat closer. 'It's silly to go out in the night air only to return again in the morning. It's already late.'

He clasped her thin hands in his, stilling their movements. 'I know, but I need to go back. Catrina buried her father today. She shouldn't spend the night alone.' He tapped the tip of her nose as she screwed her face up at the mention of Catrina.

'Well, that's the last of the decent Davies gone. God help us.'

'Grandmother,' he warned. 'Don't spoil the evening. I've enjoyed being with you.'

'And I you, dearest.' She kissed his cheek. 'The shame of it is that we could have every evening like this if you remained here, where you belong.'

He grimaced. 'With you and Catrina either side of the fire, I doubt our evenings would be anything but pleasant.'

'I'd try, honestly I would.' She slipped her arm into his and they walked to where Monty stood patiently in the yard. 'I'd do anything to have you home.'

'I'm sorry.'

'Will the brother come back now?'

'I doubt it. He'll be in America by now, free from responsibilities. Catrina couldn't even send word of George's death because we don't have a place to send it to.'

'Despicable behaviour.' His grandmother snorted her contempt. 'How long will she remain there then? You might never live here again.'

He sighed deeply and fiddled with Monty's reins. 'That is what worries me and what we have quarrelled about. I promised her I would support her in the fight to keep the estate, but I can see now that it is foolish to do so. The estate belongs to Phillip. She's killing herself with worry over it when she has no reason to. I don't understand why she won't walk away from it.'

'Could you walk away from this farm if there was the slightest chance you could keep it?' she said softly. 'I'm not

Catrina's greatest advocate, I admit to that, but she is loyal, if nothing else. Only, that loyalty is misplaced now. She's done her best, no one can deny that. However, as your wife, her loyalty should be to you.'

Travis patted Monty's neck. 'I think she's frightened of leaving the place again. The years in the Scottish Highlands did damage. She's ashamed she ran away and stayed away for so long. I think she's trying to make up for that by holding onto something that isn't there.'

'Why did she run that night?'

He paused before answering, yet he knew it was time his grandmother knew the facts. 'She was raped, Grandmother, and Phillip encouraged it.' In the quiet of the balmy night, he told her all the details. 'She was hurting, shamed, and sickened by her brother's traitorous actions. As well as confused about her feelings for me, and what was expected of her. Is it any wonder she stayed in Henley's cottage and didn't want to come home?' The love he always felt for her come gushing to the fore. What was he doing here when he should be in her arms, loving her? He prepared to mount.

'Well then,' his grandmother murmured, stalling him. 'You'd better go and be with her. Perhaps it is time a new Millard came into the world.' She smiled. 'I'd like to sit your child on my knee before I'm in my own grave.' Stepping back, she nodded in the moonlight. 'Bring her with you tomorrow. It's time I got to know her properly.'

He gave her another kiss on the cheek and mounted. 'Thank you. Now go inside.'

'Do you want a lantern?'

'No, Monty and I can find our way.' He glanced up at the clear starlit sky. 'The moon is good tonight.'

'It'll be hot again tomorrow.' She waved him on and turned back to the open kitchen doorway.

Letting Monty pick his way through the silver gloom

along the rough track that led to the estate, Travis relaxed his shoulders and for the first time in weeks felt his spirits lift. That his grandmother wanted Catrina to visit could only be a good omen. Perhaps if he and Catrina discussed the situation again, she might see his way of thinking. He just had to hold onto his temper. She might even decide to close the estate up and move to the farm. They had to talk. These last few weeks of sullen silences wore on his nerves.

The light darkened as they entered the woodland bordering Davmoor and his fields. The canopies of large oak and ash trees merged above, their lower branches brushing his head. Gorse bushes, brambles and nettles crowded for space to gain what sunlight was available between the trees during the day and which made the track narrow and dangerous at night. He cursed himself for a fool not to have taken the lantern. Monty jingled the bit in his mouth, the sound loud in the quiet. Another hundred yards would see them clear of the wood and out into open fields on the estate side.

Something rustled in the undergrowth and Monty snorted. Travis thought he saw the flash of a stoat, but in the poor light couldn't be sure. He patted Monty's neck as the horse jerked his head up and down. 'There, boy. It's nothing. Probably a rabbit.'

Peering into the murkiness ahead, he nudged Monty on a bit quicker and made a mental note to have this track cleared and widened. It wouldn't hurt to have some white-washed stones placed along the route as well.

'Stop right there!' A large man jumped out of the bushes in front of Monty's head.

'What the hell?' Travis gripped the reins as Monty shied and side-stepped. A second man leapt out from the side of him, arm raised holding a large club. Travis had no time to defend himself as the attackers struck.

* * *

AFTER FINISHING HER BREAKFAST, Catrina spent an hour playing with Ava. At first, she worried that the child would be hard to love, being a product of Phillip, but the baby was too sweet, too tiny to resemble anything of the parent who sired her. Ava had Aveline's large blue eyes, but that was all. The rest of her, Catrina told the servants, was all new and completely Ava Davies and no one else. Mrs O'Toole declared the child had the sunny disposition of her mother, for she hardly ever cried.

Her nanny, Penny, was proving to be a treasure and cared for the infant with devotion. Aveline's old rooms and been stripped of the ornate furniture and Phillip's dreadful taste in art. Mrs O'Toole instructed Ida, with the help of Freddie to wash the old, but sturdy nursery furniture and arrange that in the room instead. Penny sewed the baby's garments from good linen sheets, adding scraps of lace to them taken from Catrina's unused clothes. The young woman spent hours creating a clean and relaxed environment for the child and Catrina was thankful Cook had recommended her, despite the burden of another wage to find.

From the nursery, Catrina then worked with Mrs O'Toole on clearing and sorting her father's belongings. All his clothes were to be given to the local Almshouse and his personal effects were boxed and placed up in the attic by young Freddie. One day she would go through them but not now, it was too soon, and she didn't have the emotional strength to deal with them.

The morning's heat wilted the flowers and people alike. Catrina changed her under garments twice and drank Cook's refreshing cold ginger ale, while the older woman complained of the weather souring the cream in the larder.

Towards noon a thunderstorm rolled in from the West.

Furious lightening streaked the sky and dark, angry clouds turned day into night. Ida started to close the windows, but Catrina stopped her, enjoying the fresh smell of rain on the wind. She wondered if the storm would send Travis home, since he hadn't returned last night. On second thoughts she realised he was at home, at Bottom End. He'd never see Davmoor as more than somewhere he was temporarily living and why should he? The estate had nothing to do with him. She hated arguing with him. Somehow, they'd have to reach a compromise. Not for the first time did she wished they'd both stayed in the little lodge on the mountain. The special place where she'd conceived.

Catrina entered the conservatory, a room that usually gave her peace with its leafy green palms and white iron furniture, but the morning's heat was trapped in the glass panels making it stuffy and hot. Lightening flashed brilliantly in the marble grey sky and she watched it for a while, her mind again doing the calculations that made her believe she was pregnant. A little smile played on her lips. She was certain she carried his child. She'd had no monthly show since he found her in Scotland in March. By her reckoning, their baby would be born in November. A baby of her own. She imagined the joy on Travis's face, then her thoughts changed. Would he insist on the child being born at Bottom End?

A tap on the door preceded Mrs O'Toole, who looked anxious. 'Ma'am, *he's* back.'

Catrina jumped, her heart pounding like a blacksmith's hammer. 'Phillip?'

'No. Darius Smith.'

'Oh, lord.'

'He's brought Mr Kelthorn too.'

Her eyes widened in shock. 'Kelthorn? He brought him or did they happen to arrive at the same time?'

'One carriage.'

'Did they ask for Phillip?'

'No, for you, madam.' White lines of strain pulled at the housekeeper's mouth. 'Shall I send for Mr Millard?'

Smoothing down her black taffeta dress, she stalled for time to think, to plan and be prepared. 'Yes. I would like it if Mr Millard was here.'

Mrs O'Toole nodded vigorously. 'Right. I'll send Freddie immediately. He can run like a hare across those fields I've seen him do it before. I've put the gentlemen in the drawing room. Keep them talking as long as you can, or I can tell them to wait while you change your gown. That'll give time for Mr Millard to get here.'

'I don't have another mourning gown to change into.'

'They don't know that,' Mrs O'Toole whispered conspiratorially.

Catrina gripped the dear woman's arm for support. 'You are very good.' Taking the back narrow staircase, she went up to her bedroom. There, she washed her face and took out her hair which had escaped its combs. Lettie entered the room carrying clothes fresh from the laundry. 'Shall I put it up again, Madam?'

'Please.' Sitting on the stool before the mirror, Catrina tried to calm herself. Kelthorn was here, no doubt, to read the will, but why was Darius Smith here with him? Why hadn't they asked for Phillip? It didn't make any sense.

'All done, madam.' Lettie, with a last comb in place, stepped back.

'Thank you, Lettie.' Catrina glanced at her hair, swept neatly up into a twisted roll and studded with mother of pearl combs. Lettie had teased a few strands to hang on either side of her ears. Pulling straight her cuffs, Catrina steadied herself with deep breaths. It couldn't be helped the black mourning washed the colour from her face and the sleepless nights had given her bruising beneath her eyes.

Downstairs once more, she hesitated a moment in the hallway, and then head held high, walked through to the front of the house. Back straight, she entered the drawing room and pasted on a smile for the two men as thunder boomed overhead. 'Gentleman. My apologies to have kept you waiting.' She bowed her head graciously.

Kelthorn scrambled to his feet and jerked a bow. 'Good day to you, Mrs Millard. I am most sorry to hear of your father's sad passing.'

'Did something obstruct you from attending the funeral, Mr Kelthorn? I was expecting you yesterday.' She clasped her hands in front of her and kept her tone light. 'I hope you weren't ill.'

'No, ma'am, I wasn't...' Kelthorn flushed a dangerous red and blinked rapidly. 'My sincere apologies, madam, and I beg for your forgiveness. I had every intention of coming here to pay my respects and read the will, of course, as I aim to do so today, however-'

'The blame is solely mine, Mrs Millard.' Smith bowed smoothly before her. 'I was a rogue and kept Kelthorn chained to his desk beyond what is considered polite.'

She stared at Smith, revealing nothing on her face. 'Indeed, Mr Smith. I wasn't aware we shared the services of Mr Kelthorn.'

'We don't, madam. My solicitor and Mr Kelthorn have been working together.'

'I see.' She smiled, not seeing at all. For the two solicitors to work together it meant Phillip had something to do with it also. Her stomach clenched at the idea. 'And what brings you to Davmoor?'

'Can I say business and pleasure?' His dark assessing eyes

raked over her from head to foot. 'But first, my condolences in regards to your recent loss.'

She raised a haughty eyebrow. 'Which one, my sister-in-law or my father?'

'Both.' He bowed again, but kept his stare direct.

Mrs O'Toole entered the room carrying one tea tray and Ida carried another, which they arranged on the two small occasional tables near the sofa. Harsh rain pelted the windows.

'Please, make yourself comfortable.' Catrina indicated for the men to sit as she did. She managed to make light chit-chat with them for ten minutes while they drank tea and nibbled at the triangular sandwiches and lemon curd tartlets. With each tick of the hand on the mantle clock, Catrina grew edgier. Where was Travis?

Sipping her third cup of tea, Catrina forced a smile as she patiently listened to Mr Kelthorn's tale of his childhood escapades. She'd encouraged him to reminisce, pleased that Smith was only just keeping control of his impatience. So far, he had wandered to the window and watched the rain, studied the various paintings around the room, inspected his fingernails, eaten another sandwich, drunk his tea by the fireplace and finally paced the floor. In any other situation, she'd have laughed.

It was nearly half past one when Kelthorn finally stopped talking and looked uncertain once more. 'I must apologise for my bad manners, Mrs Millard. I fear my tongue has run away with me today.'

'Yes, quite.' Smith strutted forward, giving the man a piercing look. Saddened that Travis hadn't answered her summons, Catrina placed her teacup and saucer on the tray. 'Well, gentlemen...'

The clatter of wheels on the drive had them all looking out the rain-splattered window. Catrina rose as Mrs O'Toole passed the doorway to the front entrance and opened the door. Moments later, Ailsa Millard sailed into the drawing room, bringing with the scent of damp.

Perplexed, Catrina stepped forward. 'Mrs Millard, this is a surprise.' Expecting a cutting remark, she was shocked when the old woman grabbed both her hands.

'Tell me he's here,' she implored.

'Who?' Catrina held her thin, veiny hands. 'Who are you looking for?'

'Travis!'

Catrina jerked back. 'Travis? But isn't he with you?'

'No. Not since last night. He left about ten o'clock. I watched him go. An hour ago, old Jim found Monty in the east field still saddled, his reins trailing on the ground. The storm was scaring him. Then your lad came running for Travis and I didn't know...' She paused to catch her breath, her face as white as the hair beneath her hat.

What fragile strength Catrina still possessed threatened to desert her. She gazed into the other woman's eyes. 'He never came home. I assumed he'd stayed the night at the farm.'

'Then where is he in this weather?'

'I have no idea.' She put her hand to her throat. 'Monty must have thrown him. He might...that is...he could...'

'He's been out all night? Oh my!' Ailsa drifted sideways into a dead faint. She hit the floor before either Smith or Kelthorn could catch her.

CHAPTER 16

$\mathcal{O}$ver the pounding thunder, Catrina shouted for Mrs O'Toole while Smith and Kelthorn helped Ailsa into a chair. For a moment there was too much talking and movement for Catrina to concentrate as Mrs O'Toole rushed in with Ida. Kelthorn poured a glass of water from the drinks cabinet and gave it to Ailsa.

'Mrs Millard.' Smith came beside Catrina and gently took her elbow. 'I will help you.'

She looked up at him and blinked, his words hard to understand. 'Help?'

'To search for your husband.'

'Search. Yes.' His words finally penetrated the fog of her shocked mind and she jerked forward, needing to do something. 'Ida, fetch all the staff immediately. We need to organise a search for my husband. He may...have been thrown and is lying...somewhere...' She swallowed unable to finish as images of Travis lying with a broken neck filled her mind.

Smith stepped forward. 'Ida, is it? Good, go now. We'll need as many people as you can find. I'll meet you in the stable yard.' When the girl fled the room, he turned to the housekeeper. 'Mrs O'Toole, I think it prudent for the doctor to be called to see to Mrs Millard.' He nodded to Ailsa who sat stupefied on the chair, the glass of water in her hands was in danger of slipping to the floor.

'Yes, sir. Shall I also send young Freddie into the village to ask about? Someone might have seen Mr Millard last night.'

'Excellent idea.'

Mrs O'Toole glanced at Catrina. 'Madam, will you not sit down?'

Her stomach clenched in knots, Catrina shook her head. 'I will search also.'

Smith frowned and reached out to take her arm. 'You needn't venture out in this weather.'

'My husband is out there somewhere. A bit of water won't hurt me!'

'Mrs Millard, I—'

'I will search!' She gave him a quelling stare then turned from him. 'Come, we are wasting time.'

Rain on a fierce wind had cropped up, flattening Catrina's skirts against her legs and making it difficult to walk. Smith held her elbow but didn't' speak. Furious black clouds dashed across the sky, bending the flowers to the ground and violently tossing the trees as though they were no more than slender reeds. From the house, she, along with Smith, Kelthorn and the pitiful few staff strode off in the direction of the estate's boundary while old Jones took the carriage along the village road, in case Travis came home that way instead of across the fields as normal. They wore coats to keep the worst of the rain off them, but within minutes they were soaked.

Once in the woods separating Bottom End farm from the estate, they all fanned out to cover a greater distance. Against the wind, Catrina called Travis's name repeatedly, her eyes seeking for any sign of him. A part of her didn't want to find him hurt, but injured was better than nothing at all. Her clothes were wet through now and cold seeped into her skin. The hat she'd quickly stuck on her head in the kitchen was blown off and hurled away before she had time to snatch at it. Regardless, she continued on, cursing her heavy, awkward wet skirts and the storm which was making the task more complicated.

After they'd made a search of the wood, Catrina ordered them to start again. In a wide line they turned and walked back towards the estate. An hour of calling his name, she'd lost her voice. At the end of the second hour she started to trip over her tired feet. The hem of her wet skirt was inches deep in dirt and dragging on the ground. Her teeth chattered and when she stumbled over a tree root, Smith held her upright, his hold never slackening. He was a silent presence, unyielding towards the elements, as though he suffered no discomfort. Unbelievably, his quiet authority soothed her. She felt thankful for him walking beside her, but she didn't have time to wonder at it.

By late afternoon, they'd searched the entire estate and Bottom End. The storm had headed out to the east but left the rain behind, although it was softer now, a mere drizzle. Everyone was exhausted. Catrina saw it in their faces, the droop of their shoulders. At intervals, reports came from the house. Travis hadn't returned home, nor been seen in the village. Jones had driven the carriage along the York road and asked anyone he met for sightings, all to no avail.

'Mrs Millard...Catrina, you must rest.' Smith stopped her as she went to climb over the stile that straddled a stone wall between fields miles from either the estate or the farm.

Catrina paused, her boot on the wooden step. 'I'm fine.'

'No, you're not.' He pulled her away from the stile. 'We're

on a neighbouring property. Travis would have no need to be here in the middle of the night.'

She straightened, wincing as the cold rain fell down the back of her neck. 'Shall we try over there?' She pointed north of the village which could be seen in the distance. 'Perhaps he went...' She hesitated as Smith took a step closer to her.

'Enough.'

Her mouth tightened in annoyance. 'Mr Smith, I don't need you to tell me what to do!'

'And I don't fancy carrying you all the way home.'

'If you wish to return to the house, please do so. I can continue on alone. I'm quite capable.'

His expression softened. 'We'll both return together.'

'No. I cannot go back yet. There are more places to search. Travis could be...broken...or...'

'I understand your reluctance, but making yourself ill will not help him.'

'Leaving won't help him either if he has fallen or...' She frowned, her thoughts not coherent. 'Perhaps if we go back to the woods and check again, we might have missed...' Her words died as he shook his head.

'We missed nothing. You need food and warmth. Rest. I insist you have it.' With ease he turned her about and they trudged back the way they'd come.

* * *

DARKNESS HAD FALLEN and the villagers who'd arrived a few hours ago to maintain the search were now slowly returning to the drive in front of the house, where Mrs O'Toole and Ida served them with hot soup. Catrina looked out of the window watching them huddle in small groups, talking and drinking the soup, the persistent misty rain making the light murky and everyone uncomfortable.

'Catrina...' Mr Smith came to her side and held out a cup and saucer of steaming tea. 'Will you not sit down?'

She waved the tea away and turned her shoulder to him to resume her vigil by the window, willing Travis to come down the drive. What had happened to him? Why was there no trace of him? Had he left her? Was he tired of their strained relationship, their constant arguing over the duty to the estate? But surely he wouldn't leave her because of that? He loved her, she knew he did. She'd give up the estate and move to Bottom End in a heartbeat if only he'd come home. But no, he hadn't left her. He'd been taken. She felt it in the very heart of herself. Something had happened to him, something he couldn't prevent.

'Standing there won't bring him back, you know.' Ailsa's harsh words cut through the silence of the drawing room.

Catrina closed her eyes, hearing the blame in the older woman's tone. Ailsa had not said a word to anyone since being placed on the chair after her faint. Kelthorn had tried to soothe her, but she ignored him. Now it seemed she'd found her voice and spirit again.

There was movement on the drive and Catrina strained to see through the gloom to who it was. Her shoulders slumped on recognising the local constable riding towards the house. He'd visited earlier and received the details of Travis's movements of the night before. His return could mean one of two things, he knew where Travis was, or he didn't. Summoning her courage, she left the window and waited for him to enter the house.

Constable Den Peters, a portly man in his early fifties, and who'd been born and raised in the village, stood in the doorway and removed his tall hat. 'Mrs Millard. Mrs Ailsa. Gentlemen.' He bowed respectively to each and advanced a few steps into the room.

'Any word, Den?' Ailsa inched forward in her chair a look of hope on her old face.

'I'm sorry, Ailsa, none at all.' His expression showed his sympathy. 'I've notified York and also Leeds. They'll have their men on the lookout.'

'A lookout for what I ask you!' Ailsa snapped. 'He hasn't simply walked away from here. He's been abducted, I told you that hours ago.'

'Every possibility will be addressed, I promise you.'

'Pah!' She dismissed him with a toss of her sage head. 'You're all useless. Especially you, Den Peters, you always have been for as long as I've known you!'

Peters fiddled with his hat brim, his cheeks red. 'No one can be sure of what has happened yet. It's all opinion. There's no evidence of foul play, no blood or—'

'You think he has simply left?' Ailsa top lip curled back in an ugly sneer. 'My grandson would never leave me!' She flung a gnarled hand towards Catrina. 'He'd leave *her*, of that I'm sure, but never me or his farm.' Her eyes grew small with hate. 'If he's left it's because *she's* driven him to it with her selfish need to have her own way.'

Peters flushed deeper and shyly glanced at Catrina. Earlier she'd told him of the arguments between her and Travis. No doubt the constable thought Travis had taken himself off to a better life elsewhere without the hassle of a demanding wife and an opinionated grandmother. And who could blame him?

Tired, Catrina glanced down at the green and caramel swirl carpet, wishing everyone would just leave.

'Shall I send them home?' Smith was once more beside her, his dark gaze soft.

She nodded, not having the energy to deal with it anymore. If Travis had left her, then standing by the window wasn't going to bring him back. And if he'd been abducted then it was out of her hands also. She glanced up as Peters stepped closer.

'Mrs Millard. I will return in the morning.'

'Thank you.'

'Before I go...' He hesitated a moment. 'Are you sure your brother has gone to America?'

'As much as I can be.' She tilted her head. 'You think Philip might have something to do with this?'

'I need to consider all possibilities. Would Mr Davies have any troubles with Mr Millard?'

'No, none. They weren't friends, and didn't respect each other, but Phillip had no reason to harm Travis.' Her blood ran cold. Could Phillip be involved? Was he trying to get back at her? Her hand flew to her throat. 'Can you...are you able...to...to check that Phillip sailed?'

'Phillip Davies!' Ailsa stood abruptly on hearing their conversation. 'He's done it! I know he has.'

Peters shook his head, holding his hand up to forestall her tirade. 'Calm down, Ailsa.'

'Calm down? Calm down!' She jutted her chin forward, reminding Catrina of a ruffled hen. 'My grandson is missing!'

Smith straightened, and his presence was such that everyone turned to look at him. 'Thank you for your time, Constable.' He gave the man a small nod before glaring at Ailsa. 'Mrs Millard, I'll have your carriage brought around.'

'Who are you to tell me what to do?' Ailsa eyes flashed and if looks could kill Smith would be dead at their feet.

'You are distraught. It's late and nothing will be achieved by us all being up the whole night.' He glanced at the doorway as Mrs O'Toole entered. 'Could you have Jones bring the carriage around, please.' That sorted, he turned to Mr Kelthorn who sat silently in the corner of the room, his cup of tea balanced on his knee. 'Ah, Kelthorn, it's been a long day. Mrs O'Toole has prepared a room for you. Time to turn in, my man.'

'Indeed!' Kelthorn jumped up nearly oversetting his cup on the saucer. 'Indeed, we are all exhausted.' He bowed to the women and hurriedly left the room.

Within minutes the drawing room was empty save for Catrina and Smith. She stood nearer to the fire blazing in the hearth. The summer display of flowers and been hastily put aside and the fire lit when they came back from the search wet and cold. Had it only been hours since she'd been walking the fields? It felt like a lifetime ago.

'Here.' Smith handed her a balloon glass with brandy in the bottom of it. 'Drink it.'

She did as he commanded and accepted gratefully the fire it burned down her throat and into her stomach. She stared into the flames, watching the sparks crackle and float up the chimney. That Smith was still here puzzled her. Why had he remained? He was nothing to this family, and without Phillip he wasn't even a friend. She didn't understand it, or him. But, to give the man his due, he'd been a companion to her today. In the cold rain he'd helped her search for hours and once home, he'd organised others from the village to continue while she bathed.

Glancing up, she watched him move about the room. He drew the velvet curtains on the night, replaced cups on the tea tray and poured himself another brandy.

He stopped and found her eyes on him. He smiled gently. 'You should go to bed.'

She said nothing and just stared at him. For the first time since their acquaintance she didn't feel threatened by him and wondered at it. However, fatigue made her thoughts sluggish and the brandy on an empty stomach made her sleepy. When he offered her his arm, she took it and allowed him to escort her upstairs to her bedroom. At the door he bowed and whispered goodnight before Lettie came to comfort her and close the door on him.

* * *

FOR THREE DAYS Catrina kept her position by the drawing room window. It was fruitless to search anymore. Nothing had been found, not one single clue. From the window she could watch the drive and saw everyone who came and left. Constable Peters called each day, but his reports were the same – no one had heard or seen anything of Travis Millard. It was as though he'd vanished, like one of those magic tricks played at the fairs.

She lived in a half existence, barely eating or talking. She was partially aware of others being busy, of conversations, of new searches being sent out. Smith, she knew, was organising all that was being done, and she was happy to let him.

By the fourth morning she felt the need to stay in bed. Rainy periods continued, one minute the sun shone and then the next low grey clouds covered the sky and the drizzle fell again. Lettie hovered about the bedroom, constantly asking if madam needed anything but Catrina would only shake her head. What did she need? Only Travis. And he wasn't here. Would he ever be again?

When Lettie finally left the room to go down to the kitchen and make up a tray for her, Catrina snuggled down into the pillows and pulled the blankets up to her chin. Like this she watched the clouds drift by the window. She felt numb. It was as though all her emotions had left her the same time Travis did. Perhaps crying would have helped to get rid of the apathy which claimed her, but tears refused to fall. There was a pressure in her chest, but Catrina didn't know how to ease it. The only relief she got was to sleep and so she slept, only waking when Lettie shook her to sit up and eat, then when she'd finished she'd roll over and close her eyes again. The world beyond her bed ceased to exist and so did the pain.

* * *

SHE WAS RUDELY WOKEN one morning by the curtains being yanked back and the sunshine flooding the room. 'Lettie!'

'It's not Lettie, madam, it's me!' Mrs O'Toole marched about the room going from window to window, straightening the curtains and pushing open the windows.

Catrina struggled to sit up and blinked in the bright sunshine. 'Mrs O'Toole, please, I need-'

'You need to be up and on your feet!' The old housekeeper stood with hands on hips and glared at her.

'I beg your pardon?' Amazed at the harsh tone after days of near silence, Catrina scowled at the disruption.

'Aye, and so you should.' Mrs O'Toole raised a haughty eyebrow, her Irish accent stronger when she was flustered. 'The shame of it, wasting away in here. Now, if you don't mind my saying so, madam, tis time you got up and got on with your life, so it is.'

Anger lanced through Catrina like a blade through a boil. 'How dare you!'

'Oh, I dare, madam. Someone has to.'

'Get out!' She pointed to the door, but Mrs O'Toole grabbed the bed blankets and stripped them off her before she had time to grab them. 'What are you doing?'

'Washing these sheets. Disgraceful so they are, and I'll be having a word with that Lettie too. She assured me she was taking care of you. Well, she and I have a different opinion on that!' She bundled them up into a pile on the floor. 'Now, I've ordered you a bath and the breakfast table is set with your favourite food. Mr Kelthorn has returned and... oh yes, you can look bewildered for you've not known what's been going on here these last few days and it's time you did. As I said Kelthorn's returned, as there is the will reading today...aye today, so don't look at me like that. The poor man has been back and forwards from York for a week and is nearly insensible at the thought of having to do it again tomorrow.' She went to the wardrobe and pulled out several dresses. 'Mr Smith has been prowling like a caged animal, so he has...aye he's still here. I don't think he'll ever go, but that's nowt to do with me.' She opened the door as two young maids entered carrying the tin bath between them. 'Put it over there, that's right.'

Catrina stared. 'Who are they?'

'Maids. New ones. Mr Smith has been busy hiring, if nowt else. I don't know what to make of him, truly I don't. But if he wants to spend his brass then it's nowt to do with me. I just do as I'm told.' Mrs O'Toole ushered the girls out and told them not to dawdle in bringing up the hot water. 'Now, out of that bed, my lass, and let's see what's what.' Mrs O'Toole stopped mid stride and gaped at her as Catrina rose from the bed. 'Nay, lass...' She stared at her stomach.

Catrina glanced down and saw the round mound which had replaced the smooth flatness of her stomach.

'A baby?' Mrs O'Toole whispered in awe.

The child she carried had been forgotten in her torment of Travis's disappearance. But now Catrina could see with her own eyes the evidence of the life growing within her. Stuffing her fist over her mouth she tried to stop the sob which escaped.

'Oh, my lass.' Mrs O'Toole enveloped her in a tight embrace as Catrina cried brokenheartedly for the first time since the man she loved was taken from her ten days ago.

CHAPTER 17

*W*ith the release of her pent-up tears, Catrina felt better, more able to face the world outside her bedroom. The ache of her loss still gnawed at her, but she had to face the world at some point and she might as well start now, or she'd probably stay in her room for the rest of her life. How long did grief last? She'd seen her father grieve over her mother for years. In fact, he carried it with him to the grave. She knew how he felt.

After bathing and dressing in a black crepe mourning dress, which was considerably tighter around the waist, she ventured out of her room and went downstairs. Instantly, she noticed the changes. The carpets looked cleaner, huge copper bowls of fresh flowers littered nearly every available space, curtains hung crisply, windows sparkled. It seemed the whole house glowed and it wasn't just because of the sunshine.

Catrina slowly made her way to breakfast, her eyes widening at the new staff working about the rooms. There was an air of industry which Davmoor hadn't seen for quite some time.

A footman bowed to her as he came out of the study carrying a lantern. 'What are you doing with that?'

He bowed again. 'Taking it to be cleaned, madam. Mr Smith said I was to clean and maintain every lantern in the house and also count them.'

'Count them?'

'Yes, madam, before the electric lighting is put on as they'll then be stored away.'

Electric lighting? God in heaven was there no limits to this man's wealth? And who was he to order such a thing? A small stab of anxiety plagued her as walked into the sunny breakfast room. Smith sat at the head of the table, the newspaper in one hand and a piece of toast in the other. He looked very relaxed and right at home. And the growing awareness of his position here made her heart thud. 'Good morning, Mr Smith.'

He dropped the newspaper and toast and at once sprang to his feet, smiling a warm welcome. 'How lovely to see you downstairs, Catrina. You have been much missed.'

She smarted at his use of her first name, as she couldn't remember giving him permission to use it, but perhaps she did. Her mind lately hadn't been her own since Travis disappeared and it was hard remembering what she'd said or done for days.

Sitting down, she gazed at the two new girls waiting at the serving table. 'I see you have made some changes while I was...indisposed.' She raised her eyebrows at him as one of the girls stepped forward and offered her the choice of tea, coffee or hot chocolate. 'Coffee, thank you.' Catrina turned her attention to Smith, waiting for his answer.

'Yes, I have.' His frank stare left her in no doubt that he had been in control while she stayed in her room. 'I felt it necessary. You were...unwell...and direction needed to be taken.'

'Really? Why so?' She buttered her toast and kept her tone calm. 'I am sure Mrs O'Toole is quite capable of running the house. She has been doing it since before I was born, and it is, after all, her job. Is it not?'

His jaw clenched but he smiled slightly. 'I thought it would help you to have more staff. The house, the estate, cannot be run with so few.'

'And when did such decisions become yours, sir?' She reached for the strawberry jam, keeping hold of her temper.

'The evening Phillip signed the deeds of Davmoor Court over to me.' His smooth reply hit her hard, yet she had expected it. Why else would he spend so much time and money on the estate? She gripped the knife while he continued to shatter her world. 'You must understand, Catrina, I have no wish to hurt you. Phillip was going to sell the estate anyway, I got there first. Besides, he owed me.'

She struggled to find her voice. Damn Phillip! 'And...and what about me, or his daughter?'

'I'm sorry.' He reached out his hand to enfold hers, but she jerked back, the knife clattering onto the polished table.

For a long moment neither of them spoke. Catrina felt the waves of helplessness bash through her like she was on a storm-tossed sea. Nausea rose. All her hopes, her efforts to keep the estate together for Ava were dashed. By this man. No, that was not fair. Phillip had done this. He'd gambled away their heritage. She swallowed, fighting for courage, and to not give way to the emotions that threatened to topple her over into madness.

'Catrina.'

As though pulled by strings her head yanked in his direction, stiff and painful. 'Good Lord, you must be utterly tired of having me under your roof. I'm so sorry. We'll leave immediately.' She half rose, but he stood faster and grabbed her arm.

'No, please.'

'I must!'

'You don't have to, Catrina. Not yet.'

She didn't understand the pleading look in his eyes. He was behaving as a gentleman, of course, giving her time to absorb the news. Only, his expression was desperate somehow... 'Mr Smith—'

'Darius. I want you to call me Darius. Will you do that?'

'I hardly think—'

'Catrina, sit down. There are things to discuss.'

She sat because he put pressure on her arm he still held and also because she was unsure what to do next. She should send for Lettie and pack? Then there was Ava and her things. Where would they go? Bottom End? She cringed inwardly at the thought. Living with Ailsa while Travis was gone would not be wise. Murder would be committed by one of them for certain.

Smith settled himself back in his chair and pushed his plate away. The look he gave her was intense yet his posture was relaxed. 'I can comprehend that this news has shocked you and I'm sorry for it.'

'I was silly not to have expected it, knowing Phillip and what you told me weeks ago.' She focused on the newspaper print by his elbow. Anything was better than trying to read his face. She didn't want to see him gloat.

'Regardless of my ownership of Davmoor, this is your home. I do not want you to go.'

Catrina frowned at him. 'Not go?'

His smile was friendly, engaging. 'No. Indeed, I need you here...that is until your husband returns.'

'Why?'

'To help me bring Davmoor back from the brink of ruin. I want it to be a viable, successful estate again. The house needs redecorating, given life again. I can't, as a man, do it. It needs a woman's touch. And who better than someone who has lived here, was born here, knows the history, the feel of it.'

'I don't think it is possible. I cannot stay with you.'

'Why not?' He took her hand. 'Let the gossip tongues wag if they must, but don't let them stop you from remaining here. We can help each other. Or would you prefer to live with Ailsa Millard and her sharp words?'

'No.' She bowed her head, only to look up again as Kelthorn walked into the room. She withdrew her hand from Smith's and folded them both in her lap.

Kelthorn pushed his glasses further up his nose. 'Good morning, Mrs Millard. I am pleased to see you well again.'

'I believe there is the will to read, Mr Kelthorn?' she said softly feeling very alone and afraid. 'Shall we get on with it?'

* * *

THE SWAYING of the bunk was in gentle rhythm to the ship's roll over the ocean swell. Inside the cabin was warm, humid and filled with the stale air of two men living in close quarters. Travis breathed in shallowly for his broken ribs were bound tightly, restricting movement and his breathing. He lay on the bunk, slick with sweat and trembling. No matter how hard he tried he couldn't summon the strength to sit up.

'Ah, you're awake?'

Travis turned his head slightly to watch the man come closer, his face was in shadow, the lantern glow was behind him, but Travis knew him to be a doctor. The old man was also a drunkard.

'Water?' The doctor asked and not waiting for an answer, turned to pour out water from a jug on the table. He lifted Travis's head and put the enamel cup to his dry cracked lips.

Travis gulped greedily, not able to drink quick enough to quench his thirst before the cup was taken away.

'There, that will do you for a while.' The fellow returned to his chair at the desk in the corner of the cabin and wrote in a book.

Sighing, fighting the ever-present drowsiness, Travis stared up at the ceiling and watched a spider spin its web across the beam. He tried to count the days he'd been in this bunk, but his memory was fogged with strange details and long spells of blankness. His last memory was of his grandmother standing at the kitchen door. Then, the next he knew was of waking to a bucket of water being thrown over him and realising he was on a ship's deck.

Pain had been his constant companion at the time. He could only see out of one eye and bent double with sore ribs he'd been thrust down a steep ladder into the black bowels of the vessel. The descent was agonising, the pain from not only his ribs, but his head and stomach made him pass out before he reached the bottom. Later, an old man who told him he was a doctor and who would be caring for him, said he'd dislocated his shoulder in the fall.

Since then he'd been confined to this bed, to the doctor's slack administrations and the fret that he'd die and never see Catrina again. The thought of Catrina made him raise his head to look at the doctor. The effort brought him out in a sweat, but he had to make some attempt to get home. 'You...doctor...' His voice was nothing more than a cracked whine.

The man at the desk turned his head and stared at him. 'What? You need the pot?'

'No... Home?'

Leaving his chair, the man crossed to a small cabinet and took out a bottle of liquor, which he poured into a small glass. 'Home is it you want?' He laughed and suddenly sat on the stool by Travis's bed as though ready to share a joke. 'Listen, my boy, if you ever see your home again it'll be a long time coming, you understand?'

'No.' He blinked back the threat of tears, cursing his weakness. 'Why?'

'Simple, dear fellow, I was paid a lot of money to take you away from England.'

'Who?'

'Who?' The old man threw back the contents of the glass and then eyed him warily. 'That's none of your concern. Let's just say I owed some people money and they called in my debt. Being a doctor isn't such a good living, you know. Unless you've got high class clients, which I didn't. More fool me I suppose. I spent so many years trying to eke out a living in the poor areas, thinking I would get my due when the time came.' He stood and looked out through the porthole at the night sky. 'What a I fool I was. Good things don't come to good people, they come to people who snatch them.'

Despite his burning body, Travis studied the man and heard his dissatisfaction of the world. Yes, life could twist and turn you inside out and in his mind the bad won more times than the good. He was living proof of that. He'd never done harm to anyone, yet he was the one now in this serious predicament. Why? Who wanted to do this to him?

'Africa is out there you know,' the old man was saying. 'Africa on one side and Europe on the other. Interesting, isn't it? We'll be travelling through the Suez Canal in a day or two. I must say this heat is rather disgusting, wouldn't you agree? And it's not helping your condition at all.'

'What will...happen...?' He licked his lips, aching for more water. His fuddled mind worked overtime. Suez Canal? Where in hell were they taking him?

The doctor turned. 'What will happen to you?' He sniffed and stared out of the porthole again. 'If you survive your injuries and this fever that won't leave you, then you'll be tossed ashore once we've reached our destination. I was only told to take you with me as far as I was travelling and then to leave you there penniless. It seems they didn't want you dead...just gone. Quite bizarre, actually.' He shrugged and scratched at his balding head. 'I was happy to do it and clear my slate with them before leaving England. I didn't want to start a new life with old debts following me.'

Travis blinked, forcing his fever-muddled brain to concentrate on every world the old man spoke. Someone wanted him missing, gone? Who? He had no enemies. He hated no one...except Phillip. He closed his eyes at the realisation that Phillip must have brought this upon him. However, the old man was still talking and he had to listen.

'I'm told a man can start again there. I intend to do that for certain. I never had a chance to improve my lot. The money my father left me ran out while I was still in university, and money makes friends, does it not?' The doctor smiled mockingly at Travis before pouring himself another drink. 'So, this will be my opportunity to start again.'

'Where?' Travis croaked, half afraid of the answer for wherever they were headed meant the same distance home again and he'd already been away from Catrina longer than he cared to acknowledge. 'Where are we...?'

The old fellow grinned. 'I never introduced myself, did I? Unforgiveable of me.' He bowed his head. 'Donaldson, Doctor Timothy Donaldson.' He bowed again and stumbled as the ship rocked violently to one side. 'My, I say! That was a bit dicey. Though I suppose one should expect that on the high seas. No doubt we'll have more of those before we reach our destination. And we aren't in a very large ship, so we're bound for some rough days. But it was the best I could get with the money I had. The captain was obliging when Mr...er,' Donaldson coughed, his eye shifty. 'Yes, the captain was happy to have us, especially since this being a cargo ship he thought it a good deal to have a doctor onboard for the voyage. He didn't mind having you as well, despite your...injuries at the time, but then his hand was well greased with money.'

'Where?' His head throbbed worse than the engines below and he wished the old man would hurry up and get drunk and fall asleep, but before he did he needed to know where they were bound for.

Donaldson poured another glass. 'Why, my dear fellow, did I not tell you? It's the other side of the world we're heading for. Australia.'

* * *

'WHAT ABOUT THIS, MADAM?' Lettie held up a black skirt, an older, faded one. She'd spent the last hour unpicking the seam to let it out for Catrina's thickening waist.

Catrina nodded and separated a black bodice from the pile on the bed. 'It looks fine, Lettie. Now I need my bodices the same. I need one decent outfit to wear to visit the bank.' Sorting through her wardrobe kept her mind from thinking of Travis and her lack of finances. The reading of the will last week had held no surprises, except for the small amount of money her father had invested on her behalf many years ago. He hadn't told anyone about it, least of all Phillip and so it was untouched and while not a large sum, it was enough to sustain her for a few months or until Travis returned. She refused to use Travis's money, not that she could access his account anyway. They had spoken of opening up an account for her personal usage, for Travis had been adamant that she should never go without money again, unlike the time she fled to Scotland, but there hadn't been time to organise it.

'Jesus, Mary and Joseph!' Mrs O'Toole knocked on the

open door and entered the bedroom. 'Those builders! I swear the roof will fall down upon our necks any minute now. And the dirt and dust! It'll take me weeks to sort it out once they've left.'

'Yes, it is a trial.' Catrina listened to the commotion the builders were making as they installed the electric lighting throughout the house. Darius had wasted no time in bringing the estate up to modern standards. Besides the electric lighting, bathrooms and hot water plumbing were being installed. Outside he had begun buying fresh stock for the home farm. He'd taken Catrina up to the yards to watch the unloading of pigs from a cart, the new crates of chickens, geese and ducks. In the field's men had driven herds of cows and sheep. The dairy buildings had a new coat of whitewash, as too the laundry. Horses now filled the stables and gleaming transports of various descriptions stood in the yard attended by healthy strong grooms. Even the gardens hadn't been left out. A bevy of men hoed, weeded, dug and planted each day, turning the neglect into reborn beauty. Fountains and ponds were cleaned and maintained and colourful fish were bought to fill them. The staff number had grown, tripled in size, and he was talking of erecting more cottages to house the new families he employed.

She could not fault his choices, they were sound and just. The estate positively throbbed with renewed vigour and purpose. Noise filled the air, from the hooves clopping on the cobbles to the giggles of maids been given the eye by young labourers. The estate had never looked better, even when Catrina was a child. Darius's money, and of which he must have a considerable amount, flowed into Davmoor, and in response, Davmoor shone in the summer sun.

Nevertheless, Catrina was removed from it all. The house was no longer her home. She felt that in her bones. It was as though she was a visitor now. As Davmoor changed she changed also. Oh, the old charm of the building was there, but the essences of her family were slowly being removed. Darius was determined to redecorate every room in the house. Wallpapers her mother had chosen were ripped down, the paintings her father bought were stored away and new ones took up the space. The only thing Catrina was glad to see go were the bold colours of the east wing. Darius deftly eliminated all trace of Phillip and in the process, he was eradicating all trace of her old life too. She didn't belong here, and she didn't belong at Bottom End. She thought of going to Hugh, but was undecided. She disliked the idea of shattering his peace and burdening him once more with her problems. So where did that leave her?

Mrs O'Toole glanced at Lettie's work, though Catrina could tell her mind was elsewhere. 'I heard Miss Ava kept her nanny up all night last night.'

'Yes, Nanny told me this morning.'

'Poor mite must be unsettled with all this racket going on. Well, I'd better get downstairs and see to those new girls. I've to watch them like a hawk, so I do. It's the only way I know they are doing their job properly.' Mrs O'Toole paused by the door. 'I just wanted to see if you're all right...'

'I'm fine. Apart from this irritant.' She waved to the clothes spread out on the bed. 'Until I can get to the bank tomorrow and free up some money I won't be able to buy new clothes.'

'He still doesn't know about the baby?'

'No. I haven't told him. It's not his business yet.'

'No, it's not. Mr Smith has control of enough things here, without...well, I'll say no more on that subject.' Mrs O'Toole squared her shoulders and left the room.

Catrina walked to the window. She knew what Mrs O'Toole referred to. Darius Smith had an air about him whenever she was close by, a predatory air. He watched her when he thought she wasn't looking.

Below, the grounds were a hive of activity in the warm sunshine. Darius was standing talking to the head gardener and a new chap recently hired. She watched Darius, noted how he stood tall, head high. His expression, she knew from even this distance, would be serious yet there'd be an intelligent glint in his eyes which told people he was listening but also thinking of other things. She wondered if his mind was ever still. She'd learnt in the last several days that he couldn't abide to sit for longer than a few minutes. Only after dinner, while he cradled a brandy in his hand, did he rest and relax, but even then, she had a feeling his mind still continued to work, to plan.

As if he knew Catrina was watching him, he suddenly raised his head and looked up at her. She stepped back hastily, then cursed herself for being foolish. If he saw her he'd think she'd been spying on him. For some reason she always felt gauche in his presence. Through design she tried to make the days go past without much contact between them. When he was in the house she stayed in the nursery with Ava or in her room. They talked mainly at meal times, and she kept all discussion to topics about the estate and simple things like decorating and furnishings. He asked for her advice on such things and she gave it willingly, but never once did she allow their conversation to stray into the dangerous waters of her marriage or Phillip. She should leave soon, she had to, but while ever she remained at Davmoor she felt Travis could come back at any moment. He would expect her to be waiting for him...

'There.' Lettie examined a blouse seam she'd unpicked and smiled. 'It won't take long to have this ready for you, madam.'

'Thank you, Lettie.' Catrina strolled over to the dressing

table and idly picked up Hugh's last letter, which spoke of his sadness to hear of Travis's disappearance, and his insistence that she go to him. She'd read it a dozen times already, but she was at a loose end and didn't know what to do with herself. The warm weather beckoned her outside and the bedroom was stuffy, but with Darius in the gardens she preferred to stay indoors.

'Why don't you go for a stroll by the lake, madam?' Lettie said, sitting on the window seat for better light. 'It's a lovely day.'

'I'm not...' She faltered, annoyed with her cowardice. So, what if Smith was in the gardens? They were big enough of the both of them. It wasn't as if the man wanted to eat her! She could head for the wood on the other side of the house. Decision made, she grinned at Lettie and grabbed her straw boater. 'I will go for a stroll, Lettie. I need some fresh air and the sun on my face.'

She went up to the nursery hoping to take Ava out with her, but the baby was asleep, and Nanny dozed in a chair by the cradle. They both looked exhausted even in sleep and Catrina quietly left the room and told a passing maid that no one was to disturb Nanny for an hour.

Once outside, she breathed in the hot summer air as she walked across the lush lawns, now cut and the edges neatly trimmed. How her father would have loved to see the grounds in their present state. She sighed and tried not to think of her father or Travis. The pain of such thoughts easily sent her into depression and to continue living she had to be strong, but it was hard. So very hard.

'Catrina!' She swung around and saw Darius striding towards her. 'Where are you going?'

'For a walk.'

'Lettie told me you're in need of fresh air after sorting out old clothes.' He stopped beside her, a friendly smile warming his dark eyes. As always, he wore the finest of clothes, cut by talented tailors in Savile Row. The deep brown colour of his suit matched his eyes and showed off his dark good looks. 'Would you like to go shopping? I can take you. We can go to York. Or even London if you wish and make an event of it.'

'I hardly think so, Darius, but thank you for the offer. Shopping for mourning clothes is not enjoyable.' She carried on walking, not caring whether he joined her or not.

'If you don't prefer London, then we can go somewhere else. A holiday if you like, to get away from the worries you have.'

'My worries will travel with me. My husband is missing. It is not something I can forget, nor do I want to.' She entered the wood and felt the temperature drop a little once out of the sunshine. The woodland was quiet, peaceful, the air clean. The odd bird called high in the canopy above her head and a rustle came from the undergrowth. In spots of sunshine, circles of wildflowers clustered and in the shadow of a fallen log she saw a delicate pale orchid.

When the trees thinned, and the fields could be seen on the other side, Catrina slowed her pace. Beside her, Darius matched her stride and she sensed his tension. 'Is something wrong, Darius?'

He left the cover of the trees and walked to the stone wall which bordered the fields as far as the land stretched. Resting his arms on the top of the wall, he gazed out. 'I am sorry you are still troubled, Catrina. I would like to take that stress from you, if I could.'

'Ah, but you can't, Darius. Until I have news of my husband I am trapped in a tortured existence.' She stood beside him and gazed up at a hawk hovering high above the field.

For many minutes they stood in silence. So still were they that several birds flew down to pick in the field in front of them, even a pheasant hen came out of hiding and pecked at the soil some yards away.

'I am with child,' Catrina murmured on the warm air. She didn't look at him but from the corner of her eye she saw him stiffen. Would he distance himself from her now?

'Should I congratulate you?'

'It is a happy event, yes. If Travis was here I would be joyous, and without him...' She still couldn't acknowledge he might be dead. 'I'll have a part of him no matter what happens.'

'What will you do if he never returns?'

She sighed deeply and raised her face to the sun. 'I don't know. I don't want to make a decision yet.'

'How long will you wait for him?'

'I cannot answer that either. It is all too difficult.' She lowered her head. 'And I'm angry, so dreadfully angry that he has been taken from me.'

He turned and held out his arm. 'Come, let us return.'

Hooking her arm through his, she gave him a brief smile. 'I know I cannot stay here forever. You've been a good friend, Darius, and I thank you. When we first met I never dreamed I would one day count you as a person I could trust.'

'Friendships can strike in the strangest of occasions.' Darius patted her hand where it lay on his arm. 'And you are welcome to stay here for as long as you want to. I will not turn you away. That is what friends are for, my dear.' He brought her hand up and kissed it.

Her smile disappeared as the tingling effect of it ran through her body.

CHAPTER 18

'*W*ell, old chap!' Donaldson flopped onto the deck chair beside Travis. 'Are you as bored as I am?'

Travis ignored him and kept his gaze on the distant shoreline. From talking to the ship's crew he'd found out they'd rounded the bottom of the western side of Australia that morning. Their first port would be Melbourne – the end of his captivity. It couldn't come soon enough.

'They say we'll make Melbourne by the start of the week,' Donaldson muttered, a pipe stuck in the corner of his mouth while he searched his coat pockets for the tobacco pouch he carried. 'It's July but winter here, would you believe. The opposite to England. That's why we're having this cold blustery weather.' Successful at finding the pouch, he proceeded to load his pipe. 'What are your plans, lad?'

Travis took his eyes off the grey horizon and glared at the old man. The cold Antarctic wind was biting, but he preferred being out here than holed up in the stuffy cabin listening to this fool of a man. 'Plans? Are you stupid? I only have one plan and that is to get home.'

Striking a match, Donaldson nodded. 'Of course. And how will you go about it?'

Seething inside, Travis wanted to throttle him. Oh, he knew Donaldson wasn't behind the kidnap and as far as being a gaoler he had treated him decently enough, took care of him when he was ill and tried to befriend him as the long days stretched into weeks, but despite all that, Travis couldn't help the rage which boiled inside of him. 'I have to beg on the streets for money so I can send a telegram home. If my wife can cable me some money for my fare, I'll survive on the streets until it arrives and I can secure a passage home. Failing that... I must entreat a captain who'll let me work my passage back to England.'

'Sensible.' Donaldson sucked on the pipe as the tobacco glowed red.

'Unless, of course, you are willing to pay for me to return home?' he said sarcastically.

Donaldson coughed, his eyes squinting against the cutting wind. 'I've none to spare, my friend. I'll be hard pressed to survive myself. I have to find some acquaintances and beg for board as it is.'

Travis sat forward, his hands hanging between his knees. In the distance loomed the grey blue of a wooded shoreline. How difficult would it be to last until money was sent? It would take a few days at least for Catrina or his grandmother to wire money into an account he set up at a bank. Then he realised, he had no proof of who he was. He cursed under his breath. He had nothing to vouch for a bank account. With no character reference or personal history details why would anyone, least of all a bank manager, believe him to be genuine? Looking down at his dirty unwashed clothes, the depression in him deepened. He didn't even have a razor to shave with. In short, he looked like a ragamuffin.

Would finding a ship's captain willing to take him on be

quicker? He had no sailing experience and the fever and injuries had robbed him of some strength. He'd lost weight and the trousers he wore only stayed up if he clinched his belt two extra holes. Could he stow away? But what of food? Perhaps if he begged... The very idea of begging repulsed him. His chest tightened at the thought of what he'd been reduced to and for what reason? He couldn't understand why he was kidnapped, and it had to have been Phillip's doing, the bastard! If he ever saw him again he'd not be responsible for his actions. And what of Catrina? She must be out of her mind with worry. His gut churned, but it had nothing to do with the rise and fall of the ship as it surged over the high swell. Emotion clogged his throat when he thought of her. He prayed that she'd know deep in her heart that he'd never leave her willingly.

Standing, he sucked in a blast of cold air and walked to the rail. Below him the grey-green sea flowed past, and further away white caps littered the wind-rough ocean like debris. A few days, that's all he had to wait until they reached Melbourne. A few days and he would be able to contact his loved ones. How he was to find the money he didn't know, beg or steal, it didn't really matter.

* * *

PUTTING the letter she'd written to Hugh in an envelope, Catrina smiled down at Ava, who lay contently in a basket at her feet. 'There, my sweet, all done.' She reached down to lift the baby into her arms. 'What shall we do now? Would you like to see the ducks? Shall we take them some bread?'

Darius strolled into the morning room and smiled at her. He held a wad of correspondence. 'Isn't she too small to know what ducks are?'

Catrina nestled the sleepy baby more comfortably against

her. 'They are never too young to learn. Besides, babies need to be entertained surely? How boring it would be for them to only lay about all day ignored.'

He laughed and rifled through his post. 'She is hardly ignored, Catrina, she has a devoted nanny all to herself.'

'Yes, but it is important that we spend time together also. Anyway, soon Nanny will have another to attend to and Ava will not be so spoilt for attention.' She watched his expression alter slightly as it always did when she mentioned her forthcoming child, which she did as often as possible. She used her condition as a shield against him and the affection she now clearly saw in his eyes when he looked at her. Sometimes, the intensity of his solicitude towards her alarmed her. Soon, she knew, she'd have to leave here and travel to Hugh in Gloucestershire.

'Shall we take the carriage out?' Darius glanced over at her as he sat on a green velvet chair by the opened window and absently opened the first letter in his pile. 'It is a beautiful day. We could take Ava with us, if it pleases you. Maybe have a picnic, too?'

She was saved from answering as Mrs O'Toole knocked and entered. 'Excuse me, Madam, Mrs Millard is here to see you. Are you at home?'

Catrina was tempted to say she wasn't, but knew Ailsa would only return again if she had something to say to her, and perhaps she had news of Travis. With that thought in mind, she placed Ava back in her basket. 'Call for Nanny, please, Mrs O'Toole.' She flashed a brief smile at Darius and quickly left the room.

In the drawing room she found Ailsa standing by the window, watching the men work in the gardens. 'Good morning, Ailsa. Do you have news of Travis?'

Ailsa turned, leaning heavily on a black walking stick. She'd aged rapidly since Travis's disappearance. She looked so much her age now. The beauty she once owned stripped from her. 'No, I have not. Do you?'

Deflated, Catrina rubbed her forehead, hope dying inside. She walked over to the sofa. 'I thought...'

'Oh, you do *think* do you? I'm astonished at such an admission.'

'Pardon?'

Ailsa lips thinned in anger. 'How dare you!'

'Ailsa, I have no idea why you are here and if it is only to drag up the past and blame me for Travis—'

'I do blame you, but that is not what brings me here today!' The old woman banged her stick on the floor. 'It galls me, truly it does, to even speak to you.'

'And why is that?' Unperturbed at the woman's fury, Catrina sat down and waited for the tirade to begin. Ailsa was her one link to Travis and insanely though it seemed, while the woman was here she felt Travis was too.

'Don't you dare look at me that way, madam. You're keen to show an innocent face to the world but I see past it.' Again, the stick banged the floor. 'I am disgusted beyond words that my darling grandson aligned himself with you, but that the minute he is gone you take up with another man is beyond redemption!'

The warmth drained from Catrina's face and a fierce rage burned her chest. 'What are you accusing me of exactly?' she ground out between clenched teeth.

'Smith!' Ailsa said the word as though it tasted repugnant on her tongue. 'I hear the estate belongs to him now.'

'That is true.'

'And so he is living here permanently? With you?'

'That is also true, but not as you crudely think it.'

'The whole village thinks it, you dreadful slut!' Spittle flew from Ailsa's mouth. 'My grandson is gone but a minute and you take up with another. I could kill you. Does

Davmoor mean so much to you that you must whore yourself—'

Catrina jerked to her feet. 'Shut your disgusting mouth! How dare you come here and say those vile things to me. I have done nothing wrong. Do you hear me? Nothing! Darius has offered for me to stay here with Ava until word comes through about Travis. He is being a gentleman, a friend. So if you and your gossips want to malign me then do so, I can't stop you, but I am telling you the truth of it.'

Ailsa straightened her bent back, her eyes narrowed to slits. 'Darius, is it now?' she said, her tone a deadly whisper. 'He is not Mr Smith, but Darius?'

'He has become a friend, Ailsa, nothing more, and I am in sore need of them since my *family relations* cannot be counted on.' Catrina stared her down, unwilling to respect the older woman, for she didn't deserve it. 'Now, if you will excuse me, I have things to do.' She walked to the door.

'It will not be borne! I won't have it, do you hear?'

Turning, Catrina sighed. 'Go home, Ailsa.'

Ailsa stepped forward, her knuckles white on the cane. 'How do you sleep at night, tell me that? If he'd never gone to Scotland and brought you back, he'd still be with me.'

'True, but would he have been happy?' Catrina drew in her bottom lip between her teeth, the fight leaving her. 'I'm sorry for your anguish, but I share it too. I may not have been the perfect wife to Travis, but I loved him and he loved me and soon I am to have his child.'

Swaying a little, Ailsa's grip tightened on the cane. 'You don't deserve his child or him. I hope he is dead. For I would rather him *that* than spend his life with you.'

Shocked at the venom in the old woman, Catrina recoiled. 'Why do you hate me so much?' she whispered.

'Because you are a Davies. Worthless! Not one of them

can be trusted. I have learnt that to my cost.' With that Ailsa hobbled past her and out of the room.

Feeling as though she'd been dealt a physical blow, Catrina stumbled towards the sofa and carefully lowered herself down onto it. She was aware of Mrs O'Toole rushing in and bending before her, capturing her hands and rubbing them vigorously.

'There now, madam, she's gone. I'll not let her back inside this house ever again, I promise you that.'

'B-but why...Mrs O'Toole...why does she hate me so intensely?'

'Thwarted love will do that to a person, madam, I'm sad to say.'

'Thwarted love?' She stared at the housekeeper in puzzlement. 'What on earth do you mean?'

Blinking rapidly and a flush creeping into her cheeks, Mrs O'Toole dropped Catrina's hands and stepped back. 'Nay, don't listen to me. Forgive me, madam.' She took another step away, her gaze darting to the door. 'I'll bring you in a tray.'

Catrina saw through her performance. 'You'll answer my question, if you please, Mrs O'Toole. There is something you know.'

'As I said, it's nothing but a bit of gossip, something I'd not thought of for many a year until I heard her...' Mrs O'Toole turned scarlet. 'Forgive me, I was standing in the hallway, in case you needed me...I heard her say she hated all Davies, or at least that was her meaning and it made me think of...'

'Yes?'

Mrs O'Toole fingered the ring of keys at her waist. 'You know I'm not one to gossip...'

'I know that.' Catrina sat very still on the sofa, knowing she wasn't going to enjoy what was about to be said.

'It may be nothing and probably is, madam. Forget it, please.'

Catrina raised her chin, the breeding and years of lessons instilled by her governess in how to deal with servants made her expect instant obedience. 'You are keeping something from me, aren't you?'

'No, madam...'

'Mrs O'Toole I cannot be hurt anymore than I have been. You are doing no disservice to me by telling something I should know. So, what is it?'

'Very well. I believe Ailsa Millard was in love with...with the master.' Mrs O'Toole's tone became prim. 'It was years ago, mind you, madam, and I could be wrong in my assumptions.'

'My father?' Her mouth gaped at such a notion.

'Yes, madam.'

'Ailsa fell in love with my father? But she was married to Doctor Millard, everyone has always said she adored her husband...'

'Aye, and I'm not saying she didn't, but...'

'Go on.'

'Such adoration came after she was rejected by the master.' The housekeeper's gaze dropped to the plush carpet.

'When was this?'

'Before your father married your mother. It was after his first wife had gone to London and then later died. Mrs Millard often called...'

Catrina's eyes grew wide. 'Do you think something happened between Father and Mrs Millard?'

Folding her hands in front of her Mrs O'Toole nodded slightly. 'I do, madam. I saw them on...two occasions in the garden and they were...they seemed close. Also, I recall now that many letters passed between them.'

'I know my father was much older than my mother, but Ailsa is...what a good five years older than my father was?'

'I believe so, madam.'

'Why is this not known to me, or common village gossip?'

'Because whatever happened between them, madam, it didn't continue for long. Your father's first wife died and then he met your mother and he instantly adored her. He was the happiest man alive when he brought her to Davmoor, and I feel...I assume...he rejected Mrs Millard's affection and wished for them to be nothing more than friends.'

'They used to dine here when I was a child.'

'Yes, that's correct. But...well...the tension was noticeable, and it was said that your good mother and Mrs Millard were unable to strike up a friendship. Not long after, Doctor and Mrs Millard stopped coming.'

'Did Mrs Millard contact my father when my mother died?'

Mrs O'Toole grimaced. 'No, madam, by then the damage had been done. Mrs Millard was on a...well, a crusade as it were to blight the Davies name.'

'Her love for my father had turned to hate?'

'I believe so.'

Catrina sagged against the cushions. 'I can hardly take it in. It seems so incredible.'

'Mrs Millard, even as a young grandmother was still an attractive woman and your father had been most hurt by his first wife. She, Mrs Millard, that is, was kind.'

'Yes, of course, I can understand that.'

'Shall I get you some tea?'

'No...thank you. I think I might go for a walk.' Catrina rose from the sofa and abruptly put her hand on Mrs O'Toole's arm. 'Thank you for telling me. It explains a lot.'

Mrs O'Toole gave a wry smile. 'You know what they say, a woman scorned and all that.'

Catrina patted her arm and left the drawing room, her mind filled with startling images of Ailsa in love with her father. What must have that been like to see? And her father to have had such a secret all these years. Had Mrs O'Toole seen correctly? Perhaps it was all innocent and pure friendship they had shared. Surely they wouldn't have...been lovers?

On seeing Ida coming up the hallway, Catrina pushed all thought of her father and Ailsa out of her head and halted the maid. 'Is Mr Smith in the house?'

'He's in the steward's room, madam.' Ida bobbed a curtsy and carried on her way.

She'd forgotten that Darius wanted her to stand in on the interviews for a new steward. At dinner last night he'd asked her to be with him while he went through the applicants for the position. She didn't understand why he wanted her by his side but if it kept things cordial between them then it wouldn't hurt. It was kind of him to want to involve her in estate business, but she wished he wouldn't, for Davmoor no longer claimed her affections as it once did and she didn't care in the slightest about the new staff who ran it.

Catrina headed down the service corridor and out across the small courtyard between the house and the estate office, which also shared a wall with the laundry building. The door to the office faced towards the stables and only a square window could be seen from the house. Apparently, it had been built this way so dirty labourers could enter the steward's office without being observed by the ladies of the house.

Not wanting to disturb Darius if he was in the middle of an interview, Catrina peeked in through the partially opened window.

Darius stood with his back to her and waited as a short, powerfully built man entered, slipped off his flat cap and closed the door behind him. 'Well, Seavers, you've taken your time.'

'But you got my note, sir?'

'I did, but it was light on details.'

Seavers looked shifty. 'I thought you'd prefer it.'

'Have you heard anything more?'

'No, Gov, not since the telegram from Port Said saying the doctor feared he wouldn't last the night from the fever.'

Both men leaned over the desk in the middle of the room and studied what looked to be a large map. Though intrigued by their conversation, Catrina was about to leave, not wanting to disturb them, when she heard Darius say Travis's name.

'So Millard is dead?' Darius was leaning on one arm. 'There's no mistaking it?'

'I'm certain of it, Gov.' The square shouldered man nodded. 'Fever the telegram said. Too ill to survive.'

Catrina stifled a gasp behind her hand.

Darius pulled at his earlobe. 'Good. Although I just wanted him out of the way until I knew my own mind, now I am certain that his death will be to my advantage.'

'So you want to marry her then, Gov?'

'Yes. She carries his child, which I'm not happy about but it can easily be ignored and it proves she is not barren. Later there are boarding schools for it to attend.' He waved his hand dismissively. 'The child and her niece can fit into my plans. If I have my way the nursery will be filled with my own children before long anyway and she will have no time for them.'

'Then I wish you every happiness, Gov.'

Darius drew in a deep breath. 'I am well satisfied, Seavers. You did well. I didn't want murder on my hands. I would have found that...difficult to see her grieve and make a martyr out of him. No, this way is best. She half believes he has run away from her and that is what I'll work on. We might even have some sightings of him relayed to her. What do you think?'

'Aye, Gov. I could go to Liverpool and get a telegram sent to her?'

'Or even further afield... We could word it as though he needs time away from her...'

Seavers grinned slyly. 'And you'll be here to help her through it, Gov.'

'That's the plan, yes. I want her as my wife and I am willing to wait for her.'

Catrina stumbled backwards, nearly tripping on her skirts as she fled from the window. Her shattered mind closed down and a blackness threatened to swamp her, but she fought it, knowing she had to keep going, to get away from here. Crossing the courtyard, she stumbled up the stone steps into the service corridor. Two maids leapt back as she rushed past them for the back stairs. She took the steep narrow stairs quickly, falling twice before she reached the landing. Hitching her skirts up with one hand, the other she wiped away hot tears that blinded her and dashed along to her bedroom.

Crashing open her door caused Lettie to jump, but Catrina barely registered the girl's shocked expression and went into the dressing room to pull down luggage cases from on top of the large wardrobes.

'Madam?' Lettie stood in the doorway, her face a picture of concern.

'Pack, Lettie, immediately!' Catrina nearly screamed at her. Going from case to wardrobe, she hauled out clothes and dumped them into the cases.

'Pack, madam?' Lettie hovered a moment before quickly picking up the garments Catrina dropped.

'Yes, everything, all of it. Hurry!' Frantic, she rushed to her dressing table and scooped all the items on it into a suede travelling bag.

'We'll need a trunk, madam.' Lettie's worried gaze halted Catrina's mad dash.

'There's no time. Fit what you can. No, don't fold them, it doesn't matter.' She spun on her heel and went to the side of the bed Travis always slept on. It nearly broke her in two when she saw the books he'd been reading still piled on the little table beside the bed. The table had one drawer and she flung it open and took out the things she'd dared not look at since he left for the fear they'd bring her undone, but now it was important she didn't leave them behind. Into the bag she put his hair comb, an old watch that had been his father's, his little notebook, one of his linen handkerchiefs and a pair of gold cufflinks. Most of his other possessions remained at Bottom End, but she couldn't think about that now.

A tap of the door stilled her hands as she tied up the bag. Heart thumping, she licked her dry lips, hoping it wasn't Darius.

'Shall I get it, madam?' Lettie asked coming to her side, the look on her face clearly showed she thought Catrina had lost her mind. The knock came again and Lettie sidled to the door. 'I'll just check who it is...' She opened the door a crack and turned back to Catrina. 'It's Mrs O'Toole.'

Relief made Catrina sag, but only for a second, then she gathered her wavering courage around her like a shield. 'Let her in.'

'What are you about, Lettie, making me stand on ceremony in the hall.' Mrs O'Toole stormed in, annoyance etched on her features. 'I only want to know if you'd seen...' Mrs

O'Toole's words dried up as she looked around the room and then spotted Catrina over in the corner. 'What on earth?'

Catrina rushed to the other woman, one who she'd cared about as though she was a beloved aunt, and gripped her hands. 'You must help me. I have to leave here. Now!' The dam of tears which constantly pressed against the back of her eyes threatened to over flow once more.

'Why?' Thunderstruck, Mrs O'Toole simply stared. 'What's happened?'

'Him, Darius. He...Travis. Oh God! I can't bear it. A fever. Darius has...' She wrung her hands and spun back to the dressing room unable to accept the tragic thoughts in her mind. 'I have to go. Now. Today.'

Perplexed, but sensing Catrina's desperate need, the housekeeper peered gently into her face. 'Has he, Mr Smith, overstepped the mark, my lass? I knew what he felt for you, he's been blind to the fact you don't feel the same way, and how could you with Mr Millard hardly gone—'

At the mention of Travis's name a sob escaped Catrina's throat and she slapped her hands over her mouth to prevent anymore from doing the same. Good God how was she to survive this?

Mrs O'Toole patted her hands, her eyes understanding. 'Leave it with me.' She turned to the girl standing in the middle of the room gripping garments to her flat chest. 'Lettie, run upstairs and tell Nanny to pack Miss Ava's and her own things.'

'Lord, Ava!' Catrina felt close to collapsing. She'd forgotten about her niece. How could she!

'Sit down a minute, lass.' Mrs O'Toole crooned. 'You've got your own little one to think of as well and *he* isn't worth all this worry, that's for certain.' She went to the door and looked down the hallway. 'You, Sally, and you, Minnie, come here. Right, Sally, run down to the stables and ask old

Jones...no, not him...' She looked up as Lettie came hurrying back down from the nursery. 'Lettie, has Roddy started back here yet? Did he get his old job?'

'Yes, Mrs O'Toole, he started this morning.'

'Sally, tell Mr Jones to bring carriage around immediately. Tell Roddy that Mrs Millard is going away and he'll be accompanying her and to pack accordingly. Go now.' She turned to the next girl. 'Minnie, I want you to go downstairs and get some of the others to help you. Mrs Millard's and Miss Ava's luggage is to be taken out onto the drive and loaded onto the carriage. Quickly, girl!' She closed the door on them.

'Thank you, Mrs O'Toole,' Catrina said softly from the bed. Now that the initial shock was wearing off she felt empty of all emotion, drained and utterly exhausted. Lettie continued to pack, her movements hurried but orderly.

'Whatever is left behind, I'll send on.' Mrs O'Toole came to stand beside her. 'You'll be going to Mr Henley's home?'

A hysterical laugh bubbled up inside Catrina. She hadn't even thought to where she'd go. But yes, Hugh's home was the obvious choice. Standing, she glanced at herself in the mirror and saw the blank eyes of a stranger. Travis was dead. No. She mentally shook herself. She could not think about that just yet. First, she had to get away from here. Later, she would grieve.

While the luggage was taken downstairs, Catrina pinned on her hat, pulled on her gloves and finally collected her reticule. Mrs O'Toole had ushered everyone downstairs, including Nanny with Ava. At the door, Catrina turned and gave one last look at her bedroom, the room she'd had as a girl and then she shared with Travis as a woman and his wife. A hard knot formed in her throat for she knew she'd never see this room again, or indeed this house.

She slipped quietly down the staircase, feeling as though

she could easily shatter as a dropped glass. Her nerves were on alert for signs of Darius, but she made it to the front doors without encountering him and let out a breath. What could he do anyway, her crazed mind spoke to her, but some instinct told her that he could do a lot and she'd have to be careful and on guard. He'd gone to great lengths to have Travis kidnapped so he could get to her, so the news of her leaving could make him do anything. She shivered and stepped bravely out into the sunshine.

Out on the drive, the bright sun hurt her eyes and she shaded them with her hand before noticing that there was the odd staff member standing around. Their subdued chatter ceased and Catrina felt close to fainting for Darius would soon know of them being here. 'Mrs O'Toole, send them inside, please.'

'Now, madam,' Mrs O'Toole fussed unnecessarily with a basket she was placing inside the carriage beside Nanny's feet. 'They are the ones who's been here the longest and want to wish you well.' She sniffed and blinked rapidly.

'Yes, of course.' Catrina gave them a watery smile and waved. The luggage was tied onto the carriage roof and Roddy sat up beside old Jones.

'You take care of yourself, madam,' Mrs O'Toole stepped closer to Catrina. 'If you need me, just send word.'

Catrina hugged her tight. 'I wish you were coming with me.' She kissed the older woman's cheek and stepped back, ready to climb into the carriage when there came a shout. She turned and her heart plummeted like a stone as Darius came running from around the side of the house.

'Catrina! Wait!' He skidded on the gravel and nearly fell at her feet. It was the first time she'd ever seen him do something reckless. His dark hair, usually perfectly sleeked back, fell forward over his eyes as he stared at the luggage. 'In the name of God,' he panted, 'where are you going?'

All at once, seeing him so much not himself, and in fact more uneasy at this moment than at any other time, she lost the apprehension that he always wrought in her. She finally saw him as the calculating man that he really was. Something snapped in her brain, a freedom from being out from under his spell she supposed, but whatever it was, she felt different, and in command of herself again. 'I'm going away, Mr Smith.'

'Away, where? Why didn't you tell me?' His surprised expression brought a cold smile to her face.

'Why would I tell you? It is you I wish to escape from. You and...' her gaze roamed over the house, 'and Davmoor. Both of you have made me feel like a prisoner. But now I am free.'

'I don't want you to go. You must stay!' His voice cracked with desperation. 'Catrina, come back inside, please. We'll talk and—'

'I don't think so. I have much to do, for once I am settled I plan to speak with the authorities, the police, lawyers and see how we can have you arrested.' Her smile turned into a grimace. 'I know, you see, Mr Smith. I know you had my husband abducted...and that he...' her voice faltered, 'and that he has died from fever on some ship somewhere...'

'No, it isn't true. It wasn't me. What you heard is not true. I-I...you see...' He lunged forward and grabbed her arms, his eyes pleading. 'Catrina, I love you. I do. From the first moment I saw you. I've never felt like this towards a woman before. I can help you with this. We'll investigate...I'll tell you what I know...I was trying to protect you. Please, listen to me.' He hauled her against his chest and kissed her hard on the mouth.

The servants gasped. Mrs O'Toole dragged at Catrina's arm, but he held her imprisoned like a vice as he ground his lips against hers until she tasted blood.

'Mr Smith! Let her go! Roddy, for God's sake help the mistress!' Mrs O'Toole's demanded, pulling hysterically.

Catrina, her mind reeling against the assault, knew fighting him was useless. She let herself go limp in his arms and her weight made him stagger and release her mouth.

'Catrina, darling, I'm sorry.'

Breathing deeply, still held in his tight embrace, Catrina glared all the hatred she felt at him. 'Sorry for which part?' she murmured and with slow exaggerated movements, stepped out of his arms. She turned to a weeping Mrs O'Toole and patted her hand. 'I'll be in touch.' Then with complete detachment she climbed into the carriage.

Smith grabbed the door, his face pale and taut. 'I love you, Catrina.

'And I, Mr Smith, loathe you.' She reached over and slammed the door in his face. Resting back against the seat, she closed her eyes on the wan faces of Lettie and Nanny, who held a sleeping Ava. They could hear Darius shouting her name over the crunch of the wheels on the gravel and Catrina shivered. Desolate, she stared out of the window sightlessly as her heart smashed to pieces.

CHAPTER 19

*T*he steam whistle blew sharp and piecing, drowning out all activity on the wharf. Travis straightened his back and winced at the throbbing ache. He'd worked hard on his farm, but never this hard, and not solidly for a week as he had done. The wharfside dockies knew what labour meant. They worked from sun up to sun down and sometimes beyond if needed.

When Travis landed in Melbourne and parted ways the Dr Donaldson, he walked the streets for a day, getting his sea legs back and clearing his mind. For an hour he begged on a street corner and managed to get enough pennies to buy a simple meal. He slept that night in an abandoned shed in some alley not far from Victoria Dock where he had come ashore and where he now worked.

It had been relatively easy for him to get a job. After a near sleepless night in the shed he'd woken and walked down to the dockyards. The sun had risen over the water and a cold winter wind blew through his clothes. He'd noticed the men standing at the gate waiting to enter the large warehouses and once the foremen let them through Travis approached him. The man in charge, Willis, was a happy fellow and within ten minutes Travis was put into a section of the warehouse where grain was stored. The men he worked with were friendly and when an older fellow by the name of Higgins learned that Travis had nowhere to live or money, he took him home to his missis, who happily fed him and let him sleep on the sofa in their front room.

Travis was told he'd be paid on Friday of each week and today was his first pay day. Today he would be able to send word home.

* * *

CATRINA SAT on the white wrought iron chair and sipped the refreshing cool lemon cordial and allowed her mind to relax. Before her, in a wide sweep, lay the side gardens of Longbrook, Hugh's beautiful home. A shallow stream ran along the far end of the lawn, giving the house its name. The house itself was old, built in the Tudor times by Hugh's ancestor, and its mellow brick was weathered and covered with ivy creepers at the front and sides. Lichen coloured the slate roof in shades of green and grey, enhancing the magical feel of the place. Small mullioned windows and a turret on the corner completed the building and Catrina had loved it instantly.

That dreadful day three days ago when she learned of Darius's deceit and the truth of what happened to Travis had sent her spiralling into a pit of acute misery. However, as the carriage rolled along the pale pebbled drive and Longbrook swung into view at the end of a short crescent of ash trees, she had felt a slight lifting of her heavy heart at the sheer elegance of the house and the soft pretty gardens nestled around it.

Inside the house had reflected the timeless beauty of

outside. Square rooms decorated in pale soft colours held thick Turkish rugs and slender legged furniture in tones of honey and chestnut. Although the house wasn't as large as Davmoor, it gave the presence of grandeur with a touch of familiarity, as though a person could feel they had sat in front of that fireplace, or ate at that table, or walked up the curving staircase all before.

'There you are, my dear.' Hugh, leaning on his gold-topped cane, walked onto the paved terrace and sat down opposite her. 'You remind me of a lizard, always out in the sun.'

She smiled and placed her glass on the table between them. 'I like the warmth of the sun. I soak up as much as I can to last me through winter.' She closed her eyes and tipped her head back, not caring if she turned the colour of old leather. What did it matter how she looked now? What claims she had to any beauty was stripped from her now. Dark smudges coloured under her eyes and weight loss had hollowed her cheeks. Her arms and legs were thin and only her stomach showed evidence that she ate at all. If it hadn't been for the baby inside her, she felt she would have given up the will to live and withered away. Only, she hadn't been given that selfish opportunity. Instead she had a life to nurture as best she could in her present state of mind and also Ava needed her to keep going. But Lord it was difficult.

'How I wish I could wipe that sadness from your face, my dear,' Hugh said on a sigh.

She turned her head and peeped at him against the brightness. 'Please don't worry. You have no idea of how you are helping me, Hugh, once again.'

'I would rather you were here under better circum-stances, but nevertheless I am glad you are at Longbrook. You suit the place.'

'I truly believe I will never leave here, Hugh. Your home is like a paradise to me. I have such a feeling of...wellbeing here. You've created a little piece of heaven, do you know that?'

'I do, indeed.'

'I feel I can...recover...here.'

'And you will, my dear, I promise you. I have been in your shoes. I have lost my wife and the happy life we shared.'

Catrina reached over and took his hand in hers. They gazed at the garden basking under a late summer sun. The flower beds were less formal than most manor homes. Hugh's gardener, Turnbull, was nearly as old as Hugh and his arthritic hands and knees kept him from being as vigorous as he once was in their upkeep. Yet, none of this distracted from the glorious colour and scent that always comes from a garden long established and loved.

'Your man seems to have settled.' Hugh pointed to Roddy, who seeing old Turnbull struggle to wheel the barrow took over. 'I was talking to him yesterday and he asked if he could be of help to Turnbull. Of course I agreed, I should have retired Turnbull years ago, but the man refuses to accept he is beyond work now. It appears your man isn't in any hurry to return to Davmoor.'

'Roddy is a good worker, Hugh, and loves the things the earth produces.' She watched him as he bent to weed a wild patch of purple heartsease in amongst the roses. No, he wouldn't return to Davmoor as long as Lettie wasn't there. She knew of their attachment, saw it in the way their gazes clung to the other. Mrs O'Toole had done well in selecting him as the one to be her protector as they made the hurried journey to Gloucestershire. She had sent Jones back, of course, once they got to the cavernous train station at York, for the carriage wasn't hers, but belonged to Darius. Roddy had been a Godsend to her as he took control of them and the luggage. Naturally they had understood that the thought of facing people in the train for hours, the interruption of changing trains, of talking to station masters and avoiding passengers' kind glances were all too much for her that day. Lettie and Nanny had treated her as gently as they cared for Ava, having witnessed her reaction to Darius's declaration of love they were disgusted that she should have to put up with such sentiment when dear Mr Millard was missing.

At the thought of her darling man, the pain rose once more to tease and pull at her. She had known grieving before, for her parents when they died, for her own misery when she ran away from home, from Travis, but this unrelenting agony was like nothing she'd ever experienced in her life. When she'd left home and thought she lost everything, the hurt had been mixed with anger, anger at Phillip, at his friend who raped her, at her father for not protecting her, and at Travis for not being the man she wanted him to be. So, the depth of her hurt then had been tepid with other emotions. Also she realised now that the budding love she felt for Travis back then hadn't been the developed loving bond they now shared, or did…

She sighed deeply, wondering if she'd ever be truly happy for any length of time. She'd had snatches of it, her wedding day and the week following, before the estate demands took all her time and energy and the floating happiness she'd lived in became soured with debt demands and responsibility.

Hugh shifted in his chair. 'Mr Dowling arrives in the morning. Are you well enough to see him?'

'Yes. Thank you again for asking him to come.' She looked forward to Hugh's lawyer coming and starting the process of bringing Darius to justice.

'Don't thank me, dearest. You know I would do anything for you. And we have to get to the bottom of this dreadful business. Mr Dowling will start making enquires.'

'I feel I should travel to Port Said, Hugh.' She ran her hand over the small baby bump, which despite her lack of appetite lately was growing rapidly.

'You know I advise against it. A woman in your condition shouldn't be in foreign cities, as especially somewhere so hot and well...let us say, not British.'

'I understand, yes, but if Travis is...buried there...'

'We have no proof he is, my dear. He could have been buried at sea.' A look of sorrow flittered across Hugh's lined face. 'Perhaps once we have found out for certain...and after the child is born...'

'Yes, you are right. I cannot endanger the life of this baby, Travis wouldn't want me to do anything silly.'

'My contacts will find out what we need to know. Then later, when you're up to it we can make plans to travel there, or whatever you like.'

Catrina rose and stepped behind Hugh's chair to wrap her arms around his shoulders. 'You are too good to me.'

He brushed away a lock of her hair that had fallen from its pins. 'You're the daughter I never had. Let me indulge myself.'

She bent and kissed his cheek then rested her head on his shoulder. 'I have missed you.'

'And I you, my dear.'

A clearing of the throat made them turn. Booth, Hugh's butler, bowed and held out a silver platter upon which rested a buff envelope. 'Just delivered, sir, for Mrs Millard.'

With a shaking hand, Catrina reached out for it and at the same time Hugh stood. She opened the letter and at first didn't recognise the handwriting but skimming down to the name at the bottom of the page, she let out the breath she'd been holding. She gave a wry smile to Hugh. 'It is from my brother, Phillip. He is in New York and asks me for money.'

'Money?'

'Yes, the fool. He knows I have none of my own. He must

expect me to ask Travis…' She swallowed and continued on. 'It appears he is again 'short' as he eloquently puts it. I take that to mean he hasn't a penny left to his name and probably borrowed money for this stationary!' She strode to the end of the terrace where the paving met with the lawn. Butterflies and bees hovered over the large bushes of white daisies in the small garden to the right. Phillip's letter had splintered the tranquil peace of her surroundings. 'He has done so much wrong, yet he writes to me as if nothing has happened. He deserted his own wife and daughter.' She waved the letter back at Hugh. 'He doesn't even have the decency to ask about them.' She scanned the letter and saw the address at the top. 'Well, I will reply to him, but not in the way he wishes it! Finally I can tell him the incidents which have occurred in his absence. His wife and father's death, the birth of his daughter, the destruction of what Darius Smith has done to my life!' She gasped for breath, the tearing burning ache squeezed at heart like the choke hold of a terrier. Yes, she would let Phillip know all this. Why should she bear it alone? He needed to suffer it too.

Hugh placed his hand on her arm and she calmed a little. 'My dear, pray do not upset yourself, think of your child.'

Nodding, Catrina folded the letter. 'You are right. He is not worth the anguish.'

'New York is not the place to be without money or friends. Phillip will be sorely tested. If you send him a letter full of hate, it might send him over the edge. Do you wish to stoop to his depths? You are better than that, and it will haunt you if you take such an action.'

'But why must he be allowed to go through life without reaping the consequences of his deeds?'

'Do you really think his mind is untroubled?' Hugh's soft words sank into her tortured thoughts.

She read the letter again and it became clear that the tone

was anything but happy. Indeed, he sounded desperate and afraid. 'I cannot send him money, Hugh, not the kind he wants to scrape him out of yet another hole.'

'I understand that. No one should be made to finance his gambling or whatever else it is that he throws his money away on.'

'Then what shall I do?'

'Send him enough money to come home. Tell him I will grant him an interview, though I ask myself why...' He gave her a gentle smile, which told her that he did it for her only. 'Perhaps we can come to some kind of arrangement.'

'As in him working for you?'

Hugh stepped towards the French doors that led into the house. 'A hard day's work is just what he needs in my opinion. Don't worry, my dear, it will be an occupation fit for a gentleman.'

* * *

'Mrs Millard!'

Ailsa slowed with a sigh, all she wanted was to get back in the carriage and home to Bottom End. These days the trips into the village and a morning spent talking with friends and shopkeepers alike left her more tired than she cared to admit. The constant pains in her chest refused to go away and she'd tried every medicine she could think of, or what was listed in her husband's medical journals, to ease it. This heat didn't help either. Had they ever known such a long spell of hot weather? It was as though July was determined to go out in a blaze of sunshine and bring August in the same. She slowly turned, scowling as Mr Watling, the postmaster, ran down the street towards her waving a slip of paper in his hands.

'Oh, Mrs Millard. I'm glad to see you've not returned to

Bottom End yet as it's saved me journeying there.' Mr Watling puffed out his thin cheeks.

'How can I help you, Mr Watling?'

'No, it is I who can help you!' He smiled triumphantly. 'I have a telegram, received only moments ago.' He paused dramatically, his eyes wide with importance. 'A telegram from Australia would you believe.

'Australia?' Ailsa frowned thinking of who she knew in that faraway place and all she came up with was a distant cousin's boy.

'Yes, Australia.' Watling waved the paper nearly in her face such was his excitement. 'From your grandson!'

The warmth left Ailsa face and for a moment she felt as though she would faint. She straightened her back, irritated at this weakness of fainting that now seemed to beset her all the time. 'Travis? Are you quite sure, there can be no mistake?' Her heart fluttered, and she put a hand to it.

'The very same.'

'He's alive?'

'Indeed. Alive and writes of his need of money to be cabled to him. I can do this for you through the Post Office.' He beamed and rocked back on his heels as though he personally had orchestrated such an invention and she should be grateful for his indulgence.

'Money?' Ailsa stared at the paper as though it held all the answers of the world. 'Oh, my dearest boy.' She snatched the missive from Watling and hurriedly read it. 'I cannot believe it.' She blinked, her mind working furiously. 'He has sent this to me, not his wife?'

Watling scratched his forehead. 'Well, your name is at the top, Mrs Millard, and it is the only telegram we have received today. That's not to say another one will come later.'

'No, Mr Watling, another one will not.' Crushing the

paper into her skirt pocket, Ailsa bestow her most brilliant smile on the hapless postmaster. 'My grandson wanted me, not her, and this shows who he trusts most.' She linked her arm through his and turned him about, all tiredness gone. 'Come, Mr Watling, my good friend. We have much to do.'

CHAPTER 20

The barley fields surrounding Longbrook rippled like a golden wave as the soft warm breeze moved sluggishly across the land as though it too was tired of summer. Catrina strolled along the rutted cart track between the fields, watching as a bevy of workers helped with the harvesting. The dry heat was perfect weather to bring in the crops and, since, unbelievably, one day all this would be hers, she wanted to be a part of the event.

A horse drawn harvester was rumbling along at a steady pace and beside it men were collecting and staking the cut barley stalks. Over in the distance was Home Farm, and Catrina had just left there to walk back towards the house. She'd enjoyed talking to the farmer's wives and helping them prepare a day's worth of food and drink for the hungry and tired men, who toiled while the weather was fine in their annual race with nature.

As the sun hit directly above their heads, the men stopped and made for the cooling shade of the hedgerow bordering the fields to eat their midday meal. Thirsty herself, and hot in her mourning dress, Catrina left the lane. She made a mental note to come back with a basket and pick the blackberries she spotted further along the lane.

She cut across the small strip of woodland on the western side of the estate. The shade from the beech, rowan and elder trees gave her relief and she took off her straw boater and wiped her forehead with her handkerchief. She disturbed a thrush feeding on the red rowan berries and smiled as it fluttered up to a higher branch and peered down at her. The trees were not too dense and allowed plenty of sunlight to filter through. Hare-bells and campanulas grew wild, scattered delicately amongst the grasses. Catrina was considering picking a handful when a twig snapped behind her. She twirled around, startled.

'We meet again, Catrina.' Darius Smith leant against a tree trunk, twirling a long grass stem between his fingers. 'It is a beautiful day, is it not?'

Fear and revulsion smothered her response. She watched him push away from the tree and step towards her.

'No greeting, my sweet girl?'

She found her voice at last. 'Why are you here?'

'To see you, isn't that obvious?' He stopped a few feet from her. 'I did not want our last...meeting to be all that was left between us. Besides, I wanted to let you know that I don't hold it against you that you summoned the police, though I wish you hadn't. Most inconvenient and all that.'

'Did you think I wouldn't after what I heard between you and your...assistant?' Loathing filled her. She itched to rake her nails down his face.

'Whatever you thought you heard is hardly relevant now. The police inspector and I talked for some time. He was a likeable chap, following orders as he is meant to do.'

A sickening feeling swirled in the pit of her stomach. She'd been stupid to think Darius would be arrested and goaled immediately. The man was too slick, too in control of his dealings to allow mistakes to happen that would lead the authorities to him. The only time he lost his cool reserve was when with her. 'I can imagine the lies you told the inspector.'

'I told the truth, my dear. I had nothing to do with Travis's disappearance. There are witnesses, Kelthorn for one, to prove I was in York that night.' He shrugged his slender shoulders as if the whole episode was nothing more than an irritant, one to be easily forgotten.

'You may not have physically handled Travis, but you orchestrated the whole thing. I feel it here!' She thumped her chest, fighting the urge to scratch her nails down his face.

'Catrina, listen to me—'

'There is nothing more to be said, Mr Smith.' She lifted her skirt, ready to step away. 'Now, if you'll excuse me.'

'No, don't leave yet, I beg you.' A pained expression shadowed his features for a second before it was gone. 'Stay, just for a moment, please. I want us to be friends.'

'That is impossible, and you know it.'

'Let me explain. I know I can put your mind at rest.'

'Oh, how so?' She took a step back, desperate to put distance between them, but was caught by his tone. Her heart pounding, she waited uneasily. She never thought she'd have to look at his face again and doing so now made her feel sick to her toes. 'Do you have proof that Travis still lives?'

His dark eyes, which in the shade of the trees had turned to black, narrowed. 'He does not, and I'm sorry for it. It wasn't my intention for him to die.' He cursed and ran the flat of his hand over his black hair. His face showed his guilt.

Her eyes widened at his slip. Fresh pain broke her heart.

Emotion burned in her throat. 'No, you simply preferred him to be away for some months, so you could try to win me over, and later, if you happened to grow tired of me, you'd then allow Travis home again.' Her top lip curled back in disgust. 'Do you honestly think I would run from Travis's arms into yours?'

'I can love you better than him if you give me the chance to prove it. I can give you everything you want. Didn't you see I was trying? I am making Davmoor into a place to be proud of, for you!'

'But I don't want it,' she spat. 'I never really did. It's full of memories and not many of them are good. I was only trying to save it for Ava, that's all.' She swept her arms out wide to encompass the area around them. 'Do you see all this? This is Longbrook, and it is bequeathed to me. In the last few days here, I have felt more a sense of belonging than I ever have at Davmoor and I was *born* there.'

'Then we'll live here, together. I can be all that you want, Catrina, I promise you.' He looked hopeful.

She jerked in surprise. 'Are you insane?'

The last word seemed to push him over the edge of his control. He lunged for her and grabbed her arms, pinning them to her side. Walking her backwards until she hit a tree, he pressed his body against hers while ravishing her mouth with his.

'No!' She fought hard, pulling at his hair, pinching and kicking, anything that would make him release her, but he was like a mindless demon intent on getting his own way. His teeth tore at her lips and she tasted blood. His hands ripped at the bodice of her dress tearing it at the seam. Her chemise was next and since she wore no corset now because of the baby, he was soon gripping her tender breasts, sending stabs of pain through her chest.

'I love you, I love you,' Darius panted against her mouth, one hand squeezing her nipple while the other was lifting up her skirt and petticoats.

She yanked her head away to scream, but he slammed his body weight into hers, cutting off her breath in a whoosh.

'Don't fight me, my beautiful girl, please.' He kissed her savagely. 'You must know that this can be special and wonderful. I love you.' His hand pulled at her drawers and she thought she'd faint. She clawed at his face, but he took no notice, his eyes were glazed, his movements frenzied. In one swift move, he pulled her to the ground, covering her body with his and she couldn't breathe for the weight on her chest. His mouth covered hers halting her protests, her calls for help.

When he gasped for air, she spoke quickly, trying to reason with him. 'Darius, don't...I beg you...'

'Love me, Catrina, please.' His plea softened his features and his hands came up to cradle her face. 'You're mine, don't you know that? Mine.' For a second his kiss was gentle, loving, before it turned more demanding at the lack of her response. 'Damn it, Catrina, kiss me properly. Let me have you.'

The force of his assault on her mouth pushed her head into the ground. Crying now, she was tiring and knew that soon he'd have his way. 'Darius...the baby...please...' Catrina gasped against his mouth as he jerked her skirts up to her waist, the lust clear in his eyes. His hair, black as the deepest cellar, hung down straight over his face, giving him a wild look. When the air hit her thighs as he tore down her drawers, she could stand no more and ripped her mouth from his to scream as loud and high as she could.

His lips silenced her as he stuck his tongue into her mouth. She gagged, choking for air, yet the moment he raised his head she screamed again.

'What the hell is goin' on here?' A burly voice spoke from somewhere. 'Hey, you there, what you're doin'?'

Darius in his madness didn't seem to hear the voice at first, but Catrina did, and she saw the farmers enter the grove. Before she could call again for help, Darius was being lifted bodily from her. All at once there was noise, shouts, calls for more help, swearing as Darius fought her rescuers and then the astonished wails of the wives who'd come running.

The women bundled her up and covered her, pulling down her shirts and drawing her bodice back together. Their crooning helped calm her but she couldn't stop shaking. Her teeth chattered painfully. Glimpsed between the women's bodies, she saw them wrestle and hold Darius on the ground until he stopped moving and swearing obscenities at them. Someone was sent to fetch the police and the doctor, and another to get some rope.

The women, speaking softly, hugged her between them and started to lead her away towards the house, but she struggled out of their embrace and stormed over to where Darius lay face down. She caught herself just in time from kicking him. Instead, she bent down low, grimacing as even now his eyes lit up with hope. 'You are a stupid man, Darius Smith. I hope you live a very long and lonely bitter life, or, failing that, you end up swinging from a rope.'

'Come, madam, away from him.' A large woman turned her away and into her arms. 'He can't hurt you no more.'

She staggered between the women, the strength gone from her legs and the tears flowed. As they left the strip of woodland, the men's voices drifted after them.

'Why the bastard...'

'We should string 'im up, Alf...'

'Aye, from the nearest tree...'

'No good swine...'

'Attacked in broad daylight...'

'And us not fifty yards away...'

'The screams, God above it raised the hairs on me arms, so it did...'

'And who the 'ell is he anyway...'

'Looks foreign ter me...'

* * *

TRAVIS leant against the rail at the stern of the ship and watched the moonlight play across the disturbed water streaming behind them in ribbons of white and silver. Looking down into the wash below him, he didn't see the water but the image of Catrina's face, her smile, the curve of her cheek, the gold flecks in her eyes, the honey in her hair. What was she doing at this moment?

He thought back over the last three days ever since his grandmother sent the telegram saying Catrina had run away with Darius Smith. A great part of him wanted to laugh at the absurd notion. His heart rejected the idea of Catrina with Smith, but his mind refused to dispel it completely. He remembered every occasion Smith was at Davmoor and how his dark assessing eyes would follow Catrina. Oh yes, he knew what was in the man's looks, but had he acted on them? And had Catrina succumbed? Surely, she wouldn't, but with him gone and her not knowing why... Then it hit him. It was Darius Smith who had him abducted and not Phillip. His shoulders slumped at the realization. He should have thought of it sooner. Smith wanted him out of the way. He swore harshly into the night. Would Smith abduct Catrina too, or had she gone willingly as Grandmother said?

Once the money started arriving from his grandmother, which had been surprisingly easy through the Post Office in the heart of Melbourne, he sent numerous telegrams to Davmoor, but received no reply. In the end, with despair eating away at him, he'd book a passage on the first ship leaving for England, but even then, he had to wait an extra two days before they sailed. In that time, he said goodbye to Willis and Higgins at the warehouse and booked into a hotel.

He bought clothes, toiletries and other items to take on the ship. A long soak in a hot bath, a shave and a clean new suit gave him back his sense of self.

Each day he visited the Post Office and received a telegram from his grandmother. She was to meet him at Portsmouth, where the ship was docking. There was no mention of Catrina, and Travis tried to keep a lid on his worry. The most important thing was for him to return to England. Once there, he'd sort out the mess that was his marriage.

'Good evening, Mr Millard.'

Travis turned and smiled at Fletcher and bowed to the man's wife as they strolled by. They'd been his dinner companions earlier and thankfully Fletcher had talked all the way through the four courses about his business interests and required very little in response. 'Good evening.'

'It is a magical night, is it not?'

'Yes, indeed.'

'Makes one feel alive, what?' Fletcher sucked in a deep breath making his waistcoat strain over his large stomach.

'Yes. I agree.' Travis inclined his head as they left him. Did he feel alive? No, he felt the dead weight of fear on his back – fear of the unknown. What would he find once he was back home?

He looked along the left-hand side of the first class deck. Wealthy couples strolled in the cool night, taking a turn to stretch their legs before they retired for the night. One couple he'd met were on their honeymoon and he winced at the thought that he and Catrina didn't have one. Was she disappointed in him? Was he not what she had imagined as a husband? She'd been brought up as a lady and taught to expect the best from life, that her own husband would provide for her the standard of living that she had been born to. Instead Catrina had married him and he'd asked her to live on a farm that once belonged to her father. What a fool he'd been to think his love for her would be enough.

He gave himself a mental shake. He had to stop these doubts from eating away at him. To think positively was the only way to go or he'd be insane before he reached home. He glanced over his shoulder at the ship's wake and then squared his shoulders. No more would he be looking back. From now on he'd stand at the bow and face the future. If they made good time he'd be home in four or five weeks. He'd have the truth of it then.

* * *

ESTELLA BALDWIN CLIMBED down from the trap, shook out her new skirt of sky blue and adjusted her matching hat, hopefully the sprigs of silk flowers were still in place under the brim at the back of it. The mad dash along the lanes wasn't good for her attire and thank the heavens it hadn't been raining or she'd be covered in splashes of mud, but she couldn't help liking the thrill of speed! She did everything fast, much to the annoyance of her husband and family, but she'd always been that way and wasn't about to change now. Life was short and she intended on wringing every ounce of enjoyment out of it.

Satisfied she looked her best and not cause a negative comment from her grandmother, she gazed around the yard at Bottom End. Everything looked the same since she was last here and she sighed sadly at the thought of her missing cousin whom she adored. But as tragic as it was that Travis had mysteriously gone, she had come to visit her grandmother and spend an hour away from the demands of being a good wife - a position she was finding harder to maintain each day.

The kitchen door opened and Molly came out carrying a

bucket of dirty water. 'Good morning, Mrs Baldwin. I didn't know you were coming today. Mrs Ailsa is in the front room.'

'Thank you, Molly.' She walked through the kitchen, the welcoming smells of food cooking always made her stomach rumble. Oatmeal biscuits and jam tartlets were cooling on the table and she snatched one and bit it as she strolled down the hallway to the front of the house.

The front parlour wasn't a large room, but it was decorated in white sprigged wallpaper to give light and the appearance of space. When he bought Bottom End Travis had allowed their grandmother to create the rooms to her own satisfaction and the result was an elegant and neat décor fitting Travis's status as a small land owner.

Estella glanced about the room. Her grandmother wasn't there but on the pedestal table under the window was a pile of correspondence and some letters had even fallen to the floor. Swooping down, Estella collected the papers and then stilled as she read the words on them. She quickly read one after the other and then sorted through the ones on the table.

'Estella!'

She jumped at her grandmother's bark from the doorway and flushed at being caught snooping. 'Grandmother... I...'

'You always were a nosy child and you've grown no better despite your marriage.'

'Is this true? Travis is alive?' Estella ignored the remark and waved to the papers spread over the table.

Her grandmother bustled forward to snatch the ones out of her hands. 'Yes. He was kidnapped.'

She glanced at the telegrams her grandmother was folding into a leather pouch. 'He's been in Australia?'

'Yes, but he's coming home now.'

Estella watched the correspondence disappear into a

locked drawer of her grandmother's bureau and lifted her head. 'You are selling the farm?'

'It's none of your business.'

'I cannot believe Travis has asked you to do this on his behalf? Why?'

'He has his reasons. Now are you staying for tea or going? I'm busy today.'

That her grandmother didn't look her in the eye, which was very unlike her, gave Estella the feeling that not all was as it should be. 'How did Catrina take the news?'

'She is away apparently.'

'But she knows of Travis being alive?'

'Yes. I'm sorry, my dear, but I really must get on. I've much to do.'

They both turned as Molly entered the room. 'Mrs Millard I've brought down the trunk, do you want me—'

'Yes, thank you, Molly. That will be all.'

A tingle of unease shivered down Estella's back. 'What is happening, Grandmother?'

'Nothing, my dear. I'm preparing to go down south and meet Travis off his ship, that's all.'

Estella didn't believe for a minute that was all. Her grandmother was acting strangely, her movements jerky, her eyes averted. She was up to something and Estella had to know what it was. 'Catrina is away, is she?' Estella peered at her grandmother and was amazed to see her blush. 'She doesn't know about Travis, does she?'

'No, and you're not telling her either, do you hear me! She's no good for him, never has been and he's better off without her.'

'And what about Travis? What does he want? Or have you decided for him?'

'Stay out of this, Estella. I have his best interests at heart.

He's suffered enough through that Davies woman and I won't let it continue.'

'She was his choice!'

'And he's been a fool. Look at what has happened to him.'

'It wasn't his wife's doing.'

'We don't know that for sure.'

'Grandmother, you may not like Catrina, but she does have affection for Travis. You only had to look at their happiness on their wedding day to see it. Why won't you let them be?' She hadn't always liked the prissy Catrina Davies when they were children, but she knew Travis loved her, had done for years and his happiness mattered most to her, for he had been the only one who didn't condemn her sometimes unruly behaviour.

'If Catrina cared for your cousin then why is she living with Darius Smith? He owns Davmoor now, and yet she still resides there. They've been seen walking the park together and she's helping him to refurbish the house. Why? Why would she happily be doing that when her husband is missing?' Her grandmother bent over suddenly and rubbed her chest, the colour leaving her face.

Concern filled Estella as for the first time in her life she saw her grandmother as a fragile old woman. 'Are you ill?'

'No, just indigestion. I'll be fine. Fetch me my tonic.' She waved towards another small table by the fireplace which held a little brown bottle and spoon.

After Estella had sat her grandmother down and helped her take the tonic she knelt before her. 'Are you well enough to travel to meet Travis? Do you want me to go instead?'

'No. I must do it.' She patted Estella's hand. 'I am perfectly well for someone my age. I don't plan on joining your grandfather just yet. So stop worrying.'

'When do you leave?'

'At the end of the week. I want to do a little touring while I'm down there to see if I can find a new home for us.'

'A home? In the south?'

'We have to be away from here, for Travis's sake.'

'What about me? You'll be so far away from me.' Shocked, Estella glared at the injustice of it. 'I won't ever see you.'

'You can visit, child. Don't take on so.'

Estella flounced away, the old feeling of being second best once more coming to the fore. 'You always favour Travis over me. He's the one you love the most.'

'Nonsense. Stop behaving like a spoilt child.'

'I don't know why I bother even coming here. You aren't interested in me or what I do.'

'I won't listen to your silly remarks, girl. Go home to your husband and prattle your drivel to him.'

'Oh yes, send me home to my husband, you're pleased to do that. You couldn't wait to see me married and gone so you could have Travis all to yourself!'

'You chose to be married, girl. I never forced you!'

'I had to marry just to get away from your demands and control.'

'Was it my fault you were wild and you got yourself with child before marriage? You shamed our family!'

'And a lot of good it did me as I lost the child on my honeymoon. I married for nothing and begged you to help me, but you turned me away, not caring.' Incensed and hurt, Estella turned for the door, but then halted and glanced back at the old woman huddled on the chair. 'I feel sorry for Travis, I really do. He has no idea what he has in store living the rest of his life with you. No matter what Catrina has done or is doing, he is better off with her than you.'

CHAPTER 21

*C*atrina sat in the rocking chair and cradled Ava to her as the child slept against her shoulder and the round of her stomach. The baby had kicked at first, not liking Ava's pressing weight, but it soon settled when Catrina tucked Ava up higher and took the support on her arms instead. The baby's movements delighted her, and gave her reassurance that Smith's attack had not damaged it. She had feared she might lose the child from the assault, but the doctor assured her everything was fine, and now, a week later, she was finally breathing easily, more confident, that he was right.

Sunlight streamed in through the bedroom window and she looked out over the distant fields where labourers still brought in the harvest. Nanny, given an hour off from her charge had gone downstairs, leaving Catrina alone in the room tucked away at the far end of the house and which, for now, was a temporary nursery. The silence of the room was broken only by the ticking of the carriage clock on the mantle and the twittering of birds in the trees outside.

Ava sniffled and moved her head slightly, her sleep deep

and peaceful. Catrina envied her that. She couldn't remember the last time she had slept properly for any length of time. Despite being exhausted in mind and body, sleep refused to offer the oblivion she craved. Only, it seemed at night, when she was alone in the large bed, did her heart and mind worked overtime in misery. She wanted Travis's arms about her, to hear his soft breathing near her ear when he slept beside her. She wanted to wake up to his smile and see the desire in his eyes as he reached for her. To have had the wonder of it for a short time and then have it snatched away was too cruel, and some days she believed she would die from the ache it caused.

The door opened and Hugh quietly walked in and sat on the window seat opposite her. He was finely dressed, his suit a deep dark brown wool, the waistcoat of burgundy silk. He'd been to Bristol to find out news of Smith.

'How did it go?' Catrina watched his face closely, waiting for his answer.

'He was fined. A heavy fine, mind you, but no incarceration. I'm sorry, my dear.'

Her heart plummeted and she took a deep breath. 'Thank you for going.'

'Mr Dowling tried his best but could do no more. He is downstairs if you wish to speak to him. He can tell you all the details of the morning's events.'

'I don't wish to know. Talking of it won't change the outcome. Smith is free, for I assume he paid the fine?'

'Yes, he did. He had a bevy of men there to support him and as a gentleman he was treated better than someone from a lower class.' Hugh looked tired and as disappointed as she felt. 'However, he has been warned not to approach you or next time he'll get more than a fine.'

Catrina gazed out on the golden fields being slowly shred of their bounty. 'If there is a next time, and I'm sure there will be, Smith will be more successful in getting what he wants. The threat of gaol doesn't bother him. He'd be out of the country before the constable can blow his whistle.'

'I'll employ men to guard the grounds and—'

'No, Hugh. I'll not let Longbrook become a prison, Davmoor felt like that...at the end...and I'll not have it here.' She rocked the chair gently with her foot. 'Smith will not rule my life. He has done enough damage.' She lifted her head and gave Hugh a steely smile. 'I am not afraid of him.'

'Dearest, he is a dangerous man. You need to be guarded since the man is irrational where you are concerned.'

'I'll stay close to the house until the baby is born, but afterwards...well Smith can go to the devil if he thinks I'll hide from him forever.'

'He'll not leave you alone, especially if you go through with the investigation of his involvement of Travis's kidnap.'

'You think I should not do it? That he should be allowed to get away with it?'

'A man like Smith will have organised the job in such a way that there can be no link back to him. He is an intelligent man, determined, obviously. Dowling has found out that he moves in dubious company in London and he is not a man to cross.'

'So because of that he should be a law unto himself?' Her voice rose, and Ava woke up and stretched her little arms. Catrina soothed her, and soon enough Ava settled back into the rocking of the chair and her lashes drooped again.

'Put the child into bed, and come downstairs to talk to Mr Dowling,' Hugh suggested, standing. 'Ah, here's Nanny.' Hugh smiled as the young woman came into the room.

'Mrs Millard, there's someone to see you.' Nanny grinned and reached out for Ava.

'For me? Are you sure?' She received no visitors.

'Yes. A woman.'

'Thank you, Nanny.' Intrigued, Catrina passed the baby over to her and, wondering who could be visiting her, she left and went downstairs with Hugh.

In the drawing room, Catrina paused on the threshold and stared as Mr Dowling chatted amiably with Mrs O'Toole.

Hugh and Mr Dowling excused themselves and went along to Hugh's study while Catrina rang for tea and grasping Mrs O'Toole's hands begged her to sit down.

'This is such a surprise! I am so happy to see you, Mrs O'Toole.'

'And I you, Madam. I hope you don't mind me coming here?' Anxiety flittered across the older woman's face.

'Heavens, no. You are most welcome.'

'Thank you, Madam. I didn't know where else to go and I couldn't stay at Davmoor another minute with that man.'

'You did the right thing coming here.' Catrina squeezed her hand reassuringly, aware of the weariness in the older woman's posture. 'You should have left with me. I'm sorry that you didn't. I didn't like leaving you behind.'

'Nay, there's no need to apologise, Madam. You had to get away fast. He's...he's not right in the head, madam, Smith, I mean...' Mrs O'Toole glanced towards the doorway. 'He has such rages and then is sullen for hours. He spends time in your room, touching the bed...'

Catrina shivered. 'He attacked me, last week. Did you know?'

'He was here?' Mrs O'Toole looked around her as though he was about to jump out from behind the sofa.

'He's been in Bristol goal for a week, but this morning he was fined and released. But it is hardly surprising a worm such as he could wriggle off the hook.' Disgust rose in her throat.

'We wondered where he had got to... He's been gone from

Davmoor for over ten days. I couldn't rest, wondering when he'd return and well, my nerves just couldn't stand it.' She blinked rapidly, before taking a deep breath. 'I decided to leave before he came back. I had hoped you would give me a reference.'

Catrina smiled. 'Never mind a reference, you'll stay here. Hugh has no housekeeper only an old butler whom you'd have seen when you arrived. We need someone for the female staff. I was going to write to you and offer the position but then Smith...'

Mrs O'Toole straightened her back. 'Well then, Madam, I've saved you the stationary, so I have.'

'Oh, Mrs O'Toole,' Catrina let out a long breath, 'your coming has lifted my spirits.'

'Well, I'm glad of that. I see you have put Bottom End up for sale?'

'Pardon?'

'Bottom End farm, it's up for sale. You must be happy Ailsa Millard has gone. She packed up and left last week with no word to anyone.'

Catrina frowned, amazed at such news. 'The farm is up for sale?'

'Well, yes, didn't you arrange it?'

'No...'

'But if Mr Travis is...dead...then you, as his wife, own the farm. We all thought you had organised to sell it. That's when I knew I had to come as you weren't coming back.'

'I haven't done any such thing. This is the first I've known about it. Are you sure it is for sale? Ailsa hasn't simply gone to her granddaughter, Mrs Baldwin's home?'

'No. Mrs Baldwin refuses to speak of her grandmother apparently. The village is agog at the news of their rift.'

'Perhaps Mrs Millard finds staying at the farm holds too many memories?'

Mrs O'Toole tutted. 'Nay, Madam, don't you realise, the farm is up for *sale*. I saw the sign on the gate myself.'

Shocked, Catrina slumped against the sofa cushions, the breath gone from her body. 'I gave no authority for such undertaking. Ailsa has taken it upon herself to do this and she has no right!'

'Unless...'

'Yes?'

'Unless Mr Travis gave her permission to...'

Like a slap across her face, Catrina jerked her head aside, pain biting deep into her soul. No, it couldn't be. Travis alive... Wild joy filled her heart but was quickly smothered by her next thought. If he was alive and gave Ailsa permission to sell the farm, then he had no thoughts to return to her...

* * *

TRAVIS CRANED his neck to search the crowded dock for any sign of his grandmother. His heart thumped in anticipation of once more seeing her, when not so long ago he feared he'd never see a loved one again. Darkness was falling and the shadows and crush of disembarking passengers made it hard difficult to make out a friendly face. He followed the crowd inside a building to get his papers stamped and then headed out into an area where people waited for luggage and beyond them was the street and a line of cabs waiting for fares.

'Travis!'

He turned and there she was, leaning heavily on her stick, wearing a black coat to block out the cold wind which blew off the ocean. He ran to her and enfolded her into his arms.

'Oh my darling, sweet boy.' She held him tight, her eyes streaming tears which ran down her sunken cheeks. She looked older than when he last saw her – smaller, thinner, weaker.

'I am so happy to see you again, Grandmother.'

'And I you.' She patted his shoulder. 'It has been a trial for you, dearest, but it's over now. Come, I have a carriage waiting to take us to the hotel. Do you have luggage?'

'Only this.' He held up the portmanteau he'd dropped at his feet on embracing her.

'Right then, let us be going.' She tucked her arm through his and guided him outside where a blast of cold air hit them. 'It's been raining all day, but our rooms are comfortable and overlooking the sea. Are you hungry?'

Climbing into the first hansom in the line, Travis answered her questions about the voyage all the way to the hotel. Once in their suite of rooms he looked around but didn't really see the neat furnishings, the fire glowing brightly in the grate. He watched his Grandmother shrug off her coat and unpin her black hat. Such simple activity made her short of breath and her colour was dreadful, the shade of uncooked dough.

'I'll have something sent up, shall I?' She sat near to the fire on a brown velvet chair. 'Such awful weather. One would think it was the middle of winter, and not the end of summer.'

'Grandmother...'

'Now, you have your room just through there.' She waved towards a set of open doors on the right of the room. 'Mine is through there too, and a small bathroom, imagine that. The height of luxury it is, and they know how to charge for it too, but it's worth it after all you've suffered.'

'Grandmother—'

'Do you wish to lie down and rest, dearest, until the food comes up? Or bathe perhaps?'

'I want Catrina, Grandmother.'

Her eyes widened. 'I told you, she has run off with Darius Smith. Did you not get my telegram?'

'I got it, but I don't believe it. I've had a lot of time to think on that ship and I refuse to believe she would run off with that man.'

'But she has. They are both gone from Davmoor.'

Her words were like knives stabbing him, but he had to hold on to the notion that she was wrong, that somehow, Catrina loved him and waited for him. 'I cannot rest, Grandmother, until I have seen her.'

'No one knows where she is. Why must you pursue her? She is worthless!' She stood and gripped the chair arm. 'I forbid you to make a fool of yourself anymore, Travis. This obsession with her has to stop!'

'She is my wife!'

'She is a whore!'

Travis glared at his grandmother as silence filled the room, though their heated words still lingered between them. His chest heaved with frustration and anger that he'd been dragged from the woman he loved. 'I won't have you insult her. She has done nothing to you.'

'She has treated you contemptuously and that affects me.'

'No, Grandmother, whatever happens to me I will deal with. I don't need you to fight my battles.'

'Well someone has to, you allow her to walk all over you. All the Davies are the same. They use people and then fling them away when no longer needed. I won't let it happen again. I—' She stopped mid-sentence, her eyes grew wide and then she grasped her left arm and tilted sideways.

'Grandmother!' Travis ran and caught her, breaking her fall as he stumbled to his knees. 'Grandmother, what is it? Speak to me.'

Her face was grey as she lay in his arms. 'Oh, dear God...' she moaned, wincing, the pain evident in her eyes.

'I'll get help.'

'No.' She stopped him from rising. 'No need, dearest...'

Panic squeezed his guts. 'Grandmother, you must have a doctor.'

She tensed with pain and her eyes closed. 'George...?' she whispered.

'George, Grandmother?' Travis leaned close to her mouth, but she spoke no more and went limp in his arms. He stared down at her unable to believe what was happening. He swallowed with difficulty past the tightness in this throat. Slowly he lifted her up into his arms and carried her into the bedroom and laid her on the bed. Stepping back, he gazed at the small body, willing her to open her eyes and demand something. Her spirit, that bright robust spark that he had known all his life couldn't be extinguished, surely?

Tears burned hot behind his eyes and he sucked in a deep breath to calm himself. He must send for a doctor. He edged towards the door, not taking his eyes off his grandmother. 'I'll be straight back, I promise. I won't take a minute,' he murmured, hating the thought of leaving her.

With a bowed head and his feet dragging he left the suite to go down to the reception desk.

CHAPTER 22

*C*atrina stood with Mrs O'Toole and surveyed the mess left by the builders. Longbrook's attic, which was once a long room running the length of the house, was now separated into three large rooms, the day nursery, the night nursery and Nanny's bedroom.

'It won't take long to clear this up, madam.' Mrs O'Toole touched the newly dried plaster walls. 'A bit of paint, new carpet, some furniture and you'll not recognise the place.'

Catrina walked over to the black-leaded, freestanding stove, erected only that morning. 'Will this give enough heating though? I still have my doubts.'

'There's one in each room. They will keep the rooms comfortable, even Mr Henley agrees.' Mrs O'Toole stepped to the window and peered out. 'After a good clean, I'll have the drapes hung. Shall I get the girls up and make a start, madam?'

'Yes, thank you.'

Pausing by the door, Mrs O'Toole glanced back over her shoulder. 'Madam, why don't you go outside for a breath of fresh air? If you don't mind me saying so, you look a bit peaky.'

'Perhaps I will. I have stayed indoors too much.' She longed to stride out down the lanes and clear her head of Travis, but some days it was an effort to simply rise from her bed and dress. For Hugh she smiled and behaved normally, but inside her hopes and dreams were dying little by little, her life as she imagined it was being swept away like dust on the wind.

'I'll get the girls started then, madam. For the furniture will be arriving next week and we won't be ready for it.'

After the housekeeper left, Catrina gazed out of the window and across the woodland where Darius had attacked her. A part of her wanted to defy her promise to Hugh about staying close to the house. She wanted to lift her head and say to hell with Darius Smith, he couldn't frighten her! Why should he stop her from going where she pleased? But another, sensible side of her said it was too soon to leave the gardens alone. She must think of her unborn child, and of Ava.

With a sigh, she left the attic and went downstairs. The sun warmed the house and dust motes danced in its rays streaming through the windows. The afternoon heat made her feel lazy. Grabbing an apple from the large glass bowl centred on the dining room table, and her straw hat left on a chair, she let herself out through the French windows and onto the side terrace. From here the lawns meandered down a gentle slope, interposed with formal gardens and box hedges. The first part of the Longbrook gardens that were being wrestled into shape by Roddy and the new lad Hugh had hired to help him.

Catrina bit into the apple, savouring the fresh crunch and the sweet juice that ran down her chin. She wore a newly measured mourning dress and it flowed over her bump without restriction, as she'd thrown off the special pregnancy corset she had ordered last week when the weather became too hot to wear it. Besides, she saw no company, except Hugh.

At the bottom of the slope was an ornamental carp pond, complete with a cupid fountain in the middle. The white, red and orange fish came to the surface eager for some bread and she felt guilty for not bringing any.

'They'll want feeding, Madam.' Roddy called from where he dug alongside the gravel path. 'Hungry beasts that they are.'

'I'll remember next time to bring some bread.' She smiled back at him.

'Can I bring you a chair, Madam?'

'Thank you, but no, Roddy. I should have brought a blanket.'

'Here then, madam.' Roddy dropped his spade and collected his jacket which hung over the end of the barrow. He ran down to where she stood and spread it out on the grass. 'It's clean, washed just yesterday.'

'Thank you, Roddy, you are most kind.' She held out her hand and he took it to help her sit. 'This stomach of mine is getting larger each day.'

'That's good, Madam, means it's healthy.' He blushed furiously and stammered an apology.

Catrina grinned up at him and then sobered a little. 'Tell me, Roddy, are you happy here? Truly? I would want to know if you are not.'

'Nay, don't fret yourself, Madam. I'm most content at Longbrook. I think it the best place I have ever worked. Mr Henley is a good employer and...' his face grew even redder, 'and...'

'And Lettie is here,' she teased, chewing on her apple.

'There is that, yes, Madam.'

'You aren't playing her false?'

'No, Madam. No, not at all. I think her very fine. She's decent and kind.'

'Have you asked her to marry you yet?'

Roddy stretched his neck and cleared his throat. 'Aye, well, we've discussed it... We've wanted to talk to you about it, but well, with everything that's been going on and... well...'

Catrina nodded. 'You are both enormously generous, Roddy, but I refuse to be the subject of yours and Lettie's unhappiness. I want you to go now and speak with her. Choose a date and then both of you go to Siston and speak with the parish clerk. We'll have the banns read this Sunday I think.'

'Really, Madam?'

'Would that be your wish?'

'Aye, Madam, of course.' His eyes were round with stunned joy.

'Off you go then.' She waved him away, feeling light of heart at the happiness of such dear people. Life went on, whether she wanted it to or not.

Restless, she threw her apple away in the thicket on the other side of the pond, knowing a bird would delight in the extra food. With difficulty she rose to her feet and brushed down her skirt. As she bent to pick up Roddy's jacket, movement up the slope caught her eye. Frowning in the sunlight, she shaded her eyes with her hand and tried to work out who the man was standing on the terrace.

Suddenly her heart jolted against her ribs and the fine hairs prickled along the back of her neck. A whimper sounded in her throat. Travis.

He started to walk down to her and she felt rooted to the spot. He wasn't dead, but very much alive. As he came closer he slowed, and she saw the devastation written on his face.

'Catrina?' His hoarse enquiry was filled with doubt and he stopped a few feet from her.

Her gazed raked over him. He was so thin, his cheeks hollow and his eyes haunted. He was so unlike the man she loved, the one who'd held her with powerful arms, whose healthy and energetic body had made love to her for hours. He seemed troubled, stricken.

'Have you nothing to say?' His voice was low and he held his shoulders stiff as though braced for the worst. 'Will you tell me the truth?'

'The truth?' Her heart raced so fast she thought it would leave her chest.

'You and Darius Smith. Is he the one you want?'

'What? Good Lord, no! Never.' She searched his face. 'How could you think such a thing? I love you. I carry your child.'

His eyes widened when he realised the shape of her body beneath the dress.

A sob broke free from her and tears blurred her vision. 'I'm so sorry if I gave you cause to doubt me.'

'My love, no.'

She fell into his arms and cried broken heartedly as he crushed her to him. She gripped his shoulders, his head, not knowing how to hold him tightly enough.

Travis rained kisses over her face. 'Oh my darling, my beautiful girl. I've missed you.'

Catrina sobbed into his neck, her arms wound around him. 'I love you so much. I thought you were dead. Then when I heard...the farm was for...sale... I thought perhaps you...weren't...dead... and that you'd didn't want to be with...me.'

'It's not true...I love you...' He kissed her hard on the mouth as though to remind her of his devotion. 'You're all I want, I promise you.'

Catrina kissed him back, eager to show him how much she missed him.

For a while they were content to simply hold each other, to kiss and soothe, reassuring the other of their love. But as the tempest of the reunion abated, tiredness overwhelmed Catrina and she sank onto the grass and Travis did the same.

He ran his hands over her swollen stomach, his eyes wondrous. 'A baby. I'm to be a father.'

'Yes. I had planned to tell you after Father's funeral, but we quarrelled...'

'I'm sorry.' He kissed her hands and then bent to kiss her stomach, touching it lightly.

She stroked his hair, noticed the odd strand of grey that now threaded through it. 'I'm sorry too, my love. For everything. I should have done as you asked and lived at Bottom End. If I had, none of this would have happened. I am to blame. It was wrong of me to ask you to live at Davmoor, to give up your home, and—'

'Shh, darling. What's done is done.' He kissed her forehead.

'You have suffered so much. Can you tell me about it?'

Travis stared into her eyes and gave her a sweet smile. 'I would rather talk about you.'

'Please, darling, I need to know what Smith put you through.'

'I will tell you, all of it, I promise, but not just now. Later, tonight, yes?' He slipped off his jacket as the sun blazed down on them.

She took his hands in hers and leaned forward to kiss him softly. 'Yes. We have the rest of our lives to talk.'

'Come here.' He pulled her onto his lap and cupped her cheek, kissing her until they were out of breath. 'Lord, I've missed you,' he whispered, nuzzling under her ear. 'I've dreamt of this moment so many times.'

'I never want to be parted from you again.' She sighed against him.

'We won't be. I can promise you that.'

They sat quietly for a while happy to be just together and then Travis helped her up and arm-in-arm they strolled through the gardens as the golden glow of dusk coated the countryside.

'Grandmother is dead,' Travis spoke finally.

Catrina stopped and stared. 'How do you know that? She's not at Bottom End.'

'She came to meet my ship when it docked. She died that evening. We were arguing...'

'About me?' Catrina guessed, knowing Ailsa as well as she did, the older woman would have done her best to turn Travis away from her.

He hesitated. 'Unfortunately, yes.'

'Again, I am sorry. Through me you have suffered greatly.'

'Grandmother was at fault too. She wouldn't let go of her ridiculous hatred of the Davies family.'

'She loved my father, Travis. They had an affair.'

His jaw went slack, and he scowled. 'An affair, Grandmother?'

'She wasn't always old, you know. It was before my father met my mother. So over twenty-five years ago.'

'Good lord. I never knew.'

'Nor did I. Mrs O'Toole told me. It was a great secret that not many people knew about.' She went on to tell him what Mrs O'Toole had said.

'That is why she said George as she lay dying and not my grandfather's name.' Travis mused, ducking his head under a low arbour from which a rambling yellow rose hung.

'She called for my father?' Catrina could hardly believe it. 'She loved him still?'

'That's why she was so bitter, I suppose. How sad.' He

sucked in a deep breath. 'She loved Estella and me very much. Wanted only the best for us.' He paused, controlling his emotions with a hasty swallow. 'I took her body back to Bottom End. She would want to be buried in the village with Grandfather. Estella and I talked after the funeral. She was distressed because she had argued with Grandmother and not made it up with her before she died.'

She rubbed his arm, wishing she could take away his pain. 'You must ask her to visit us here at Longbrook. Estella is your family, and I welcome the chance to become better friends with her. We must put the past behind us.'

'Well now, isn't this interesting!'

They both turned at the voice coming from the right. Darius Smith stepped away from the yew hedge that bordered the drive and faced them.

Catrina moaned deep in her chest.

Travis quickly stepped in front of her, dropping the jacket which he'd slung over his shoulder. 'Don't take another step, Smith.' His tone was low and dangerous.

Darius's sly grin was at odds to the cold darkness in his eyes. 'You made it back, Millard. How clumsy of my men to not see the job through to a satisfying end.'

'What end would that be, Smith? My death?'

'Come now, at the beginning I never wished for that.' Smith, wearing a tailored suit of chocolate brown, tilted his head to one side and smiled more warmly at Catrina. 'Come out from behind him, dearest, I will not hurt you. I never wanted to hurt you.'

'But you did, Darius.' Catrina stepped alongside Travis and he wrapped his arm around her waist. Comforted by his presence, Catrina's fear of Smith evaporated. 'You may not have meant to hurt me, but your very actions did just that.'

'I can give you a better life than he can. We became friends. It could have been so much more if you let it.'

Darius's fingers tapped his thigh but other than that he stood completely still.

'No, you don't understand.' Catrina spoke softly to him, as though he was a child. 'I love my husband. I carry his child. You would never have been first in my affections even if Travis had died.'

'In time I could have. I would have showered you with riches, made you forget him.'

She shook her head sadly. 'I don't need your riches.' She swept her arm back towards the house behind them. 'Long-brook is mine, Darius. It always has been. I didn't need Davmoor. I didn't want it. I thought I could keep it for Ava, but I was wrong.'

Darius, his handsome swarthy face wan, moved his arm and within a heartbeat Catrina and Travis were looking down the barrel of his pistol. 'You have played me for a fool.'

Travis dragged Catrina behind him once more. 'Put that away, Smith. This will solve nothing. Go home. Leave us in peace, you've done enough.'

'I'm not even close to finishing what I started, Millard.' He cocked the pistol. The sound seemed dreadfully loud in the shimmering afternoon heat.

Sweat trickled down Catrina's back, her knees seemed to lose all their strength, but she remained upright, gripping the back of Travis's shirt.

Travis stiffened, his body immovable. 'Will shooting me get you what you want, Smith? I seriously doubt it.'

'Perhaps not, but I'll enjoy it nevertheless.' Darius's arm straightened, the pistol pointed at Travis's chest.

She screamed and all at once the world seemed to go mad. Travis pushed Catrina to the ground as the blast shattered the peaceful garden. Birds flew out of the trees nearby screeching in alarm. The smell of grass and earth was in Catrina's nose, her hair, fallen out of its pins, covered her eyes and she quickly pushed it aside to see Travis lying beside her. She looked over him to see Darius also lying on the ground. There were other sounds, people shouting, moaning, crying, was that her?

She struggled up, reaching for Travis, praying he wasn't mortally wounded for she wouldn't be able to stand it.

He turned at her touch, his gaze searched hers. 'Are you hurt?'

'No. Are you?' She looked for blood but saw none.

'He missed.' Travis managed to say before they were surrounded by people all talking at once.

Catrina was helped to her feet by Travis and a young gardener hired to help Roddy. Mrs O'Toole was taking charge, ordering weeping maids to stop sniffling and do her bidding. Everyone was in shock, out of breath from running, murmuring, yet the whole time Catrina was aware of one thing, Hugh.

He stood away from them, a rifle held in his arm as he leaned over Darius, watching him. She could see Darius writhing on the ground, grasping at his chest where blood seeped through the fine material of his suit, staining the brown to black.

'Come into the house, my love.' Travis took her in his arms, but she shook her head and walked over to Hugh.

The rifle he held pointed to the grass beside Darius and the expression on Hugh's face was resigned.

'Hugh,' Catrina whispered, touching his arm.

He looked up at her, his shoulders bent, head bowed. 'I didn't think I would get him in time. I couldn't get a clear shot from the terrace. I had to move to the right so I wouldn't hit you or Travis.'

They gazed down at the man who had tried and failed to ruin their lives. Darius's eyes rolled in his head, his breathing grew irregular and every now and then he swore in agony.

Catrina watched him unmoved. If it hadn't been for Hugh's quick thinking, Travis would be dead at her feet. Instead, it was this wretched man dying and she felt no remorse, no emotion, only a gratefulness that it was over and Smith was no more.

Travis clasped Catrina's arm in support. He ignored Darius and with his other hand gently took the rifle from Hugh. 'The doctor has been sent for and the police. You're not to worry, Hugh, you were protecting us. There are witnesses. No court in the land will send you down for that.'

'It doesn't matter if they do, lad,' Hugh said softly. 'I've lived a good life.'

She reached up and kissed Hugh's whiskery cheek. 'Thank you for saving us.'

His eyes softened in response. 'I knew he wouldn't rest until he'd done more damage. I've been on guard.' Hugh looked at Travis. 'Now I can rest for you are here with Catrina, as is only right. Longbrook has been sleeping, but the both of you will bring her back alive.'

The three of them turned and watched as Darius Smith groaned and then lay still, his life finally extinguished.

Hugh's old butler came alongside and threw a blanket over the man and said he would stay until the doctor came.

With her arms linked through Travis and Hugh's, Catrina led them up the slope to the house as the sun slid down on the horizon.

There would be an investigation ahead of them, but she knew without a doubt that they'd weather it, and on the other side, lay a new life full of promise and hope.

The baby kicked, and she sighed in relief that her fall hadn't hurt the precious child she carried.

On the terrace, Hugh squeezed her arm, and went into the house first with a bustling Mrs O'Toole worrying over him. Catrina hung back and gazed at Travis, who quickly took her into his arms.

'It's all over, my sweetheart,' he murmured into her hair.

'I want to spend the rest of my life loving you and raising our children.' She rested her head on his shoulder. 'A simple life, Travis.'

'Here at Longbrook,' he added.

She raised her head to stare at him. 'Can you be happy living here? If you don't think you will be, we'll leave. I'll go wherever you wish me to, and without complaint.'

'It's a fine estate, Catrina, one any man would be proud to call home. Besides, Hugh has saved my life. I owe him to take care of Longbrook.'

'It's ours, not just mine. You'll be in charge as is only right.' She waved towards the distant fields and Home Farm. 'I cannot do it alone. I don't want to. I need you by my side always.'

He kissed her softly. 'I'll never leave you again, I promise. We'll be a family soon and it's all I want. I want to sell Bottom End. I can no longer live in the shadow of Davmoor. Instead, I'll put my own stamp on Longbrook. Together we'll make it the perfect home for us and our children. A fresh start.'

'I like the sound of that.' She smiled, kissing him.

ABOUT THE AUTHOR

If you enjoyed my story please leave a review online, it helps an author very much, and we appreciate them more than you know.

Thank you
AnneMarie Brear

Australian born AnneMarie Brear writes historical novels and modern romances and sometimes the odd short story, too. Her passions, apart from writing, are travelling, reading, eating her husband's delicious food, reading, researching, and dragging her husband around historical sites looking for inspiration for her next book.

Please visit her website to join her newsletter and hear her latest news. www.annemariebrear.com